Finch Books by J.S. Frankel

PORT ANYWHERE

J.S. FRANKEL

Port Anywhere
ISBN # 978-1-80250-960-1
©Copyright J.S. Frankel 2022
Cover Art by Erin Dameron-Hill ©Copyright June 2022
Interior text design by Claire Siemaszkiewicz
Finch Books

Published in 2022 by Finch Books, United Kingdom.

PORT
ANYWHERE

Dedication

To my wife, Akiko, who makes my life worthwhile. To my children, Kai and Ray, who bring me joy, and to Eva Pasco, Sara Linnertz, Joanne Van Leerdam, Gigi Sedlmayer, Emily Akimoto, Anna Casamento Arrigo, Rachel Glickler, Schuyler Thorpe and so many more, thank you for your support.

And to my sister, Nancy D. Frankel, a special thank you for your unwavering belief that I could write and write well.

Chapter One

New Arrivals

Randorran Galaxy. Sometime around noon.
Earth Year, 2134

"Is that griddle clean, yet?"

Nerfer's call emanated from the storage room, a question that went past impatience but stopped just shy of outright anger. Deep and harsh, his voice sounded like it belonged to a giant, but he stood on the short side of one-hundred-sixty centimeters. His actual height was contentious at best, as he was essentially pink jelly encased in a clear plastic containment suit. But the commanding tone was unmistakable.

In days gone by, people would have called him Spam-In-A-Can. Perhaps calling him 'crushed fruit in a suit' would have been more appropriate. But after thinking about it...no. It wouldn't have worked.

With a sigh, knowing he wouldn't believe me, I answered, "Yes, it's clean. So are all the other tables. Come see for yourself." I doubted he'd take my word for it. Nerfer was notoriously difficult to please.

"I will. Give me a second."

He could have a second—or ten. My journey to spotlessness on the bridge continued. The bridge itself took up a third of the total space, with a captain's chair and a console in front of the main viewing window, an interstellar communicator, which sat on the console to the left of the captain's chair, and helm controls to the right.

Behind the helm was the other two-thirds of the bridge. That was the restaurant. The glass that made up our main window to the stars was spotless, and it offered an incomparable view of the heavens.

If the view was incredible, so was the restaurant, in its own way. My late father had designed it after looking at countless vid-photos of diners from the mid-twenty-first century. For some reason, he'd had a fascination with that era.

Our restaurant had plush leather booths—ten in all—a counter with eight stools and a syntha-fridge that could synthesize any kind of food, but only in its raw form. I still had to cook it. We also had a combo grill-fryer where the food got prepared by me, Rick Granger, co-captain of *Port Anywhere*, our ship's name.

This place was where I belonged, where my focus was. As the co-captain of this ship, I had a duty to guide our ship among the stars as well as to be on guard for anything that might threaten the safety of—

"Coming out," Nerfer said, interrupting my dreams of a full captaincy.

The door to the storage room opened. It housed numerous old food crates and doubled as his sleeping quarters. He came toward me, his semi-solid body undulating in his containment suit as he moved along. From what he'd told me, he was a member of the Gliddod race. His people came from a distant galaxy, one so far away that no one really knew where it was.

He'd shown up here six months ago in a spacecraft that had fallen apart after he'd docked with ours, and he'd asked my father for a job. My father, being the decent person he had been, had given him the position of running this restaurant while he went off to attend to the daily mechanics of operating this ship. Oh, and he'd also made him co-captain.

Did that piss me off? There was an old saying—'Did a one-legged duck walk in circles?' In a private moment, I'd asked my father, *"Dad, why'd you hire this guy? You don't know where he's been or if anyone's chasing him or what. Weren't you training me to be the captain and the head cook?"*

"When it's time, you'll be both," he'd answered.

Thanks for your confidence in me, Dad.

After a while, though, I had to admit that our new pink crewperson had proved to be an excellent cook, and after my father's death from Bridorran Fever, Nerfer had also ended up being a more than capable captain. It still bothered me at times, though, being relegated to the 'also-ran' position.

In a quick, economical motion, Nerfer moved around to check each table. Finally, he finished his inspection with a grunt that sounded like a bubble popping underwater. "Good job, kid."

Finally, a compliment. A pseudopod shot out from his suit—the suit was porous in a sense, and it allowed him to do that—and he pointed to a table. "Number six has a spot on it. We got Janoorians comin' in soon, and they hate dirt."

Compliment given, compliment withdrawn—and with that, he went back to the storage room. Fine, I'd clean the table—again. We had only ten, but he'd spotted a tiny imperfection one-fifth as large as my pinky fingernail on one of them. In days past, people had called it being anal. These days, people called it attention to detail.

Our vessel, an Earth-class freighter, had been converted from a freighter-slash-exploration vessel to an exploration-vessel-slash-interstellar restaurant. So, when we entered a new galaxy and if some alien life forms contacted us, once they found out we weren't armed, they'd either drop in for a meal or tell us to keep moving.

Usually, they partook of a meal with us, we chatted, then they departed after paying us whatever they could. You could call it a precarious living, because we never knew who'd come our way. My parents had always believed in randomness, and my existence here was as random as it got.

We called our ship *Port Anywhere*, mainly because we went everywhere, to every galaxy and beyond. We had self-sustaining ion-conversion engines, and the great thing was that they left no radioactive residue upon the stars, unlike other ships. Recycling was cool. 'Go green,' the old saying went. We were in space, so, 'go non-radioactive'.

Our journey had started two years before, just after I'd turned fifteen. We'd lifted off on a bright, sunny day in June from a flight field located near Salt Lake Flats, Utah. A sudden surge, the G-forces had pulled me back, and soon, we'd been in space.

After that, our voyage to wherever continued unimpeded. The ship didn't have a wormhole device, not exactly. Unlike other, newer ships, it couldn't go very fast, but it had a recyclable fuel supply, it was safe and from that point on, I'd learned almost everything there was to learn about spaceships and fixing them.

My parents were first-rate engineers as well as designers, and they'd willingly taught me everything I needed to know about the ship, save the engines. *"They're self-sustaining,"* my father had once said. *"All you have to do is keep the place clean."*

Of course, I learned about other things, such as basic repairs to the hull, space walking, electrical wiring and more, but, by and large, my parents handled things.

The first six months had been cool. Outside of my cleaning and service duties, charting the stars and training against battle droids had taken up most of my time. On occasion, we'd touch down on distant worlds, but like desert nomads, we were always on the move, except we moved among the stars and not sand, although the grains of the universe were always there.

On the surface, everything was wonderful — up until my mother had died from cancer a year ago, just after I'd turned sixteen. Modern science could cure a lot of things, but it still hadn't gotten around to curing that.

The picture in my cabin showed a tall woman with long, flowing brown hair, a pretty face and a pleasant smile. My father had also been tall, around a hundred and eighty-two centimeters, with an aquiline nose, short brown hair and brown eyes, traits which I'd inherited, although I wasn't quite that tall — yet.

In all honesty, I'd never thought much my looks. After all, there were no girls here to date, and the closest I ever got to female companionship of my age was watching old holo-vids. Decades back, they'd been called movies.

"I'm sorry about your mother," my father had said to me after her funeral. He'd encased her in a metal coffin, we'd said our goodbyes then he'd pressed the button that ejected her into space. *"She was a good person."*

Yes, she had been, and from that point on, he'd rarely spoken of her. Grief was a powerful thing. Still, we'd soldiered on, and our lives had continued among the stars...

"Rick, you wiping those tables down again?"

Nerfer had poked his head out of the storage room to ask me that question. I gave him the standard answer. "Yes, captain."

His standard grunt came my way. "Fine."

He moved to the captain's chair while I finished doing the tables and gave the grill another touch-up job as well.

We'd been in the Randorran Galaxy for three days. It was the home to Janoorians, Melattans and Sillosians, among others. They were traders, they got along with each other, but they didn't keep company very often. Something about a guild operating here...

"Rick!"

Nerfer's voice — loud and stern — made me jump. I'd been spacing out — literally — and while it made me laugh silently, it also confirmed that I had to pay attention more. A good captain paid attention to everything. "What?"

"Check the computer. Company should be coming soon."

Sure enough, the interstellar com-link device crackled to life. "This is Vadda, of the Janoorian people. We have a reservation. Your Captain Nerfer agreed to this."

Captain Nerfer. Captain. What about me? However, I had to act professional. "Acknowledged. Co-captain Rick Granger speaking. How many in your party?"

"Three. We requested that you prepare one of our planet's delicacies. We will bring the raw form of it. Can you make it to our satisfaction?"

Well, if I were about to be roasted or grilled, I'd scream, too. "C'mere," Nerfer said, and his pseudopods quickly grabbed the plant and crushed its root. It gave one final shrill cry then let go.

"You're on, kid," Nerfer said as he tossed it on the griddle that already had a coating of oil on it. "Start 'er up!"

Showtime, and I went to the griddle to take out a knife and a spatula and start cooking the mess. A horrible odor came from it, and why couldn't alien plants or meat smell decent like bacon and eggs...or grilled cheese? Rhetorical — they couldn't.

While I suffered through a stink that was a combination of wood alcohol and crap, the Janoorians went wild over the odor, undulating their squishy bodies this way and that. "Ah, the young man is a master chef," one of them said. "He knows our tastes!"

They could have their tastes and keep them. Once it was done, it resembled fried rocks. I divided the portions just so, slid them onto plates then served our guests. Did they use utensils?

No, they simply bent over the mess and ingested it...noisily. Once they'd finished, Vadda leaned back. "A fine meal! The tenlos is a foul plant on our world. It attacks our people from time to time, so please, do not feel bad for killing it."

I didn't feel bad for cooking it up. I would have felt bad, though, if I'd had to eat it. Vadda then got up and pointed to the door. "We are sorry not to spend more time here, but we must be on our way. We are delivering cargo to another sector in the galaxy."

"Not a problem," I said, attempting to keep my stomach's contents inside.

His friends also rose, getting ready to leave. Vadda slid a pseudopod inside his body, took out a red jewel and handed it over. "Take this as payment, please. Should you visit this sector of space again, we will most certainly partake of a meal with you."

Oh, please don't.

But I said nothing and led them to the airlock. While I waited for it to pressurize, I asked him about the jewel.

"It is called *energa*," he said.

Energa? "What does it do, exactly?"

"It has the property of reflection and is considered valuable on our world. Please use it as you see fit."

Reflection? Maybe it was a mirror. It was shiny, anyway, and I bowed, out of respect. "Thank you."

They departed, and once they were free of the ship, I checked out the jewel. It sparkled, but that was about it. Out of curiosity, I walked into a storage room nearby, found a small hand-laser and did my best to slice off a tiny piece. The beam simply deflected away and burned a hole in the door. "Oh, so that's what it does."

Interesting…and a call that came over the ship's intercom interrupted my thoughts. "Prepare to shift. Prepare to shift."

Why now? The computer never gave a reason, although the sensors detected another vessel approximately four thousand kilometers away, its purpose, unknown. No communication came from it, so…

"Shift occurring. Shift occurring."

With all haste, I ran to the restaurant where Nerfer was in the process of putting all the dishes and cutlery away. "Get ready," he said. "Shift's in forty-five seconds."

"Right."

I parked my butt in a booth, wrapping my legs around the table support. The shift was simply the interspatial move of this restaurant-vessel from one quadrant of space to another. I had no idea why it happened, and neither did Nerfer. It simply did. After my father had died, the shifts had begun.

And when we shifted, talk about massive! The energy of the movement flung us far and wide, and if I weren't sitting down, I'd end up on my back or head at the far point of any room I was in.

Good thing we had our interstellar computer. It held all the information on the various galaxies we'd visited thus far. Our ship had no weapons, but it had powerful sensors that could map out any planet's dimensions and details almost instantaneously, and while it couldn't tell us about the inhabitants' culture, it gave the basics on what to expect. It could also translate any language instantly.

Still, face-to-face communication had to be done, and in my almost two years on this interstellar barge — a flying brick that was one-hundred-twenty meters in length by seventy-five meters in width—I'd seen sludge, rock-people, lizards and other life forms that were too difficult to describe. I'd spoken with them all, and it was interesting to learn their ways. But I still missed Earth.

Nerfer's race—so he said—could learn languages much faster than humans could, within a couple of hours. Very useful for him…

"One," the computer said, bringing me back to reality.

Then it came, that great heave from here to wherever. I kept my head down on the table and waited it out. "Hey, Nerfer, how are you doing?"

"Still in one piece."

When we stopped shaking, I asked the computer for more information.

"We are currently in the Madlia Galaxy," it said in its tinny voice. "Scanning. We are orbiting a planet known as Rattan One."

"Display information on the planet."

Whir...click. "Displayed."

A hologram popped up with the pertinent information. The planet was similar in size to Earth, with approximately fifty percent of its surface covered by water. Oxygen-nitrogen atmosphere, suitable for breathing. Rich vegetation.

As for the people, they were around two meters in height, slender yet muscular, with oversized hands and feet. Hairy all over, they resembled the cavemen on Earth that I'd studied when I had been younger. Two mouths, one on top of the other. Tiny ears. A slit for a nose. Gray-skinned. In a word, ugly. I wondered if they were warlike and if our entrance into space would provoke them...

"Unidentified vessel, respond."

The crackling of the interstellar com-link and the voice — deep, raspy, and unfriendly — made me jump. "This is *Port Anywhere*," I answered.

"What is the nature of your vessel and your visit?"

"We're a, uh, a restaurant ship. My name's Rick Granger, and I'm in charge of—"

"You are in orbit around our planet. We have the right to inspect any alien spacecraft or repel it if we wish."

Jerk. If I'd had a space cannon, I would have decimated that slime, but we had nothing to defend ourselves with. "Understood," I answered, striving to enhance my inner calm. "I'll send the coordinates for our docking site."

"Does your ship not have a landing bay?"

It did, but it had only enough room for one of our ships, a reconnaissance vessel. "We do, but it's probably too small to accommodate one of your ships."

Silence...then, "Very well. Send your coordinates."

The voice cut out, and I dutifully sent the coordinates to our—*ahem*—hosts. Nerfer was hard to read, mainly because he didn't often form expressions. He invariably relied on his voice to make his thoughts and intentions known, but now, his mushiness formed itself into a frown and his voice was full of grave misgivings.

"Rattanians don't take no for an answer. Deal fairly with them and they'll be nice, but if you cross them in a deal, then you won't be worth *vellora* spit."

In space, vellora were akin to maggots, the lowest of the low. "I'll be careful."

He bobbed back and forth. "Good. Did they tell you what they wanted to eat?"

"No, they only wanted to look around." That was what bothered me.

Nerfer grunted. "Fine, they can look around, for all I care."

Yeah, that reminded me. "How do you know everyone, Nerfer? You never told me, and you've been in charge here for six months."

His frown deepened. "My world no longer exists," he said after a time. "A plague hit us. It broke down our cellular matrixes."

"Which means...what?"

"It means we dissolved into organic ooze. There is no treatment, no cure."

Geez, no wonder he was impatient and angry much of the time. Even though I hadn't seen Earth since I'd been just past fifteen, at least I had a home. He didn't. Nerfer continued in a voice devoid of self-pity.

"I got out, just in time. After that, I became a courier. I delivered goods and sometimes arms to other worlds. Had my own ship, did well, but then I pissed off a warlord and he blew my ship out. I managed to make it here, and..."

The com-link crackled. "Alien vessel, this is Commander Kulida, leader of the Rattanian space forces. We are nearing your space dock."

Nerfer shut down his bio, formed a finger and punched the intercom-link button. "Understood. Our representative will meet you at the airlock. You are welcome here."

He clicked off, and had he had eyes, he probably would have rolled them. Instead, he only muttered, "Welcome like hell. I don't like this one bit. Kid, you be careful."

Kid, it was always 'kid'. I'd turned seventeen about a month before, and he still thought of me as an infant. It was enough to make me scream in frustration.

A few seconds later, a dull thud signaled that Kulida's ship had docked with ours. I ran to the airlock and punched in the command for the airlock doors on the visitor's side to open. Three tall beings wearing gray containment suits entered. Two of them carried a large metal crate. They looked around the eight-by-eight-meter room with interest.

There wasn't much there, only the walls and some *shodokutan* lights which used concentrated light to destroy any possible pathogens from alien races. I pressed the button to start the decontamination process. Their world may have been similar to Earth, but pathogens were pathogens.

"Activating decontamination procedures, Captain Kulida," I said. "Just a few seconds."

"Acknowledged," he responded.

After ten seconds, the process finished, and the readout showed no pathogens. I opened the door to my side, and three massive men stepped out. "Thank you for allowing us aboard your vessel," said the person who didn't have his hands on the crate.

He took off his helmet to reveal a gray skull of a head with deep-set black eyes and a visage so gaunt that it appeared that he was suffering from malnutrition. Perhaps everyone on his world looked like that.

With a sniff, he examined the ceiling of the hallway then turned his gaze upon me, as though he were viewing a particularly ugly species of insect. "I am Commander Kulida. I come bearing cargo. We need to talk."

Chapter Two

Left Behind

Up close, Kulida presented an ugly package. Clad in a spacesuit that matched his skin color, his face was pockmarked with scar tissue and pitted with craters. Maybe he'd had acne, if his race suffered from that adolescent affliction.

As for the scars, he'd probably been on the losing end of a few fights, but that was only a guess. If he shaved, I'd have classified him as not being able to use a razor correctly, but that didn't matter.

"You are the captain of this vessel?"

His voice, harsh and raspy, with a challenging tone, grated on my eardrums. He was pissed off about something, but what? "I'm one of the captains."

Eyebrows that looked plucked right down to their roots arched high upon his forehead. "You speak our language?"

I pointed to the back of my head. "No, I have a universal translator implanted. It works on interpreting brainwaves."

His look of surprise disappeared, and he tapped a blue band on his left wrist. "This is our version of a translator. No matter. We can communicate. What is your name again?"

"Rick Granger. Nerfer is the other captain."

A look of incomprehension flickered in his eyes. "What manner of creature is that? For that matter, of what race are you?"

What an arrogant SOB. His superiority complex reeked. Oh, wait, it was the stench that came from him, a smell that combined a hundred waste disposal pits with the stink of rotting food being slowly roasted over an open fire. My nose hairs wilted, but I consoled myself with the fact that they'd grow back...probably.

"I'm human. I'm from Earth, if you want to get technical. Nerfer is a Gliddod."

Kulida grunted and waved his two subordinates over. They were just about as large as he was and even uglier, if that were possible. With great ease, they carried their crate past me but then paused and one of them asked, "Where is your cargo hold?"

'Asked' wasn't quite the right word. 'Demanded' fit better. Politeness clearly didn't factor into their vocabulary. "What are you carrying?" I asked.

He glanced at his commander. It must have come as a surprise to him that someone smaller and less powerful talked back. "I do not see that question as being worthy of an answer."

Oh, it was more than worthy, and what was his problem? I wheeled around to stare him down. Big deal—this guy could have kicked my head in without breaking a sweat. But pile of junk or not, this was *my* ship. Nerfer may have been nominally in charge, but my father had re-outfitted this ship, and by rights, it had become mine.

Furthermore, I'd be damned if anyone would walk in and claim dominion. "Oh, really? You're a visitor, mister. Maybe that's your space outside, but inside, this is *my* space. We have to guard against pathogens, got it?"

While they'd already gone through the decontamination process, this was a matter of principle. Our war of the eyes continued, then Kulida interceded, waving his man back and addressing me in a slightly friendlier tone. "My apologies. It is cargo. It contains items that we use to trade with other worlds — machine parts, amplification jewels...things you need not concern yourself over."

Uh-huh. Half of me wanted to tell this Rattanian to get off my ship, but the other half said to wait, mainly because there were three of them and they were armed. I wasn't. Still, I balked. "Why do you have to store it here?"

One of the men grunted with displeasure. "Boy, you are in no position to —"

"Hold your tongues, Saddel," Kulida cut in. "I am in command, and it is you who is in no position to demand anything. Frandil, you as well."

The one called Saddel glared at me, but he bowed his head and backed off. Frandil, the third man in the party and the smallest of the trio, comparatively speaking, also nodded. He hadn't said a word thus far, but clearly, he knew where the chain of command started and where it ended.

Kulida swung back to me with an absurdly pleasant smile on his lower mouth, a total contrast to the permanent snarly ugliness of the upper one. "Once again, you have my apologies. My men are, er...overzealous. We are not a particularly patient race. We have much to learn from other cultures."

That sounded better. "The hold is this way," I said, jerking my thumb behind me.

It paid to be polite, and now that I knew what they were carrying—sort of—my curiosity grew. Kulida clapped his hands once and his men proceeded to heft their cargo and follow me to storage room number one. We had nine on the ship. It wasn't an overly large room, some twenty by thirty square meters.

We held certain foodstuffs there, memorabilia of my parents, old clothes that I'd never gotten rid of and many replacement parts for the ship, along with the two battle droids I used to train against.

Huey and Dewey stood silently next to each other at the far wall, two-meter machines waiting to for someone to reactivate them. They'd been in storage since my father had died. I didn't see the need for them anymore, but I couldn't just eject them into the void. In a way, they were family, voice-activated members of the Granger clan.

I found an empty space and Kulida's men gently placed the crate there. "Thank you," Kulida said as we exited the room and the door shut behind us. I gestured for them to follow me.

As we walked, the Rattanian commander said, "We are, er…attempting to make a deal with another group of traders. The deal concerns the cargo we have brought with us. We were discussing the matter with the traders when your ship entered our space. At first, we thought you a hostile force, hence our overly cautious and somewhat ignorant response."

"Um, I'm going to assume your ship has sensors. If you do, then you'll find out this ship isn't armed."

He nodded. "We are aware of that. Our first act upon spotting your vessel was to scan it. It is true what you say. That is why we contacted you. We were hoping to make this a neutral venue, a place in which to conduct our business. Naturally, we will pay you for your time and effort."

Hmmm...thinking it over, it wasn't a bad idea. A little extra money or jewels that could be traded for gold or platinum or some precious metal would be welcome. They could conduct their affairs, I'd serve up a meal, then they'd leave and everyone would be happy. "I think you could talk business over lunch."

By now, we'd reached the restaurant-slash-bridge, and I was beginning to believe Kulida — sort of. He offered another disarming smile from his lower mouth. "I will contact them."

Another clap of his hands summoned his subordinates, and after they huddled up to confer with one another, the two lower-ranked men hustled off to make a call through a small, wafer-thin device that Saddel carried.

The commander turned first to observe Nerfer, who stood at the grill. Not one muscle twitched in Kulida's face. He then shifted his gaze to the inky darkness that lay beyond the shatterproof glass, and he nodded at the sight. "This place offers a most marvelous view. I think your patrons would be most pleased to dine in such a fine establishment."

For a tough guy, he had a certain way of ingratiating himself. Compliments always worked. Being honest about it all, I was rather proud of the viewing area myself. I'd helped my father build it, and it did offer a clear, panoramic view of space. "Thank you, sir. It's, uh, one of the selling points of this place."

"Then I shall hope that the food complements the view."

At that point, the interstellar com-link crackled, so I excused myself to answer it. "*Port Anywhere*, Captain Granger speaking."

That got a laugh from Nerfer, and the snickering continued as he fired up the grill. *Smartass.*

"This is Captain Cradd of the vessel Nujiri. I understand that a Commander Kulida may be present."

A glance at the commander showed him nodding, and he waved his hand as if to say go ahead. "Uh, yes, he's here, and he says he'd like to discuss business with you."

"We shall be there shortly."

With that, the com-link went silent. A few seconds later, the air shimmered and three large yak-like men stepped through a portal. Roughly the same height and breadth as the Rattanians, they had long and straggly dark hair, swarthy features and they wore animal skins.

Moreover, they smelled just as bad as Kulida and company did. Even Nerfer's body wrinkled at the unpleasant aroma. Good thing this room was well-ventilated, because my nose was getting the olfactory beating of the millennia.

"I am Captain Cradd," the largest of the three yak-men said, then he turned to regard Kulida. "Ah, our trading partner! Let us talk."

Kulida nodded. "Over a meal."

That was my cue, and I went to help my boss prepare things. "Act normal," he whispered. "We'll talk after they leave."

Act normal? What was he talking about?

Nerfer didn't offer me an answer but instead raised his voice. "Gentlemen, what can we get you?"

Kulida conferred with his men as they sidled over to a nearby booth. "Whatever you wish to prepare for us," he answered. "We are a most adaptable people."

Cradd echoed his sentiments. Fine, they'd get burgers and fries. I set about working the grill while

Nerfer took out a package of frozen French fries from our syntha-fridge and got the oil hot and boiling.

Soon, the smell of grilled meat and deep-fried potatoes filled the air. While keeping an eye on the meat grilling, I sliced the onions and tomatoes, chopped the lettuce and got the condiments ready.

"A most unusual, though pleasing smell," Kulida called out. "I approve."

Glad you do. "This is called hamburgers and fries," I said after I'd put everything together on plates and carried the food over to his table on a massive tray.

Everyone eyed the food with apparent hunger. I carefully served each man, but no one touched the eats. Kulida's men waited for his orders. "Eat up," I urged. "Trust me. It's good."

Kulida was the first to sample things. He picked up his hamburger, sniffed it and proceeded to inhale the concoction of meat, bun, sauce, lettuce and tomato in one massive bite from his upper mouth.

Call that a major *ick* moment. The upper mouth did the eating, while the lower one did the talking. I was not interested at all in how they processed their meals.

His men did the same thing with their food, and the yak-guys dug into their meals, masticating them with obvious relish. "That…was most palatable," Kulida said with satisfaction as the last bit of bun went in. "Another!"

Five more plates got prepared, then ten more. As they feasted, terms of payment along with some mild disagreements filled the air. Those mild disagreements soon segued into a few shoves between the two parties. That is, Kulida and Cradd sat back and watched while their men got more physical.

"Well, that escalated quickly," I murmured to Nerfer as the pushing-shoving match continued and the voices grew more heated. I just hoped they wouldn't smash up the place.

"Do nothing," he counseled, laying a pseudopod on my arm to keep me from inserting myself into the mounting argument. "The Rattanians and the Yeltens, they're rivals, but this is the way they do business. Under their laws, if you interfere, they've got every right to kill you."

"Their laws?" What was he talking about? That was total garbage.

A face formed on his mushy body, and the expression held concern. "Yeah. This is their space, their negotiations and their laws—and they're armed. Don't forget that."

More yelling came from the negotiators, then, just as quickly as it had started, it ended with Kulida slamming his open palm on the table, making the plates and utensils dance. "We agree!"

Cradd and his men relaxed. All was forgotten, and a general air of bonhomie reigned with the men complimenting the opposite side on their ways of doing business and their overall manliness.

Manliness was a totally overrated factor here. Acting like a tough guy was just as likely to get a person killed as win them a fight. I'd met several aliens in the past while my father and mother had been around, and while some acted aggressively, there was always someone bigger, stronger, meaner or better armed. Space was the ultimate equalizer. Shove a person into an airlock, suck out the air and their toughness soon melted away.

A buzz came from somewhere on Kulida. He fished around in his suit and pulled out another wafer-thin device. "Speak," he said into it.

A deep voice babbled something on the other end of the line, and I caught the words of, "Your presence is needed, sir."

Kulida acknowledged the request, then he shut his communicator and put it away. With a bow, he excused himself from his comrades and walked over to me. "A most pleasant meal, Captain Granger. However, I have just learned that there is something amiss with my ship. My men and I must take leave of your vessel for a short time while we attend to the problem. We shall entrust you with the cargo."

Nerfer oozed his way in our direction. "Commander, we're not in the habit of holding cargo. That's not the purpose here—"

"We understand."

Kulida clapped his hands twice. Frandil pulled out a green card from his pocket and handed it to his commander, who in turn handed it to me. "What is this?" I asked, looking at the card. It had the image of a rat-cat mix on both sides.

"Payment," replied the commander. "This card is a sign of our people. Our world is, by its nature, a war world, but we are also traders. We are tough but fair in negotiations. We are also merciless toward our enemies. Think of that card as protection against anyone who would think of doing you harm."

For me, it came off as a bogus answer, but Nerfer stepped in and formed a smile on his jelly-like face. "That's very generous of you. We'll honor this card, and we'll make sure your cargo is safe."

Kulida nodded. "We will leave this ship, but our party as well as the Yelten party shall return within a few minutes to take back that which we have stored with you."

It sounded good, but then I thought about the shift. "Uh, sir, there's something you should know. This ship tends to shift — to move through space — at the weirdest moments. I can't figure out why, and Nerfer doesn't know, either."

For that comment, I got a blank stare. "Then I shall hope you learn how to control it. This is your vessel, is it not?"

Kulida had a point. "Yes, sir, but if we shift, we don't know where we're going to end up. That's my point."

The commander didn't bat an eye. "Understood. We will be finished shortly."

Well, that was that. He didn't seem overly concerned with the cargo, and as for the card, what the hell kind of payment was that? In the past, on the rare occasions we'd gone to Class M planets, we'd traded for goods with the inhabitants or with other visitors who'd stopped by, but that card? It was worse than useless.

While I was mulling over the unfairness of serving guests and waiting on tables, Cradd also complimented me on the meal, then he and his men beamed out. I took Kulida and his men to the airlock. They left without saying another word.

All right, now that our official business was over, I needed details. Back at the restaurant, Nerfer was in the process of scrubbing the griddle, and as he scrubbed, he said, "Kid, I don't know about Cradd and his men. They're junkers, from what I figure. They find stuff wherever they can and sell it, and junkers to me are scum.

"As for those Rattanians, what I said before goes. Do business with them fairly and they'll act nice, but just 'cuz they gave you their protection card don't mean they're gonna protect you. And by that, I mean they'll shoot anyone who wants to kill you first, but then your ass is theirs, if you get my interstellar drift."

Yeah, that part came through clearly. "So, is that why you hate them?"

"Hate's too mild a word," he replied while scratching off a particularly tough piece of gristle and tossing it into the trash.

He stepped back to survey his work. I waited for an explanation, and sure enough, it came. "I already told you about my world being gone, right?"

"Yeah, you did."

Sadness entered his voice. "Yeah, well, imagine losing everyone who meant everything to you. You lost your parents. That's tough. I lost my family, my friends *and* my planet.

"So, after that, I drifted around from place to place. Got a job as a courier, and sometimes, the people I worked for traded with them Rattanians, a bad-tempered, mean lot. Their word is about as good as a used tissue, if you know what I mean."

"They're not going to kill us, are they?"

Oh, that sounded brave...not. Nerfer shifted his body side to side, which indicated that he was thinking of something. "They never kill without a reason. They're what you call justifiable killers. Give 'em a reason, and they'll atomize you."

Wonderful, killers with warped ethics — that's what we had to contend with. Nerfer finished cleaning the griddle, and at that point, a shockwave hit us. "Hey, was that the shift?" I asked.

Nerfer oozed his way over to the captain's chair and punched a button on the console. "Scanning... No. Look!"

A pseudopod formed from his body and pointed at the viewing screen. Sure enough, Kulida's ship was

firing bolts of energy at another squat-looking vessel—
Cradd's ship. So much for the business deal—this was
trouble.

Cradd returned fire, and just as it appeared as
though they'd reached a stalemate, a brilliant flash of
light lit up the inkiness of the heavens that practically
blinded me. When the flash disappeared, only Kulida's
ship remained. Pirate... He was nothing more than a
pirate. Oh, wait! He was a murderer as well.

Another shockwave hit. "What is that?" I asked.
"Them?"

Nerfer wiggled his body from side to side, and a
note of alarm sounded in his voice. "Shift. It's
happening faster than usual. This computer's gone
haywire. Better call Kulida so he can get his cargo out
of here."

A third jolt hit, and I made a beeline for the
interstellar radio and tried to signal Kulida on his
frequency. "Commander, this is Rick Granger. Can you
hear me?"

"Acknowledged," he replied. "What is happening to
your vessel? It is vibrating."

What did he think was happening? "That's what
happens when we shift. It's happening earlier than
expected. What went on out there?"

Silence, then he answered in an incongruously
happy voice. "There was a disagreement between me
and the commander of the Yelten forces. The man you
spoke to—Cradd—was most disagreeable."

Most disagreeable? He'd just gotten blown out of the
sky...

"Hey, kid..." Nerfer called out, but a massive
shockwave hit that tossed me away from the console
and onto my butt four meters away.

Bruised and embarrassed about not being ready, I made my way back to the com-link and tried signaling Kulida. At first, his voice sounded faint — then angry. "Captain Granger, our cargo...current position...find you..."

Static interrupted the conversation. I tried again on a different frequency — no luck. I still got static. "Hey, can you hear me? Sir? Is anyone there?"

Another lurch sent me flying — again. It also must have dislodged an electrical wire or six at the grill as sparks flew then a small fire started. "On it!" Nerfer called out.

Pseudopods shot from his body to a shelf overhead where we kept a portable fire extinguisher, a small pistol that shot out a blue gel in a wide, watery net. Said net could douse any blaze around.

Back at the com-link, static dominated. In a sudden fury, I slammed the button, shutting it off. A third lurch from the ship tossed me on my face. Nerfer had already put out the fire, but the movement caught him off-guard and sent him into the far wall. His containment suit tore, and he slid down, muttering, "That wasn't nice."

With a series of ear-splitting curses, he began the process of picking himself up — all the pieces spattered by the force of the ship being slammed backward, sideways then forward — and putting them back into his body. "I'm going to need a new containment suit," he remarked after he'd calmed down.

I looked at the spots on the floor where bits and pieces of his body remained, along with scraps of food. "I'm not cleaning that up."

A sour look formed on the area where his face should have been. "Fine. I'll do it."

Nerfer grunted and inhaled deeply. As the stray parts flowed into his body, I checked out the computer. "This shouldn't have happened."

"Tell me about it."

Humor was something I didn't need at that moment. In fact, all I needed to know was where we were, but the computer had decided to take a vacation. No matter what I did, nothing worked. It remained an uncommunicative hunk of metal and wire. Nerfer finished re-forming and called out, "I'll fix it. Let me get myself back together first."

He oozed his way into the storage room, and I heard grunts as well as a sloshing sound as he poured his essence into a new suit. While he did so, I looked out through the view screen, trying to place the stars. Nothing made sense, as I couldn't decipher any pattern. Nothing! Frustration hit hard.

"I have zero idea where we are," I called out. "We've never had that big a shift before. It must have thrown us clear across the galaxy."

A grunt came from him, signaling his return. A sigh followed the grunt, and it sounded like a bubble popping underwater. "There's always a first time for everything. Hey, kid, they brought something with them, right?"

Oh. "Yeah, the crate."

It must have been valuable, and Kulida and his gang would not be happy that we'd suddenly disappeared with it, even though it hadn't been our fault.

Nerfer waved a pseudopod in my direction and bent over to eye a space near the refrigerator for a repair kit we had. "You check out our cargo. Once I get the computer up and running again, I'll find out where we are. This is a region of space I don't recognize, and I've been pretty much everywhere."

By your command. I ran to the cargo hold. Every item on the shelves had been tossed hither and yon, and I spent the next twenty minutes cleaning things up and making the room clear to walk around in.

The crate came next. Upon further examination, it resembled a cage more than anything else. Rustling sounds came from inside. Animal? Vegetable? Mineral? I'd heard all three types speak before. Every single galaxy had its own forms of life that simply didn't correspond to anything remotely human, so, *"Let's hear it for diversity,"* as someone once said.

Cautiously, I crept closer and peeked inside. Something green and humanoid was in there. It was moving around…a person…a woman? It was dark, but I made out a slender figure with small, shell-shaped ears, green skin, long, raven-black hair, orange eyes — and were those fangs I saw?

They were.

In a lunge that was almost too quick for me to follow, the she-creature hit the bars and tried to get through them. Failing to do so, she hissed at me. In a lightning-fast move, she thrust her hands through the opening in the bars, and they had claws three centimeters in length, which looked capable of tearing through just about anything.

Immediately, I backed off and raised my hands. "Hey, I'm not going to hurt you."

The hissing continued then segued into a low growl. If that didn't indicate anger and a desire to maim, then I didn't know what did. "Look… Can you understand what I'm saying? Can you talk? Give me a sign or something."

No signs — I got only hissing sounds combined with mutters of what had to be hatred. Still, whoever or whatever was inside withdrew her hands. But those sounds of supreme anger continued, and that made me back off to reassess what was going on.

Reassessment meant kicking myself mentally for committing such a boneheaded mistake in allowing Kulida to come aboard. I should have tossed his smelly butt off as soon as he'd come through the airlock—but I hadn't.

And it wasn't because I hadn't gotten a bad feeling from Kulida. I had. My late father had once told me that captains had to run with their feelings at times, whether it was to inspect a new world, take on a guest or try a new kind of food without any knowledge of what it could do a person's body.

Some captain I was. This was my ship and I'd buggered things up by not listening to my instincts. Still, at the time, where we'd been half an hour ago—that was Kulida's section of space.

However, even if he'd had the right to come aboard, and even though he and his men had been armed, they'd lied to me and Nerfer. He'd destroyed another vessel as easily as someone would crush an insect under their boot, and we'd just taken aboard a person who was about to be traded for money, jewels or something else. Kulida and his gang would undoubtedly come looking for her.

All that spelled trouble.

We now housed an interstellar refugee. Some days, it simply wasn't worth meeting the scum of the universe.

Chapter Three

First Contact

Back at the bridge, Nerfer had already gotten into a new containment suit. He sat in the captain's chair without acknowledging my existence, his gaze fixed on the sea of stars ahead of us. He must have known I was there as I cleared my throat twice.

Finally, after I gave my third phlegm-inducing growl, he turned around with a disappointed expression on his jelly-like face. His me-time had been interrupted. "What is it, Rick?"

"We've got trouble."

He swung back to stare out at the inky blackness in front of us that seemed to stretch on forever. It probably did, and I wondered if the universe was truly infinite. If not, what was at the end? Did it somehow recycle itself and send any new arrivals in the opposite direction? No one knew, no computer knew and chances were, I'd never discover it. "What kind of trouble? Something I'll have to clean up later?"

Oh, right, what to say that wouldn't piss him off and ruin his day? "Uh, not really, no. It's, uh, more important than that. Life-altering…mission-altering, in fact."

At that comment, he swiveled around to nail me with a glare. "You know, Rick, when your father let me stay on, he said you could be a little vague at times. Just say what's on your mind, will you?"

Fine, be direct. "Kulida and his buddies brought a green-skinned alien on as cargo."

A surprised expression formed on his body. "At least you got right to the point. Let's go see."

In the hold, our passenger's mood hadn't improved. Once Nerfer got within range of the bars, she shot out a hand to rake his face with her claws. Her gesture was accompanied by that familiar hiss of rage. He pulled back, just in time. "Well, she's not being overly friendly, that's for sure."

Yeah, that was obvious. The women continued to hiss, and her orange eyes narrowed with extreme fury. Nerfer cocked his head to one side. "Think she understands us?"

Why was he asking me? "I tried talking to her before, but she just hissed at me. Maybe she's part snake."

I remembered studying that kind of reptile on Earth, its movements and sounds, even though it was on the endangered species list. Nerfer grunted again and gestured at the cage. "Maybe she's hungry."

Fine, she might be hungry. She could act more pleasantly, though. "I'll make her something to eat."

Sandwiches and a glass of milk seemed best. Granted, it was simple, but considering our new houseguest wasn't being overly communicative, I had to go with something basic. Tuna salad sandwiches were basic. Hopefully, she wasn't allergic.

Back at the restaurant, I prepared things accordingly and brought the food to the cargo hold, placing it within reach of the cage door. Another hiss greeted me. Wonderful—our relationship was moving along swimmingly. "I hope you like fish."

A couple of hours later, I returned to the hold and found that my carefully prepared meal now decorated the walls and the floor. With a sigh, I grabbed a rag from one of the shelves, cleaned up the mess then went back to the bridge. Nerfer's first comment was, "Finicky eater?"

"Very funny." I went to the sink to wash out the rag and the dish and dumped the remains of the shattered glass in the garbage. "Maybe she's allergic to tuna."

"Try eggs. They're pretty bland."

Eggs it would be, but if she tossed them away, the smell would linger. "I don't suppose you've got any advice?"

Nerfer blew out a deep breath. "Rick, try seeing it from her point of view. Let's say she doesn't understand you. She's been kidnapped from her world, brought here as cargo—slave bait, more than likely—so no wonder she's going to lash out. We'd probably do the same thing. I know I would."

Yes, that made sense. "Now, let's say she does understand what you're saying," he continued. "She may be testing you to see if she can trust you. Go with it."

His was a voice of reason, and it made me realize that my attitude also needed an adjustment. Trust was a five-letter word that stood for belief, a six-letter word. I'd been burned before in terms of relationships. Back home, I'd been friendly with one of the other boys in my neighborhood, a guy named Todd Carthage.

I'd been living in Salt Lake City at the time. I'd been born in Chicago, but my family had moved all over the country from the time I was little, due to the demands of my parents' jobs. We'd never stayed in any one place for more than a year or two. Never enough time to make good friends. No roots. Impermanence had ruled.

Anyway, with Todd, from day one, I'd recognized that he had the gift of gab. Short and stocky, he'd had absurdly small features, totally out of proportion to the rest of his body. But it hadn't been his looks that had gotten people interested in him. It was his personality, one that lulled others into a sense of security.

However, over time, I'd come to understand that it had been a false sense of security and that he hadn't been after friendship.

No, in his case, he'd always wanted something. An electronic book reader, an information disc, food — anything he could talk someone out of, he would do it. He'd done that to me — once — and it had led to the breakup of our friendship.

It hadn't been over an info disc, either. It had been over a girl we'd both liked. Her name was Sarah. From what she'd told me, he'd gone up to her and told her that I'd said it was okay if she dated around. *Say what?*

Naturally, she'd come to me, all upset at what he'd said. *"Is that true, Rick?"*

Anger had hit me like a solar storm hitting a small planet. *"No, it's not. I'll settle this."*

Confronting Todd with his BS had been easy enough. I'd thought that getting him to admit it would be difficult. Oddly enough, though, he'd owned up to it right away and acted like it was no big deal. *"Yeah, I thought it was worthwhile."*

"Why'd you do it?" I had been mad enough to punch him in his tiny nose.

"Because I could," he'd replied with a smile. *"That's why."*

His smile had disappeared in a shower of red after I'd punched him in his mouth. So had three of his teeth vanished. A follow-up punch had crushed his nose. He hadn't fought back. He couldn't, and even after a few of the kids had come around to pull me off him, even after they'd said it was a silly, juvenile thing to do, it hadn't mattered.

And I'd never regretted it.

Shortly afterward, my parents had taken me along on their journey and all contact with my old life had been broken, but the sense of being betrayed had remained. Now, I was being asked to put my trust in an alien who could tear my face off.

Mentally heaving a sigh, I prepared more sandwiches and returned to the storage area. I carefully placed the plate down and said in the most cheerful voice I could muster, "Hi. Uh, my name's Richard. You can call me Rick. I made you these. They're called egg sandwiches. I hope you like them. We're not slavers out to sell you. Those other guys? They wanted to. We're not like that."

It sounded hollow, and why would she believe me? Still, there was hope, and sometimes, hope was all a person had. I left her, then, and when I returned an hour later, the plate was empty. Not a crumb remained.

"Well, glad you liked it," I muttered as I took the plate away.

Before I could pull it out of range, though, her hand shot out from the cage to encircle my wrist. Seven fingers, all long and tapered, held me in a vise-like grasp. For a moment I was scared, but then I realized that if she'd wanted to hurt me, she would have used her claws. She didn't.

"Uh, I don't suppose you could let me go. I don't have a key."

Immediately, she released me. All right, she understood, and what was more, she could reason. As I turned to go, a voice, high-pitched and feminine, said, "I am sorry for how I acted before."

Lo and behold, there shall be communication! I swung around to find her gazing at me through the bars. She wore a curious expression. "Of what race are you?"

"I'm human—from Earth. Listen… If you want out, then relax. I'm not the one who put you in there, all right?"

Quiet reigned, and the person regarded me with a calm air. "I understand. I do not know of your world, and I am sorry for how I reacted before. You must have thought of me as a beast. I thought you were with them, and I was not sure if I could trust you. I have never seen your type before."

Call that a given. Nerfer was right about the trust thing, and when the girl mentioned 'them' she'd meant our gray-skinned visitors. "You mean, Kulida and his men?"

"Yes."

Anger and loathing entered her voice. "They brought me out here as…as a kind of bargaining chip. They were going to hand me over to those hairy beasts, and I did not want that."

Oh. Slavers, interstellar procurers—they sold flesh as well as material goods. *Sick bastards.*

The person then asked, "How is it that I can understand you?"

"I have an interstellar translator in my head." I turned around to show her the position of the translator, even though it was too small to see. "It makes it easy for me to download your language. It also translates my language to yours."

"Yes, that is convenient," she replied. "My people, we have something similar implanted in our wrists. Many years ago, when our people first reached out to the stars, our scientists invented such a device so that we could communicate with others who came from different worlds. All our people have such a device within them."

She then added with a touch of impatience, "Please, can you get me out of here? I have to relieve myself. Our species is capable of holding in our waste products for a long period of time, but now, I must go, and I do not have any clothes to wear. They took mine and threw me in here before they set out to sell me."

Oh—again. I risked a look and found a female form staring back at me through placid orange eyes. Even though she hadn't hurt me before, the fact that she had fangs, claws and was semi-feral made me cautious.

She'd said that she was a slave. "If I let you out, you're not going to slash me or anything, right?"

An expression—a mix of petulance, impatience and resignation—flitted across her face. Still, her fangs had disappeared. She'd also retracted her claws. "No, I am not going to kill you. You must trust me."

Decision time—and I went with my gut feeling. "Okay, hang on a second."

I searched around for something to open the cage door with and hoped it wouldn't be the last thing I ever did.

Chapter Four

Strange Cargo

"Do you have a name?" I asked.

"Merlynni," she said softly. "I am from Kagekia. Our people have only one name. That is mine. It means 'she-who-is-different'. Does your name carry any meaning?"

Her name came out as Mer-lin-nai, with the accent on the last syllable. She spoke very formally, not unlike Kulida and his men, although she was probably more intelligent, as well as more decent.

Oh, answer the question. "Uh, it means 'a strong and brave leader'."

Truthfully, I was neither of those, although I'd never been in a situation where I'd had to demonstrate those qualities. Merlynni simply nodded her head. "I see."

Now I knew how to pronounce her name, but as for her home world, I had no idea where that was. The universe was infinite, and there were a lot of star systems out there that hadn't been explored. There were far more that I'd never been to. While I turned the name over my lips, she tapped the bar with her knuckles, bringing me back to reality. "Please, hurry. I really must go."

"Hang on."

The lock was like a Mechani-Fast, an army-made and industrial-strength type of lock used on containers that held hazardous materials. Locks such as those needed a code to get them open.

I had no such code available and was doubtful that Kulida would call and tell me. I did the search-the-shelf thing, found a small hand-laser then hustled back to the cage. "Move. I have to burn the lock off."

Merlynni shied back as I flicked on the laser and sliced the lock apart. "Okay, it's open."

She emerged and stood, shaking out her arms and legs and shifting from side to side, along with squeezing her thighs together. A bit taller than me, she had a lithe, toned body. Humanoid, she was humanoid—and naked, with emerald-green skin.

Considering she'd been cooped up for what had to be at least a few days, I expected her to stink. She didn't. As for the rest of her, I couldn't help but stare. Her torso from the breasts down to her waist was translucent, and her organs showed, but they didn't appear like a human's organs would.

Rather, they appeared more like planets and stars, mainly because the inner part of her stomach sparkled. It made for an interesting effect, and embarrassed though I was, I couldn't tear my eyes away. That, and the fact she had three belly buttons, artfully arranged in a vertical row.

"Bathroom," she said, not attempting to hide her form. "Show me. Oh, and clothes, please."

Totally flustered by now, I covered my eyes with one hand and pointed to the washroom door that was seven meters away with the other. "Over there. The brown door. You go. Uh, there's a toilet...I, uh, I guess that you know how to use—"

"I will figure it out!"

Immediately, she tore past me. While she was gone, I hunted around and found some of my old clothes—T-shirts, jeans and an old white jumpsuit that I'd never worn—stored here. Would those clothes fit her? We were roughly the same height, although her build was different...

"I have returned," a voice said from behind me.

Holy crap, that made me jump. She'd walked up so silently that I hadn't heard her. I tossed the jumpsuit over my shoulder. "I think this should fit you."

The rustle of the fabric as she got into it broke the silence, and a moment later, she said, "You may look. I understood how to use the flushing mechanism, and I am now dressed. I washed as well, although I would like to use a proper cleaning device later on, if that is possible."

After I turned around, a rather pretty picture greeted me. She'd tied her hair into a neatly done ponytail that hung halfway down her back. Her skin color made for a nice contrast against the suit's plain white background. It seemed to be a little tight across her chest and hips, but then I reminded myself that she was a guest and not a holo-pic of the women I'd been interested in...

"Your eyes are sticking out," she observed. "Is that normal for your race?"

"What?"

She affected a bug-eyed look, which was both amusing as well as embarrassing, and I had the sneaking suspicion she meant me. "That is how your expression is right now."

Yup, suspicion — confirmed.

"I do not know if it indicates surprise or some illness," she continued. "Are you unwell, by any chance?"

"No."

"Then please do not stare. It makes me uncomfortable."

"Oh."

Call that a major burn. One person's simple glance turned out to be another person's way of staring. In other words, I'd been rude. A burst of heat swept through me. Then, again, since I'd been on this ship, I hadn't met another girl my age, although it was hard to tell how old Merlynni really was. I'd had a girlfriend once, but that had been two years and a lifetime ago.

Now, I was face to face with someone who went beyond attractive, and I was acting like a lovesick fool. What could I say that wouldn't offend her? Probably nothing. People often got offended over perceived insults. They'd had what was called the 'Politically Correct' movement about a hundred-and-twenty years ago.

People were people, though — human. Merlynni was humanoid, but not human, even though that didn't matter to me. I'd always been raised to tell the truth, so…tell it. "Uh, well, I'm human, and you're pretty," I answered. "Sorry for staring."

A tiny smile emerged. "I have not met a human before. We sort of resemble each other, except for the skin."

"You have fangs. You also have claws like a cat — not that there's anything wrong with that," I added hastily then immediately kicked myself upstairs for mentioning her resemblance to an animal. Did she really need to hear that?

Merlynni briefly examined her fingernails. "A cat? I do not know that thing. Is it an animal?"

"Yeah, we keep them as pets. They're small and furry, but they've got sharp teeth and claws…"

I stopped speaking then, feeling totally ridiculous. Merlynni didn't seem to take offense at my social faux pas, though. She merely nodded at the description. "My fangs and claws only come out when I am threatened. I am sorry for that. I did not know you at first. I was frightened. It is a natural response for our people."

A natural response. *Fight or flight. Instinct.* With those weapons Merlynni possessed, I really couldn't see anyone being stupid enough to fight her, armed or not. Kulida was big, and so were the ex-yaks, but it had probably taken at least two men to hold Merlynni down and cage her. Considering their faces had been so torn up, it showed she was a vicious fighter.

Her stomach growled, and where were my manners? "You're hungry?" Even though she'd eaten an hour or so before, it was a given that she probably hadn't had anything substantial before that.

"What made you say so?" Another tiny smile accompanied her question.

"Lucky guess. I hope you like bacon and eggs."

Call that simple, but it was one of my late father's favorite dishes as well as mine. I'd grown up eating not only common food like that—comfort food, many called it—but also more esoteric kinds of foods if and when my mother could get her hands on the right ingredients.

Once we'd gone into space, though, I'd tried alien food and it was great, too, except for *lorges*. They looked and tasted something like bananas, but they contained parasites that messed up a person's insides, and since they attached themselves to a person's lower intestines with tiny hooks that did *not* want to let go, they were difficult to get rid of. It involved six weeks of taking foul-tasting medicine, constant trips to the toilet and a butt-load of pain.

I'd also gotten no sympathy from my parents after the initial diagnosis. *"You should always ask about what you're going to eat,"* my mother had said to me in the infirmary after I'd drunk a few milligrams of a powerful purgative. *"I'm not being insensitive. I'm simply telling you to be careful."*

A horrible twisting feeling in my lower intestines had compelled me to get off the table and make a mad dash for the nearest restroom. *"Thanks, Mom,"* I'd yelled as I'd run and hoped to make it to the toilet on time…

However, that had been then. This was now. Merlynni and I went to the restaurant. At the door, she balked when she saw my boss, but for his part, he greeted her with all the friendliness and aplomb a pink blob possessed. "Nice to meet you. You're from — "

"The Cidlennan Galaxy," she cut in. "My world is called Kagekia."

For his part, Nerfer didn't seem unduly disturbed by the sight of her. Merlynni picked up on that right away. "You do not stare. That is — "

"Nerfer's been around the universe a lot," I said. "He's seen pretty much every kind of life there is. He knows where most places and galaxies are, and he knows more about different cultures than I ever will.

The translator we have helps, but if yours or mine ever breaks, he's our go-to person. He picks up languages fast."

Merlynni's mouth hung open, but then, as if remembering her attitude toward me, she clamped it shut and took a seat in one of the booths. "I'll get something ready," Nerfer said in a friendlier manner than he'd ever demonstrated with me. "What do you want?"

"Bacon and eggs," I answered. "Please."

Bob-bob went his body. "On it. You two kids talk."

Talk? About what?

Merlynni turned her attention to our restaurant, marveling at the concept of owning and operating such an establishment in space. "It is most unusual. Then again, I have never been off my world."

As she sat in a booth, she stared at the stars. I'd done the same thing for the past two years, although in my case, it'd gotten old after the first few months. "Our people have the capability of space travel, although not to deep space. It is limited to going to one of the three moons that orbit our world. I am impressed."

She then leaned over the table to impart to me with a confidential air, "I am also impressed at your attitude and Nerfer's. You take my difference in appearance in stride. Not everyone is so...understanding."

Not speaking for Nerfer, but it didn't bother me at all. "You seem like a nice person."

While that didn't count as the pithiest answer around, it was an honest one. After all, she'd been kidnapped and transported as cargo for some unknown reason. Slave? Bargaining chip? Booty? After our initial rocky start, I'd gotten no bad vibes from her, and a measure of trust had to be given.

As for her being impressed with my so-called position in life, would she still feel the same way if she found out that I was a captain in name only? Would she be impressed to learn that I had no way of controlling where this ship went?

Probably not. I wasn't into talking about myself much. I'd embarked on this voyage with my parents, a voyage that I really hadn't wanted to go on. I'd only set foot on planets a few times in my life, never for very long — only long enough to restock, take a few pictures then leave.

The last time I'd touched down on solid land had been a year-and-a-half ago, just before my mother had gotten sick. The world's name was Shurinda. It was a tropical world, and I'd started to sweat as soon as the door opened. After ten minutes, I'd felt totally dehydrated.

Fortunately, the natives there had been friendly and one of them had offered me a bluish-brown cup full of something he called kerand. *"You will like it. Drink only a little, and drink it slowly."*

I had drunk the entire cup's contents down and promptly passed out. I'd woken up in the infirmary, hooked up to a life-support device with tubes running into both arms. My father had come in and told me that I'd drunk too much and almost died. Worry lines had etched his forehead.

My head had hurt like someone had set off a bomb inside my skull. That was space's version of a severe hangover and the ensuing alcohol poisoning of a habitual drunk...

"Food's ready," Nerfer said, bringing me back to reality. He put two plates in front of us, along with forks and knives. "Eat up."

My gut was empty. I hadn't eaten breakfast, and the smells of Kulida, the late Cradd and their men had spoiled my appetite. Now, though, I was hungry. Merlynni watched how I handled the utensils, hesitantly took the fork in her right hand and scooped up a tiny portion of the meal…and subsequently, she wolfed everything down. "This is good!"

Glad you like it. Over her second helping of eggs and bacon sans toast, though, she told me about her unfortunate incarceration. "Our world is one of industry and agriculture. We are not a star-faring people, although, as I said, we do have ships that can reach the stars. But they were no match for the ones that the Rattanians employed. They came to our world, said that they had scanned us, then they started to fire on our cities indiscriminately."

It got worse. In less than an hour, they'd reduced most of the major industries in her home city of Nelvok to ashes. After that, they'd laid waste to her planet, killed a number of men and women who served in their armed forces, and they'd kidnapped her. "Why you?"

"Because…I am from a very influential family."

Influential. "Does that mean you're royalty?"

"No."

"Rich?"

"No."

"Famous for a talent?"

"No."

Okay, this was getting to be frustrating, and playing this kind of interrogation game wasn't my idea of fun. The Rattanians had obviously kidnapped her for a reason, and it had to be an important one. "That what was it?"

"My father is a scientist."

Uh-huh...that was the first thing she'd said that made sense. I put down my fork. "So, let me guess. He was working on an experiment that could change the galaxy — and perhaps the universe."

A somewhat sad smile came from her. "You are halfway right. I was the experiment, and I was his universe. Or, rather, part of the universe is in me."

At first, I stared at her, unable to comprehend what she'd told me. Then I remembered what she'd looked like naked — her internal organs sparkling like the stars outside and at least three planets next to her intestinal tract, and it hit me like the proverbial meteor shower, the facts clanging around my skull...

"Oh, wait a second...your body...those stars... You mean that —"

"Part of the universe is in me," she finished. "I am his experiment. What you saw was — and is — a laboratory-created galaxy."

The concept of a galaxy existing inside someone was a mind-bender in and of itself. "Don't get me wrong, but does that mean you're some kind of god? I mean, I've read about people with special abilities, but —"

"Let me explain, first."

She reached out to gently touch her hand to mine. Contact — and her fingers, warm and powerful — got me flustered. "Is something wrong?" she asked.

Yeah, she'd picked up on it, all right. While she wore an innocent expression, and while her gesture was innocent enough, she had to know how I felt. However, that was my problem, not hers. "No, nothing's wrong," I stammered out. "Please, er, let me...I mean, tell me."

Merlynni's father was a top-flight quantum physics researcher. He'd theorized that since matter could be compressed in nature, much like a black hole compressing and trapping matter and emitting no light, he could simulate the same thing in a lab.

"I am not much of a scientist," she admitted. "My father has the genius to do such a thing. He developed a kind of ray that, once emitted, shrank objects to a fraction of their size. He continued to experiment on bigger objects."

Her story continued, and it got more fantastic as it went along. He'd managed to create a small galaxy in his laboratory. He'd then reduced it to a very tiny one, roughly half the size of a human's pinky finger. Stars, planets, even a sun—a miniature galaxy with no life—yet—but one that existed all the same.

"My father was never able to duplicate the process," Merlynni said. "He encased it inside a minuscule container. That is what you saw inside me."

Then, as the old saying went, things got weird. Kulida and his band of rogues had shown up on her world without any warning—or so she'd thought. They'd known about the experiment. Word had gotten around fast, it seemed, and they'd wanted in. "How did they find out?"

Her face tightened at the question. "My father had an assistant, a man named Laddan. He was greedy, stupid and a fool. While he knew of my father's experiment, he wanted credit for it, and my father had denied him that honor. Laddan had done nothing to merit it."

It seemed that greed was a universal concept. "So, let me guess, he ratted on your father to the wrong guys?"

Merlynni nodded. "If by that, you mean he contacted the Rattanians, you are correct. He made a deal with Kulida."

Things had escalated quickly after that. Kulida had visited her world, bombarded it with intense fire and demanded the secret. Merlynni's father had refused to help them, and as a way of hiding his invention, he'd placed it inside his daughter with her consent. Kulida had bullied and threatened him with execution if he didn't cough up his secrets, but her father had still refused.

Then Laddan had made things worse. "He wanted more money than Kulida was willing to pay," Merlynni said. "Kulida executed him in front of us, as a warning of what would happen if we did not accede to his demands."

If that wasn't enough, the raiders had decided to make things worse. Merlynni had told her father to run. "I yelled at him to escape. He carried the secrets of my newfound life with him. He went, and I do not know where he is. It is better that he does not find me."

Sadness permeated her speech. To be torn away from your parents... I'd been through the same thing, and I shut that memory down. This was too important.

"So, Kulida kidnapped you?"

Merlynni nodded. For Kulida and his kind, if they couldn't have the secrets of creating life on a universal scale, then they, along with the yak-guys they'd later vaporized, decided to hold her for trade purposes.

Obviously, Kulida and his people weren't scientists. They'd developed weapons of war and traded, but they didn't have the knowledge to do what they wanted to do. They were profiteers, plain and simple, and they had put most of their time into searching for Merlynni's father.

"And what about the yak-men?" I asked.

"Cradd and his men had the knowledge — or so I'd heard," she said. "In reality, they are as stupid as the Rattanians are. They did not bother to think on a larger — and smaller — scale. They never thought that a galaxy could be hidden," Merlynni said, tapping the end of the table with a gracefully tapered fingertip. "They never thought to look at me."

Astonishing. "But what happened to your father?"

She shrugged. "Nothing. As I said, he is in hiding, and I hope he stays hidden. Without him, those Rattanians cannot duplicate the process. Furthermore, they do not know where the galaxy is. They think I am only a kidnap victim with knowledge of the whereabouts of the galaxy. But they do not know what is inside me. The Yeltens whom Kulida destroyed — they did not know, either."

Nerfer took that moment to ooze his way over to us. "I couldn't help but overhear. Look... I know how hard it must be to get kidnapped. It's got to be hard on your parents not having your around, but you being on board this ship is dangerous. No offense, but we have to find you a safe place to stay."

"Now, hang on," I said. "What about the galaxy inside her? She —"

"It is perfectly fine where it is," she interrupted. "There is only one way to remove it safely, and the means to remove it lies inside my father's laboratory. There, he has specialized equipment, and he is the sole person in the universe with the knowledge of how to remove this creation of his."

If the bad guys caught her, they could slice her open. As if reading my mind, she said, "Yes, it is possible to simply kill me and take out that which is inside. But it would only lead to their demise. Without careful removal of the sheath which protects me as well as the planets and stars inside my body, it would expand to its former size in a matter of minutes. According to my father, the galaxy inside me is roughly one thousand parsecs at its largest size. It is an experimental model. Therefore, it is extremely small.

"It also has the capacity to displace other worlds from the space—another galaxy, I mean—it enters. Therefore, it is imperative that it be kept safe."

I wasn't much of a physicist, but it unnerved me to think of what would happen to a region of space and the gravitational pull of worlds if a new galaxy was suddenly introduced. Even if it displaced the worlds already existing there, it had the potential to cause chaos on an apocalyptic scale...but that was only a guess.

In order to avert a possible interstellar disaster, it was necessary to keep Merlynni safe and away from Kulida and his gang of ghouls as much as possible— that and somehow get her father to remove the pocket universe from her body.

"So," she said with a smile, "I am safe here, but I do not understand about the shifting process of this vessel."

That made two of us, and Nerfer did his best imitation of a shrug, which meant blowing his body up around the area where his head and shoulders should have been.

"I'm a good engineer, and Rick is a fair mechanic," he said. "I'll be honest, though. I don't know why the shift occurs. Rick's father refurbished this rig, but I don't have blueprints for it. If I could find the mechanism that turns the interstellar shift on and off, I'd fix it, but his father could have hidden it anywhere."

"So, what shall we do?"

Merlynni turned a million-watt smile on me, and I melted. Even Nerfer uttered a sound of disgust and turned away with the edict of, "Whatever, kid. She's all yours."

"Well, for now, you can stay with us," I said and motioned to the hallway.

She arched her eyebrows in a very human gesture, one that indicated coyness with a certain amount of suggestiveness. "Stay? As in, I will be provided with a bed, meals and clothing?"

Okay, that came out badly. "I mean, stay, as a guest, as a friend…that kind of thing."

"And what would you expect in return?"

Was she thinking that I'd want something? Aw, she would have to go there. My face got hot. "Nothing. I mean, if you help me clean up the place, I guess that's enough."

Merlynni folded her arms across her chest. "And that is all?"

This time, I locked gazes with her. "Yeah, that's all."

She studied my face as if looking for deception, then she bobbed her head. "I accept."

Acceptance – noted. We began walking in the direction of my quarters. "I, um…look. We have an extra room, so it's no problem. Do you need anything special? I mean, food, medicine, clothes…that kind of thing?"

She shook her head. "I am healthy. The clothes you provided are acceptable, and I am able to process most kinds of food. Your bacon and eggs were very good. Does all Earth food taste like that?"

"Pretty much."

We soon arrived at my room. It wasn't overly large. The bulk of the ship was taken up by storage rooms, as well as bulkheads that contained the internal wiring and other circuitry.

My living quarters was a five-by-five-meter affair. It had enough room for a bed, a dresser for my clothes, a small combo toilet-shower and a bookcase. It held only a few science-fiction books, holdovers from Earth, but they were woefully out of date compared to the era I was living in now.

"It is small but suitable," Merlynni observed as she reclined upon my bed, undulating her body upon the sheets like she was swimming. Her hair lay like a puddle of black ink around her head.

For some reason, her statement bothered me. Small but suitable—what did she expect? This rig may have been a flying brick, but it was *my* flying brick. "Sorry if it isn't luxurious enough. I'll have a throne installed tomorrow."

Sarcasm—achieved. She sat up and glanced around the place, as if familiarizing herself with each object. Then she offered a contrite look. "I apologize. I meant no harm in what I said. This is your ship. You should be proud of it."

Her words made me feel as though I'd overreacted, but all the same, I'd made my point, and now it was time to let things go. I leaned over to grab my holo-computer. "Fine, I'll be across the hallway."

With that, I walked out and into my new room— formerly my parents' room—I sat on the bed and thought about the happenings of only a short time ago. It had been a very strange twenty-four hours.

And I had the feeling that more was in store for us. The science-fiction books I'd read always had that cliché in them. However, this was reality, and since Kulida and his men were out there — somewhere — it unnerved me more than a little.

Chapter Five

Remembrances and New Beginnings

"Remember the days that happened not so long ago," the sages on Earth used to say. *"Forget them not or be doomed to repeat them."*

As dire and old-fashioned as those words sounded, they'd made sense, and my parents had often told me the same thing when I'd been growing up. *"We should always remember the past. It gives us instructions on how to act for the future."*

Morality aside, studying history offered a window into the times that no longer existed. Back then, they'd had movies. There'd been actors and actresses and a place called Hollywood where magic happened using cameras, props, computers and special optical units.

Movies seemed to be the most amazing things. In those healthy days of long ago, people would line up for hours outside a theater to see the latest and most popular cinema epic. They had called it 'a blockbuster'. Inside the theater, they'd eaten food and watched the moving pictures as though they were real and they — the audience — had lived the adventure with them.

Delving further into the past, maybe a more innocent time, our ancestors also had things called amusement parks where a person could ride on mechanical horses and other creatures. They'd even had places where others congregated to procure items. I searched my memory for the term... Oh, yes... shopping malls.

While those activities sounded charming as well as exciting in an antiquated sort of way, at the same time, those places no longer existed.

Limpenzi's Virus had seen to that. It had been named after Anthony Limpenzi, the virologist who'd discovered it and also been its first victim. I was born in twenty-one-seventeen, a little over a decade after it had happened.

Historians often said that in every era a momentous shift occurred, either in nature or in learning or both. Twenty-one-o-six had been a year that had gone down in history as the worst in modern human existence, mainly due to a happening that had almost ended everything.

In short, it had been a pandemic that had lasted four years, wiped out ninety percent of the world's population, and it had spared no one.

A neurological disorder, it had paralyzed the body, first in stages. It'd hit some people more slowly, some faster, but it'd hit them all the same. Numbness had started in the lower extremities, then it had gone on to paralyze the torso. Anything above the shoulders had still functioned — for a time.

Respirators had helped slow the illness, as had injections of stem cells, but that had proven to be a stopgap, not a cure. Had the paralysis been the only thing, that would have been terrible, yes, but still livable — or so the experts had said. Personally, not being able to move would have been the pits for me.

But things had gotten worse. The virus had progressed internally — as after it had shut down the body, it had proceeded to shut down the mind... forever. For the poor, death had occurred within a month. Outside of the stem cells, which only the rich could afford and which prolonged life for only an extra month or two, there had been no cure, and while the disease progressed, it had been horrible to see. One doctor had compared it to lights in a large room being turned off one by one.

No one knew how it had started, much less where. Of course, the blame had gone back and forth between the major countries of the world. That had been a given. In the end, though, any potential military conflicts had stopped because there was no reason to fight. Survival had become the number one *raison d'être*.

When the epidemiological experts gave their testimony, they had given the facts. At first, the presidents and prime ministers of the major countries hadn't wanted to believe them, but eventually, they'd had no choice but to believe in their doctors and go with the truth.

And the facts had been as follows — the disease traveled fast, and it spared no race, no religion and no creed. From its start, it had taken less than a week to infect roughly half a million people.

Social contact had been the cause, as the virus had been airborne. The more people there had been, the more quickly people had contracted it. Countries with large populations, such as China and India, had suffered terribly, but even in countries with smaller populations and large areas, like Canada, the virus had decimated the population.

People on business and vacation had contracted it unknowingly, and they'd proceeded to transmit it to friends and family and coworkers when they'd flown, taken the train or had met up after work. The symptoms hadn't begun to show up until two weeks after someone had contracted the virus, and the mere act of speaking to someone had been enough to ensure transmission.

Within six months, even with social distancing— that had been the term they'd used back then—over three billion people had died. After the year had ended, the tally had gone up to almost six billion. After four years, our world had ended—mostly. Out of fifteen billion people total, our world had been left with less than eight million.

Call it catastrophic, a disease-induced mass extinction event. Everyone had been to blame, yet no one was. Some people had turned to religion, prayed for guidance, got none and they'd turned to science. In the end, neither of those things had mattered. People had still contracted the illness and they'd still died.

Isolation had been the only answer. It was something that should have been done at the outset, but the governments of the world, particularly the American and British governments, had initially refused, citing herd immunity.

Morons—that's what they had been. No such thing as herd immunity had existed, not with that. People had died by the thousands. Then the tally had run into the millions. Only after the American President had contracted it—and subsequently died—had the rest of the US population change its mind.

"That's how your mother and I met," my father had told me. *"We were young then – eighteen – and we ended up in quarantine together. I'd been accepted into university as an engineer. Your mother was in the same position.*

"We both ended up studying in isolation. We dated, and after four years, the experts said it was safe to come out. By that time, we'd gotten married, and we went to work for Rocket Y Corporation."

The history vids and audio commentary told me the rest. Once the quarantine had ended, everyone had discovered that the old rules no longer applied. Most of the farms, the livestock and the fisheries in the world had failed, due to lack of human care.

On the flipside, while many domesticated farm animals had perished, wild animals flourished, and once mankind had gotten on its feet again, they'd turned to restarting the farms, fisheries…everything.

However, all those things had taken time. When people had begun to starve, riots had broken out, violence had claimed more lives and the military elements in each society had taken over, including those in the United States.

Draconian as it had been, the military guys had gotten the scientists to do what they hadn't done before. They'd turned to creating a range of synthetic and palatable food products to feed the hungry. Factory owners had quickly developed synthetic clothes to garb the needy.

I'd grown up in a society that had functioned only on the essentials. There had been no time for activities that didn't contribute to progress. There had been no shopping malls, no libraries and no gatherings of more than ten people at a time. Social distancing had become the norm, rather than the exception.

Oh, we'd still had freedom, to a degree. Freedom of speech and action had remained paramount, as long as it didn't ruffle too many feathers and no one spoke out against the government or the laws.

"*Fascism,*" my mother had once said to me as we'd walked around the outskirts of our house in Salt Lake City. "*That's all it was and is.*"

She'd never mentioned it again, but I'd known. Everyone had. While my mother hadn't talked about repression, she'd talked about space travel, as had my father. "*After the Great Collapse, scientists turned to the stars,*" he'd said.

"*The Earth wasn't dying, not yet, but we came close to dying out as a species. We could never go back to the way things were. So, our governments and our private companies built and sent out spaceships to distant galaxies. Some came back, saying they'd found habitable worlds on which to live. Others never returned.*"

Rocket Y had funded roughly half of everything in conjunction with the government—the government meaning the armed forces. The corporation had been a visionary one, one that had taken chances and rewarded its employees handsomely if they came through with new, viable ideas.

"*Headed by billionaires who found out money meant nothing if death could reach up and snatch them,*" my father had added with a grimace.

Apparently, he'd had no love for his employers, although he'd never mentioned why. "*Once the virus finished its run and burned itself out, they put us to work right away on creating starships, just in case the virus came back or another killer virus took its place,*" he'd said. "*Your mother and I got the go-ahead to do our own thing.*"

It had turned out that they hadn't needed to build a ship. They'd already had one, a converted cargo freighter that had run supplies from the Earth to the moon, where a base had been established years back. The colony had been big, but living there wasn't an option. People had wanted to walk outside, and the scientists hadn't figured out how to create an artificial atmosphere, hence our journey to the stars.

Like all the other vessels, theirs had run on ion power, something that was ages old, but under the military's aegis, they'd modernized it, so that it left little contamination. It had thrilled me to see the immense dry-docks where the ships were built.

We'd lived about five kilometers from the space base where the retrofitting had gone on. I'd ride my minibike out to see my parents working on it, never dreaming that one day I'd be up among the stars.

The spaceship was an ugly thing, really, "*a flying brick*", as my father had put it. It had been used numerous times to transport supplies wherever they had been needed. 'Helping out' had been suspended when the government had taken over, and from that point on, they'd called the shots.

So, my parents had slaved away, planning, building and working with the construction crews. Most of the time, they'd had to work on other projects, and that meant their work on the upgraded spaceship had needed to be postponed. It wasn't something they'd wanted, but other projects took priority, and the military had demanded results.

As for me, since my parents had left me largely unsupervised, I'd spent my days studying, for the most part. My holo-teacher had made sure I did my lessons and turned them in on time. After that, I'd practiced preparing food in the kitchen. Most nights, my parents had been too tired to cook, so I'd ended up doing it.

Our conversations had usually been about their work. On occasion, they'd asked me about my studies, but for the most part, no. They had been exhausted from their day's labors, and while I had been disappointed in their lack of interest, I'd told myself that they were doing important work and that I could take care of myself.

Taking care of myself had meant setting my own parameters. In turn, that had meant partitioning off time segments for sleeping, cooking and meeting up with the few people I'd called friends. All the while, though, I'd wished that my parents would set aside a little more time for me...

"Rick, we're thinking of taking a trip," my father had told me one night at dinner.

It had been two weeks after my fifteenth birthday, and the concept of a trip had interested me. *"Where to, Dad?"*

Guam would've been nice. It had been one of the few places untouched by the ravages of the virus from years back, although access had been limited to those with pull. We hadn't had pull.

As for the virus, most countries had never recovered from it. The USA had, but not to its former glory. Like many other nations, it had limped along, gaining traction here, losing it there. We'd gotten by.

In answer, my father had pointed to the window. It had been after seven p.m., and the stars had been shining their eternal light. *"It would be for only one year. It's a special mission, and we want you with us. The head of the agency cleared it."*

Space. I'd sat back in my chair, weighing the consequences of going versus not going. Not going would have invited ridicule. Moreover, I'd had no relatives to stay with, and I hadn't really been close to anyone in my age bracket.

On the other hand, going had meant giving up my comforts. I'd had my holo-computer, some electronic book devices and I'd had real gravity. Being in space…artificial food which I'd would probably hate, artificial gravity and only two other people to spend it with…

"Just a year?"

My father had nodded. *"Guaranteed."*

Had I known that he'd been lying about the 'guaranteed' part, I'd have said no. Being young, trusting and kind of stupid, I'd agreed, and from that day on, I'd prepared to become the world's youngest astronaut. Prep time, drills on safety, maintenance of the ship and general cleaning had taken up most of my time.

As the days had fallen away until liftoff, the tension and excitement had grown. Some of the other kids had caught wind of my impending journey and they'd pressed me for details.

Secrecy had been the catchword. "Say nothing," my mother had told me numerous times. She'd seemed nervous to even say that much, but I could keep a secret as well as the next person. "If you have to say something, tell them that it's a research mission for the government."

I'd gotten the message and had kept my mouth shut. Soon, the other kids had stopped pestering me. Training continued…six months to go… Three… One…

Finally, D-Day—Departure Day—had rolled around. The blast-off from Earth, the climb into the stratosphere and beyond, the semi-weightlessness of space, and when the ion-powered engines had come online, the smooth and effortless journey had begun.

"Earth to Cargo Vessel Twenty-Seven," the interstellar com-link had crackled, addressing us by our ship's official name. Other star-faring vessels had names like *Barella, Thunder, Star Seeker* and more. We'd gotten a number.

"Captain Orville Granger and Mary Granger in command," my father had answered in a terse manner. *"Orbit established, but we're moving out, soon."*

"Acknowledged. Godspeed, and keep us —"

"Granger out."

My father cut the transmission and off we'd gone. Once we'd moved out of range, he'd breathed a sigh of relief and asked my mother, *"Any stragglers?"*

She'd been manning the sensors and had replied without looking up. *"Nothing. No one's following us. We're on our own now."*

At that point, my father had relaxed somewhat, and I'd wondered why all the secrecy? It had all been very hush-hush, and my mother had simply said he was a little edgy due to the newness of being in space and so on.

Uh-huh. I'd gotten the idea and gone to my room. Along the way, though, I'd stopped at one of the portholes to look outside and marvel at the depths and beauty of the universe. I'd wondered if the other kids were interested, then I'd decided not to think about it, anymore. It hadn't been worth it, and our journey would only be for one year.

Ion propulsion had moved us along slowly but steadily. Travel to Mars in days of yore would have taken months — at least five on the short end, orbit-wise, and around three hundred days on the long end.

In our case, it had taken only a week. We'd journeyed beyond Mars, seen the red spot of Jupiter and gone beyond the confines of our galaxy. That had been where we'd lost communication with Earth.

At first, it had been somewhat disconcerting to hear only static. Then about a month into our journey, we'd met our first aliens, multi-limbed beings that had been friendly, curious and above all, kind. My father hadn't yet invented his universal translator, so we'd had to make do with hand gestures, pictures, smiles and nods.

Overall, that had been a cool experience, although my mother had said that it had been the scariest moment of her life. *"I thought they were going to eat us. They looked — "*

"Like cockroaches," my father had finished. *"Well, I was scared, too, but they were okay, and we're still here."*

Yes, we had been, and that had become part of the problem. Soon after our encounter with the different kind, the thrill had left. For me, life had become one long and dull routine. Up at six, train with the battle droids — large, powerful machines that had hit hard and continued to hit until ordered to stop — then cleaning, maintenance and virtual piloting exercises had made up my morning.

Cleaning had been a necessary evil, but it hadn't thrilled me. Being on the bridge had. It had been where my parents piloted the ship and where we'd had our meals. It had offered a great view of the stars, as the viewport was one long piece of reinforced glass, something called 'tomeikan' glass that had a special alloy of incredibly thin titanium and another alloy called 'mentatum', a metal that was stronger than steel and practically impervious to damage.

Still, since I had been the junior member here, in the afternoon, study-time had called. At times, though, my father or mother would summon me to the bridge. I'd enter, salute either one or both—depending on who was present—then they'd say, *"Take over."*

"Yes, sir," I'd say. That, or *"Yes, ma'am."*

After that, they'd say, *"The helm is yours, Captain Granger,"* and they'd disappear into the bowels of the ship for an hour or so. It had been my chance to command, and I'd wanted to make the most of it.

To be honest, handling the helm of the ship hadn't been difficult, considering the onboard computer had done most of the work. All I'd had to do was course-correct occasionally. That had been fun...until my mother had gotten sick and died.

Cancer—an insidious six-letter word meaning death, a five-letter word. Earth's technology had allowed us to venture into deep space. It had allowed us to build plasma weapons, attack spacecraft and universal translators.

However, Earth's medicine still hadn't figured out a cure for cancer, and neither had any of the alien species we'd come into contact with. And my mother's case had become too advanced. Exactly one month after she'd told us, she'd succumbed to the disease, and my father had sent her to be among the stars in a specially designed coffin that had kept her body from deteriorating.

After that, my father had withdrawn into himself. While I'd taken care of the cleaning and maintenance tasks on the ship, he'd spent most of his time on the bridge, refitting it. Although I'd helped him from time to time, my job had consisted of putting various parts together. *"Just leave them at the door,"* he'd say. *"I'll take care of the rest."*

I'd wondered why. Then one day, a few months after my mother had passed away, I'd gone to the bridge to find that it had been turned into a retro nineteen-fifties diner-type of place, with checkered floors, plush leather booths and chrome railings — and a lot of Formica tables. I'd seen the pictures on my holo-computer, and they had been interesting memories of a now-gone age, but still...

"Uh, Dad, what's going on?"

He'd turned around, a rag in his hand and a somewhat cryptic smile on his prematurely lined face. *"Oh, just refitting everything. I think that since we're so far from Earth, if we meet anyone who wants to stop in for a meal, we might just as well offer it to them."*

His answer had made no sense, and it was then that I'd realized he'd gone a little mad. Not space-happy insanity, but mad in the sense that grief had overwhelmed him. *"Dad, I know that you miss Mom, but — "*

"Rick, trust me. This is what your mother would have wanted. We had happy times around the dinner table, yes?"

My father had said that with a measure of desperation. One look at his eyes had shown the loss he'd suffered as well as the hint of instability. Would it go any further? At that point, it had been up in the non-air, so I'd had to humor him. We had been a long way from Earth and not quite ready to settle down on another world.

Still, he had been right about one thing. Our happiest times had been our meals together. We'd talked of the day's doings, creatures we'd met, the composition of space and its infinite possibilities and more. Still, was that all there had been? *"Yeah, but – "*

"But nothing. Look… I rigged the interstellar com-link to send out a message in all the known languages that we're open for business and that we mean no harm. And that's part of this mission."

I'd bobbed my head once. He'd had a point, even if it had verged on the desperate and the delusional. *"Okay, Dad…"*

My father had kept working on his interstellar translation device, perfected it and had implanted it in me and himself. It worked. As time had gone by, other races had dropped by to see who and what we were. They'd partaken of meals with us, paid us, and we'd all gotten along. Then had come Kulida and the cargo he'd carried…

A knock at the door interrupted my trip down memory lane. "Yes?"

"It is Merlynni. May I enter?"

Oh, crud, the room was a mess. "Um, just a second."

In a whirlwind of speed, I grabbed my used and rank clothes and stuffed them into a small machine the size of a stool called a 'wesser' – a combination washer and presser. The machine did everything and all I had to do was to wait.

I pressed the button to start the process. Then I smoothed the sheets on my bed down and ran to open the door. It slid aside, revealing Merlynni in my uniform. Her hair was tousled, as though she'd been sleeping, and her next words confirmed it, accompanied by a yawn. "Your bed was so comfortable that I lay down and fell asleep. I hope you do not mind."

Why would I mind? She'd only taken over my room, one I'd had for the last two years. "Uh, no, that's okay. You might as well stay there."

Merlynni glanced around the place. I stood in front of the wesser to hide it. It made an odd thrumming sound, but fortunately, my guest didn't bother asking about it. "Is this also your abode?"

"No, it's my parents' room. They're dead, so now I'm staying here."

An uncomfortable silence descended, broken only by the hiss of the recycled air through the vents in the ceiling as well as our breathing. Bedhead or not, she looked terrific, and I had to remind myself that she was a person and not an object. Although we'd entered the twenty-second century, the old ways of guys objectifying women hadn't entirely faded away. They probably never would.

However, this was a different situation, and it wasn't like I was used to it. Whether Merlynni knew it or not, she was having some effect on me. Finally, she asked, "You are bothered by my presence?"

I looked at her and decided to tell the truth — partially. "What makes you think that?"

A tiny smile flitted across her face. "When we first met, you stared. I thought it was due to anger. On my world, staring indicates such.

"However, now, you are shifting from foot to foot, and your eyes do not make contact with mine. I am not an expert on humans, but I have observed other humanoid species when they visited our world, and your gestures indicate nervousness and perhaps shyness, as well."

Oh, wonderful. I hadn't realized that I was moving around, and she'd managed to sum up my character in less than twenty words. Forcing myself to stay still and make eye contact, I said, "Well, yeah, you make me nervous."

Merlynni bit her lip. "Have I done something wrong?"

In a slow, almost-seductive move, she sat down on my bed, a meter away from me. Her breath smelled sweet, and it played around my nostrils in a light, breezy manner. "I did not wish to offend you. After all, you have given me sanctuary."

Should I tell her that I was interested in her? No, it was too soon. Like I had any experience? Not really, and in any case, business came first, the business of operating this ship. "No, it's me. It's, uh, well, there's no one my age here, and you're pretty. I'm not very good around pretty women."

There, I'd said it, and while it didn't sound offensive, who knew how she'd react? For a moment, she said nothing, then her face flushed a light-yellow color. "You told me before that I was pretty."

Oh, yeah, I had. "Well, yeah, and—"

"I...I have never been called pretty before," she said in a halting manner. "Thank you."

Awkward, this was getting awkward, and right now I had nowhere to put my hands except to shove them in my pockets or swing my arms around my back. Either way, it made me look stupid.

"You're welcome. C'mon. Let's get something to eat."

Chapter Six

Contact

Nerfer greeted us with a smile. "Well, you two seem to be happy about something."

In his case, a smile meant a faint upward curvature in the center of his jelly-like body. As his containment suit was transparent, the image came across as odd and somewhat disturbing, but there was no sense in saying anything about it. Was he being sarcastic?

No, he wasn't. From his expression—such as it was—he seemed to be genuine, but from the way he'd said it, it sounded like Merlynni and I had done something illicit. We hadn't. I caught sight of my reflection in the window. It sported a goofy grin. *Busted.*

"Just making friends, Nerfer," I replied, trying to force my facial muscles into a mask and probably only partially succeeding. "Can we get something to eat, please? I can make it, if you want, and—"

"No, you two take a seat and let the best cook in the universe make something for you."

Best cook in the universe? Call that a pride-slam! When my parents had been around, I'd done all the cooking. It happened to be something I was good at. Goodness knows I'd practiced enough when they'd gone off to work.

Since Nerfer had come onboard, though, he'd handled a lot of the cooking duties, and it bothered me a little that he thought himself king of the grill. I was about to go over and show him who was the best, but his pseudopods shot out and waved us to table number eight. Merlynni and I sat and watched as our pink host prepared burgers and fries for us. She sniffed the air. "What is that smell? It is good."

"Burgers and fries," I answered. "Stuff that I can make, too."

Oh, that sounded desperate. *Shut it, already!* I was acting like an ass — and an immature one at that. Did it really matter? Nerfer knew what he was doing. He could have made pizza, spaghetti with meat sauce, cannelloni, grilled cheese sandwiches and soup or some other quick and delicious meal. It would have been fine.

He could have also made some more esoteric dishes. In the past, when my parents had been around, we'd tried suckling pig, couscous, falafel and all the variants on French haute cuisine. My parents had had a thing for old-time recipes.

I stuck with the former. Comfort food truly made my day. Decades ago, the expression had been that 'it rocked'. These days, no one used that expression, but it seemed to sum up what I loved most about Earth, outside of my parents.

Additionally, it provided my one, last, remaining link with my home world — that, and my heritage.

Ethnically, my parents were Welsh, and their ancestors had come from small villages in Wales that had long and unpronounceable names and which no longer existed.

Food-wise, while most of Earth's population had ended up eating synthetic food, my parents had always given me the real thing. Working for their quasi-government company had meant receiving a few perks. One of them was hydroponically grown vegetables and fruit, along with meat and poultry from privately stocked farms.

Call it privilege. I knew it, and so did everyone else. The head of the corporation, a man named Robert Hutchins, had told us that his employees' health was number one. *"We realize that some people won't like the idea of you getting fresh food, but you are valued employees. This is what we do for you."*

Whatever the case, I had eaten my share and no more, and my parents had liked me to have a balanced diet. Working out helped to keep me in shape, and at home, we'd had a small gym where I could lift weights and ride a stationary bicycle.

Once in space, I often ran through the corridors of the ship. As well, in the past, the battle droids had prepared me for the rigors of fighting, should it become necessary. It was all very twenty-first century, but it did the trick.

"I'm almost ready," Nerfer said, interrupting my reverie.

As Merlynni and I waited, I thought about the wonders of space travel. While cooking was a contentious issue between Nerfer and me, with flying, he had me beat, and he often told me that he knew more about piloting a starship than anyone. He could fly — so he said — over fifty types of starship.

In contrast, I'd flown only two, our ship as well as a scout vessel we had. Practically speaking, though, our ship was on automatic most of the time with the computer doing the work and guiding us away from danger zones, mainly asteroid belts and black holes.

"Captains know when to cede control," he'd said when I'd pointed out to him that he wasn't doing much. Our captain's chair was in front of the main viewing screen, a luxurious leather contraption that offered a perfect view of the heavens and quick access to the console. It was also incredibly comfortable. *"Captains and automatic control go together."*

I had no answer to that.

I also had no answer when, at the grill, Nerfer handed over the food and said in the most deadpan manner possible, "If this isn't the best burger you've ever eaten, I'll eat my hat."

Right, pink organic matter was telling me that it could make Earth food better. Laughable — he had no hat. He didn't even have a head, not really.

"I'm still the best cook around," I replied, only half-amused.

His next comeback, though, I did not appreciate. "Uh-huh," he said as he slipped the apron off his containment suit. "Well, then, best cook, clean up. I'm going back to my cabin."

"Why?"

He wanted to slip out of his suit for a few hours.

"Baring it all? Say it isn't so!"

Nerfer grunted, and no, he did not appreciate my sarcasm. "In our natural state, we don't have any form," he said to me *sotto voce*, so that Merlynni wouldn't overhear. "We look like what you'd call an organic puddle of primeval matter. That's our constitution, believe it or not."

In all the time he'd been aboard this vessel, he'd never mentioned that little fact. Now, it became an image that wouldn't leave. "Thanks for sharing that with me, Nerfer."

I hoped he got this bit of sarcasm, but he merely bobbed his body back and forth. "Glad you see how the other side of creation lives."

Maybe that was sarcasm back at me, so, whatever... "You like the girl," he said in an offhand manner as he scraped some burned bacon off to the side of the grill then put the spatula down.

Yeah, I did, and it was interesting how quickly he'd picked up on that personal fact. He seemed to read my mind, as he said, "I see how you look at her. I don't know much about humans, but I've seen how males and females looked at each other in over a thousand different races across thirty galaxies."

"Is that right?"

Bob-bob. "I used to talk to your father about you growing up here without someone female your age around."

Call that another personal matter. It wasn't quite an invasion of privacy, but at the same time, it demonstrated that my late father had liked to divulge family details more than he should have. "He told you about that?"

Bob-bob. "He did. Don't take offense at it, okay? He was your father, and he wanted the best for you."

I glanced at Merlynni. She was aimlessly drumming her fingers on the Formica table, staring out at the stars.

"Okay, then why did he design the ship to dropkick us to a different galaxy?"

"Who knows?"

That was the first time he'd ever been stumped. "You really don't know?"

Nerfer did his best imitation of a shrug, bloating up his shoulder area with his essence. "No, I don't. I have no idea why the engines act that way, much less the computer."

It was a mystery, but that mystery would have to wait for another day. Nerfer excused himself, and I went over to ask Merlynni to take a walk with me. She raised her eyebrows. "Where?"

"Tour of the ship? I mean, you're going to be with us until I can get you back to your world, somehow."

She blinked. "Why can you not return me now? I gave you the proper coordinates before, did I not?"

It was a fair question, and it deserved an answer. After my father had died, I'd found out that the computer wouldn't allow it. We'd entered a region of space that was far beyond what Earth could detect, the Kindaaran Galaxy.

On the bridge once, I'd looked out at the stars for the umpteenth time and thought about my transient lifestyle, I'd come to a decision and told Nerfer. I'd used the words '*go home*' and used them quite succinctly. His response had been, *"You want out, kid?"*

I'd watched my father die and had had to officiate at his service, I was feeling lousy, alone and helpless, so, yeah, going home would have been great. *"Yeah, that's a good way of putting it."*

"There's a lot to see out there," Nerfer had said as he stacked the dishes. *"It's a hell of an adventure, and —"*

"Stop right there."

I'd heard that before. It happened to be my father's pat phrase. Always something new to see, somewhere new to go. Nerfer had stared at me through guileless eyes that had formed in his flesh. *"What?"*

"Those were his words, not mine. His dream, not mine. His ship — not mine. And he thought of you as the captain, not me."

With that, tired and angry and fed up with having nowhere to go, I'd opened a line to the central computer. *"Computer, what's the distance from our current position back to launch point Earth?"*

Click-click. *"Forty-seven-point-six parsecs."*

"Estimated length of travel back to Earth under ion power at maximum speed."

More clicks, then, *"One-hundred-eighty-four solar days."*

Six months. I could go for that. *"Computer, set course for launch point Earth and initiate."*

A series of loud beeps had greeted me. It had been a warning. *"Command…not accepted. Command…not accepted."*

Now that had pissed me off. *"Why not?"*

My reply had sounded like a spoiled child asking why he couldn't have more ice cream, but since I'd asked…

"This unit cannot comply with the request. This unit's sub-command was activated when the life form of Orville Granger ceased to function."

How had the computer known? It couldn't have known unless…unless it had scanned the coffin we'd ejected into space, or…wait. An uncomfortable thought had hit me. *"Computer, what is your prime function?"*

"This unit's purpose is to continue to serve this ship. Its primary function is to continue exploration. Its mission cannot be altered. Any attempt to do so will cause the entire

function of this unit to cease. All life-support, food and bay-door functions will cease. This unit cannot comply with Richard Granger's request."

Now, my anger had gone incandescent, and like the proverbial spoiled child, I'd stomped my feet in rage. *"Who gave you that order?"*

"Orville Granger and Mary Granger."

With a shock, I'd realized that I had become a prisoner of this ship, and I'd have to journey upon the stars until such point as I could get away. My father had had his reasons for doing what he'd done, but all the same, it'd bothered me that he'd never included me in his thoughts.

After I'd recounted my tale of being stuck here to Merlynni, she regarded me coolly through those orange eyes of hers. "I accept your explanation. Perhaps it is best that I do not return now. I would not wish to endanger my father or the rest of my people."

"Good idea."

She nodded. "In any case, I would like to see what the rest of this ship looks like."

If she were expecting it to be a thing of beauty, she would be sadly mistaken. It was functional...nothing more. We walked along the dimly lit corridors, the lights low to save on power wherever possible.

I slapped my feet softly against the metal underneath us. Merlynni padded along in bare feet. Like her hands, she had seven long, slender, tapered toes, and she walked softly, barely making a sound. Only the hiss of air from the ventilation system, as well as the hum of electricity that surged from the lights overhead, kept us company.

So did dust, as it sifted from the ceiling from time to time. Additionally, rust showed on some of the joints of the metal beams and plates where they'd been fused together. That necessitated more cleaning as well as repair, so I made a mental note to do just that when I had time. Right now, I had nothing but time to fix things up.

"I guess this ship isn't much to look at," I said and swiped away some dust on a nearby wall-intercom. "Your planet must have better looking spaceships, right?"

Merlynni shrugged. "Perhaps they are more aesthetically designed. I am not sure. This ship is still your home, is it not?"

It was a good point. Bucket of bolts or not, this ship had been my living place for quite some time. To be fair, shifts aside, it had always held together, always been reliable. I still stopped short of calling it home, though...

"Our world is modern," she said, interrupting my thoughts. "Perhaps we are not so different from your people in terms of our economies. We are only technologically more advanced."

Call that a given. She spoke of her early life, that being one of study. "On our world, we are expected to learn and to obey our parents. I imagine you would call me a dutiful daughter."

She uttered a self-deprecating laugh, as if being dutiful was the most boring thing in the world. For her, maybe it was. "My mother died when I was small, so I spent most of my time assisting my father. In our culture, it is not unusual for children to assist one or both of their parents in their daily work."

Well, that was one thing we had in common. I'd helped my father run this ship after my mother had passed away. As for hobbies, I wondered about hers. I didn't have any, not really, outside of keeping in shape by jogging and lifting weights three times a week. I kept them in one of the storage rooms. They were simple barbells and dumbbells. Call them primitive, but they worked.

"You are in excellent condition," Merlynni observed. "Our people are generally small and lean."

A compliment…yes! "Thanks, but, uh, you have fangs and claws," I replied as we stood by a porthole to gaze out at the inky darkness. "That's sort of a game changer."

She glanced at me. "Game changer? If by that, you mean it can alter the outcome of a fight, the answer is yes. I do not like using them, but in a fight, they are necessary. Other races that have visited our world in the past commented on them…negatively. They thought us barbarians."

Merlynni didn't strike me as being a savage. She spoke very formally, yes, but her attitude and her way of carrying herself—quietly and with dignity—made me think that alien races were not all the same and could be friendly. "I guess you miss your world."

"In a way, I do. Do you miss yours?"

Nice deflection, but there was no reason for me not to tell the truth. "Yeah, I'm, uh, I'm not much for living in space. I want ground under my feet, a real sun to look at—that kind of thing. Living here is just, uh…too random for me. I want permanence."

She nodded but continued her inspection of the heavens without looking at me. "I understand. I would like the same thing, although not on my world."

"No?"

Merlynni turned to face me. "No. I was not happy there so much, but it was my home, and my father must be worried."

Whoa, stop, go back. "Define 'not happy'."

She inhaled then blew out a deep breath, as if ready to make some grand confession. "As a little girl, I was not accepted. I…I lied before."

"Lied?"

Merlynni bowed her head. "You see, the fangs, the claws—they are rare among our people. So is the transparency of my torso. I am an anomaly. The majority of our people do not have this trait. I was called a freak, an aberration."

Her voice shook and a single tear traced its way from her right eye down her cheek. "My parents loved me— that much I know. But they could not fix what I was born to be. On our world, such thinking is that people like me cannot get married or ascend to higher positions in life, no matter how intelligent or gifted we are. I had altercations with the other children when I was small. That is how things were. That is how I learned how to fight."

A low and mournful sigh burst from her. "When I was seventeen—that was a year ago—one of the more prominent families in my city asked my father to introduce me to their son. It was an unusual request, but he honored it."

Introductions meant that they went to a garden and sat among their florae. First, the parents spoke of their children, their schools and their hopes for a blissful union. It all sounded so contrived, but that was their world, not mine.

"I did not like their son," Merlynni said. "He was fat and ugly, and he had a horrid smell about him, like dirty water. But my father had hopes that I would marry. I met this boy, and he and I took a walk in our garden. It was there that he kissed me. His thick lips, his stench… He said that he liked me. I felt nothing for him but revulsion."

Her voice grew hushed. "It was impolite, yes, but him touching me… I felt violated. Honesty is best, so I showed him my…my condition."

Strange that she'd term her transparent stomach that, but whatever. To me, it was how she'd been born. Another tear slipped from her left eye and traced its way down her cheek. She made no effort to brush it away.

"His face changed in an instant, and he said that he could never be joined with someone who was abnormal. This man, who smelled like a *yagult*, would not have me."

I didn't know what a 'yagult' was, but it probably wasn't anyone or anything I wanted to meet. Anguish coated her next words. "I did not wish to be born this way. However, I have come to accept what I am."

Her way of speaking, so honest and pure and tinged with sadness and loss, hit home and part of my heart broke for her. It didn't matter what she looked like. It mattered what she was. "I'm, um, fine with how you look."

While that sounded clichéd, I meant it and hoped that she wouldn't consider me to be a hopelessly naïve twit — which I was.

"You are?"

She sounded skeptical. Gaining her trust would be difficult but not impossible. Once again, I told her the truth. "Look… If I didn't like you, I would have left you in that cage and I wouldn't have given you food — or my room. I don't expect you to believe me, but —"

"Thank you," Merlynni interrupted. "I do not trust others so easily, not after what happened. I am especially mistrustful of my own people."

"Well, I'm not one of your people. And, uh, I'm open to having, you know, someone nice to hang out with."

If that didn't sound pathetic, I didn't know what did. Merlynni arched her eyebrows so high that they almost met her hairline. "Hang out with? I do not understand."

"Oh, it means to be, um, friends with, talk things over…that kind of thing."

She narrowed her eyes as if assessing the truthfulness of my statement, then she bobbed her head once, as if arriving at a momentous decision. "I see. I am grateful for your help…and your friendship."

Friendship… In the old days, they'd used the term 'friend zoning'. Had I just been relegated to the also-ran status? Hopefully not, but no… She took my hand in hers briefly and squeezed it. "And I need a friend."

Time to take a chance. "How about something more?"

Merlynni gazed at me before flashing a brief smile. "Yes, perhaps something more. We shall see."

Our moment of relating or bonding or whatever got interrupted when a message came over the intercom. "Rick, we've got company."

Nerfer—he would have to interrupt. I went to the wall-com and punched a button. "Friendly or unfriendly?"

"In the middle, from what I know. They're Cloradians. I can tell from the design of their ship."

Cloradians? "Uh, have you done business with them before?"

His answer came quickly. "Nah, but I heard about them from some other people I worked with. Cloradians are salvagers. Lots of their people salvage old vessels and sell them on the private market. They want to come aboard and parlay for business. That's their word — 'parlay'. It's not mine."

What to do? "Is their ship armed?"

"Yep."

Damn it! "Are they near this ship?"

"They're going to dock with us, soon."

Double damn! "All right."

Like I had a choice? I gestured for Merlynni to follow me, and we went to the airlock. Sure enough, just as we reached our destination, a dull thud signaled that the Cloradian craft had docked with our vessel.

The screen monitor showed a rather smallish ship, perhaps thirty meters in length. Most of the length was in the nose, long and needle-like. The rest of the ship was round. It was an odd-looking thing, but in the past three years, I'd seen all kinds of strange.

The door on their side of the airlock slid open and two of them entered. They reminded me of a picture I'd seen in my old holo-vids of a dung beetle rolling its prize along the ground — only they resembled the dung. "Stand by for decontamination."

"Hurry!"

That came from the lead alien who wore a light blue bodysuit that bulged in all the wrong places. *Impatient jerk.* "Commencing…now."

It took only ten seconds, but to them, it must have seemed an eternity. The readout said no harmful pathogens, so we were safe. On the other hand, when I got a good look at our guests, my concept of no-harm faded.

Both stood in the realm of a hundred and sixty centimeters. They were squat and pale, and they looked vaguely humanoid. And, like the precious cargo of the dung beetles, they stank even worse than Kulida and his men had. Did they not understand the concept of bathing?

Obviously not, or else that was their natural body aroma, in which case I pitied my nose hairs. They'd only just recovered since their encounter with the Rattanians and the yak-men, and now they had to go through the same torture again.

Were these Cloradians a threat? In Nerfer's words, maybe. Salvagers were nothing more than high-end junk pickers, and they had a rep of defending their booty by using violence first and reason second.

Sizing them up, perhaps hand to hand, I could take at least one of them—maybe both. On the other hand, the guns they carried—long and spindly—marked them as people not to trust. Nerfer would have to be right. "Where is your cargo?" one of them asked in an odd, buzzing tone.

"We don't have any," I answered, looking at their weapons and sizing up how much damage they could do. Undoubtedly, a lot.

"Guys, you can put the guns away. This is a restaurant ship. You get a meal, and whatever payment you can afford, that's fine. We don't carry anything valuable."

Virus number two jabbed his gun into Merlynni's shoulder, which provoked a squeal of rage. "You lie! We have scanned your ship. You have ion propulsion engines."

What an idiot! What did he want, to take the engines? "Hey, first off, you don't jab a member of my crew."

He glared at me. "And?"

Moron. "And…you don't. Period. Next, you said you were here to parlay. That means making a deal, where

I come from. You don't come on board and act like you own this ship. You don't."

Apparently, he thought he did, as he brandished his weapon in my face. "You will let us take your specifications. If we are pleased, then we will take one of your engines."

Say *what*? I tried to phrase my answer as nicely as possible so as to not antagonize these morons any further. "Guys, this ship needs both engines to function. If you take an engine, we'll have no way of getting around."

I hated myself for sounding desperate. Dung heap number one shook his head. "That is no concern of ours."

No, it wasn't. Merlynni hissed out her answer. "Scum! You are scum! You are nothing more than ravagers!"

A grin suffused the leader's face. "We are, and we are proud of such an appellation."

He raised his gun and pointed at her gut. Oh, no, if he fired, that would be the end of us all. "Enough!" I yelled.

He looked up in surprise as I charged him. The impact caused him to bang into his friend. They both fell to the ground, but in doing so, their guns went off simultaneously and the blast opened a hole in the ceiling. There was nothing to protect us. In fact, we had no shields.

Crap, they're going to kill us! The alarm went off, a shrill clanging that caused my eardrums to vibrate. A nearby intercom buzzed. "Rick, what's going on?"

Nerfer—he'd been listening. "We've got a breach, airlock area," I yelled. "Hurry!"

The breach had been small at first, no more than the size of my fist, but then the vacuum of space took over and started to pull the metal apart and it all happened quickly. *Oh…crap, the air's going!*

"Merlynni, move!"

She froze, but I grabbed her around the waist just as her feet left the ground and we hung onto the railing on the wall. The vacuum sucked out the aliens and their weapons in an instant. I held on for dear life, hoping Nerfer would come and do something about it.

My grip was giving out, and Merlynni yelled her rage and terror into the void that lay only a few meters away. Her claws came out and dug into my arm, causing me to grunt in pain, but long-term survival overrode immediate injury. I gripped the railing even more tightly and we both cried out, "Nerfer!"

"Hang on!"

Nerfer's voice came from behind me. He slogged forward in his containment suit, carrying a long gun that resembled an old-style bazooka. Although he moved slowly, there was a reason—he'd weighted his suit down with magnetic devices that clamped onto the floor and kept him stable. "Hang on," he repeated and fired at the hole.

A glob of reddish-green slime shot out of the muzzle, covered the hole and the awful, gut-wrenching, fear-inducing and air-sucking vacuum stopped. We dropped to the floor, our chests heaving, and Merlynni clung to me and whispered, "That was…awful."

Tell me about it. "Thanks, Nerfer," I said. "You came just in time."

While that was a horrible cliché, my co-pilot didn't seem to mind. "Least I could do. I'd hate to be alone on this tin can for the rest of my life."

That was the closest he'd ever come to admitting he liked me. He burbled out, "I'm going to my cabin," and moved off, while my female co-passenger reluctantly let go.

"I am sorry for behaving this way," she said by way of an apology. "I mean, holding on to you. Do you think it improper?"

Was she kidding? The answer, of course, was no—even if she'd pierced my arm with her claws. "Uh, it's okay. I kind of liked it, to be honest."

That admission prompted a smile. "I liked it as well."

She then looked at my suit and her smile disappeared. "There is blood on your arm!"

I checked it out, and…oh, yeah. It didn't hurt much. "That's okay."

Merlynni glanced at her hands. "I am sorry, my claws—"

"Don't worry. We'll go the infirmary."

That we did, and after I'd fixed myself up, we made our way back to the bridge. Nerfer had probably left a mess. As we walked along the corridors, I asked her if she wanted more adventures like the one we'd just had. "I would rather go home."

"I'd like to send you back, Merlynni."

It hurt me to say so. I didn't want to be alone, but she had a life, too, and I had no right to force her to stay. Her next words, though, put my mind and heart at ease. "For the moment, I am here. I wish to help."

"Thanks, Merlynni. I appreciate that."

She ducked her head shyly. "Please call me Lynni."

It came out as Lee-nai, with the accent on the second syllable. "Lynni?"

"My mother used to say that. It was her special name for me."

Lynni it would be. "Well, I guess that we need a first mate."

"What does that mean?"

"You're now part of the crew."

Chapter Seven

A Question of Bravery

Fortunately for us, the Cloradians didn't have any more men in their ship, although their vessel remained locked onto ours. Once we'd gathered on the bridge, Nerfer spoke to the computer. "Computer, disengage alien vessel from our dock."

Whir...click. "Impossible to disengage," it answered. "Unable to override their own computer commands."

Marvelous. "So, what do we do now?" I asked.

Nerfer pointed to the window. "I'm going to have to do it manually."

"You need help?"

His body went from side to side, meaning no. "Rick, this is a one-person job. I'm more familiar with alien tech than you are. If something happens, I'm expendable. You're not."

With that, we went to the airlock, where he suited up and went inside. Once there, he attached a tether line to the wall and opened the airlock. He floated out, his body undulating gracefully upon the weightlessness of space.

Lynni watched with me as he worked. Curses floated over the airwaves, and she blushed as he compared the circuitry and the mechanisms he had to work through to various organs and systems of elimination. "Do all people speak that way?" she whispered in the voice of someone who was truly innocent.

"Only if they're dicks," I answered, using an expression from long ago. That earned me a hard shot to my shoulder. All right, she wasn't *that* innocent. She understood slang, so that meant that I'd have to watch the sarcasm around her.

At first, Nerfer tried using a laser to burn through the clamp, but when that didn't work, he used the mini jetpack on his suit to pop over to their main hatchway and cut his way in. A few minutes later, he emerged with a triumphant "I got it" that echoed through space.

A tiny thump followed by a brief tremor signaled that the Cloradian ship had been disengaged from our docking site. It floated free and slowly moved out of range. After Nerfer had zipped back to our ship, he entered our airlock in short order and called out, "Decontaminate."

Once the protocol was over, he came through the door and reached inside a pocket of his suit to take something out. "Got something for you," he said as he tossed a rock at me.

A souvenir? It failed to impress, as it was only a small brown rock half the size of my palm. It didn't give off any sensation or sound—nothing at all. Finally, totally underwhelmed by the souvenir, I gave in and asked, "What is this?"

"A last-ditch resort," he answered as he shucked his suit. "That, there, is a *guller*."

"A what?"

He picked up his suit with one quickly formed arm and tucked it under another formed arm. "I've seen this before. It's a last-ditch resort," he repeated. "When all is lost, you use it."

That answered nothing and left me confused. "So, what am I supposed to do with it?"

I figured it would emit a cloaking field or some kind of energy. It had to have secret properties to it. From what I knew, all alien tech did.

"You throw it at something that's attacking you," he tossed over his shoulder and strode off down the hallway.

Throw a rock. Right, like that was going to help. Lynni giggled at his answer. Some help she was. Fine, I tucked Mr. Rock away into my pocket and made for the bridge. My stomach growled, which meant it was time for lunch. "You want something to eat?" I asked. "I'd like to cook something for you."

"That would be most enjoyable," she said, almost as if she were confessing to something illicit. "I enjoy food. I particularly liked that circular bit of meat your captain prepared."

Circular bit of meat? "You mean the hamburger?"

She blinked. "Yes, that was it. I forgot the name. Thank you. Your captain has quite a talent. It was quite delicious."

My captain – thanks a lot. Her reply soured me on the let's-make-something concept, but I'd promised. "Let's go."

It didn't take me very long to get our meal ready, but halfway through, the computer interrupted our feasting to warn us about an approaching vessel. "Name of vessel and point of origin," I said.

"Unknown."

Was it dangerous? I had no idea if it was or not. Academic, anyway, as the computer reported, "Shift occurring."

A nanosecond later, a violent surge tossed us and our lunch—spaghetti, this time, along with meat sauce—into the next booth, along with a mess of lettuce and dressing.

"Is that standard on this vessel?" Lynni asked while swiping bits of lettuce and pasta from her shoulders. She proceeded to check her hair and pulled out a few stray strands of spaghetti.

"Sometimes, yeah."

The shuddering stopped, and where were we now? Lynni excused herself and went off to the washroom, while I asked the computer to give me a readout of our surroundings. "Computer, which galaxy is this?"

It whirred and clicked, then gave its answer. "Preliminary data suggests that we are in a quadrant of space known as the Orulian Galaxy."

Orulian? That was a new one. While I pondered the wheres and whys of shifting, Lynni returned with her face and hands freshly washed. "Have you made any progress in discovering our whereabouts?"

Always so formal. We'd have to work on that. "Orulian Galaxy."

"I'm getting a bit tired of this shifting," Nerfer called out as he entered the room.

"Does it interrupt your beauty sleep?" I teased.

A harsh grunt greeted my question. "You know that I don't sleep. I rest. Computer, show us a map."

Obediently, the computer threw up a hologram. A red dot depicted us among the bright white lights that denoted the stars.

"From what we just heard, the computer called this place the Orulian Galaxy," Lynni replied as she examined the hologram, her fingers tracing the outlines of the constellations, whatever they were. "But I have never seen this star cluster. I was rather good at astronomy in school. It was my favorite subject as a little girl."

Bottom line — we were lost. In the past, we'd always been tossed hither and yon throughout the known galaxies, distant though they may have been. Now, no. However, at the very least, we were orbiting a world, one that looked like Earth, although what was on it was anyone's guess. "Computer, readout of planet below us."

Click-click went the computer. Clearly, it wasn't used to this part of space, although the area we'd landed in didn't seem to be threatening in any way. No bending of matter, no hallucinations — all seemed normal, as normal as it would ever get around here.

With a tiny hiccup, our computer resumed its smooth function. "Planet is Class M, oxygen-nitrogen atmosphere. No major cities detected. No evidence of movement on the surface."

Class M...that meant it could support human life! Then, the information hit me. "No movement?"

"None."

"Clarify."

"No animal movement. Sensors detect forests and mountainous areas, lakes and rivers, but no indigenous animal life, humanoid life or evidence of insect life."

Great, so either it was a paradise or else the animals were hiding somewhere. Was it possible that a planet could have no animal life at all? It didn't seem possible, yet this was a different part of the universe. Perhaps the laws of biological development were different, or they didn't apply — or something.

Lynni nudged my shoulder and I turned to face her. "What?"

"Is that a place for you to live?"

She was nothing if not perceptive. I had to think about it. "Maybe we could visit."

Nerfer piped up with, "What's this about a visit?"

While I washed up, we talked over the prospect of going down to check it out. He didn't think it was a great idea. "You don't know what's really down there."

His answer would have to be negative. "Oh, come on, Nerfer. Why not? The computer gave us the readout. It's a Class M world. Oxygen-nitrogen atmosphere, good air, right? It's got lots of trees and lakes. We'd only be gone for a couple of hours. Then we'll come back."

Eyebrows formed in his formless matter. "*We?*"

I gestured to Lynni. "Us, I mean."

Bob-bob. "And...you're going to take the scout ship down there?"

Lynni turned to me in surprise. "You have a scout ship?"

We did. It was called a Darter. My father had gotten it from the US Air Force. He'd refurbished it while on Earth and we had it stored in the landing bay, which was on the far side of the ship. In one of the few instances since I'd known Nerfer, a doubtful expression formed on my pink friend's faceless form. "Rick, what about the shift?"

Fair question, so I addressed the computer. "When is the next shift? And how long will it take to get to the surface of the planet via the scout ship?"

"This unit has no information on that possibility," it replied. "This unit knows only the estimated travel time from this vessel to the planet's surface."

"Which is?"

"At maximum speed, twenty-five minutes."

Now, that kind of computation I could work with. "We'll be back before long," I said, doing my best to keep a wheedling tone out. I hated begging for things, and getting his permission was really a trip down embarrassment lane. Wasn't I the captain of this ship — at least, one of the captains? Didn't I have a say in things?

Apparently not, as Nerfer stood with his pseudo-arms folded across his lumpy chest. "C'mon," I begged and hated myself for it. "A short trip. We'll take samples if you want."

He shifted his body this way and that, as if weighing the options, then he waved a pseudopod in our direction. "Go. Never mind the samples. Just be careful. I'll monitor things from up here."

That was all I needed to hear. Lynni gave me a questioning glance, but she dutifully followed me to the landing bay. There, the Darter waited. As the name implied, it was a gray, dart-shaped missile that was an upgraded version of an old space shuttle the US Air Force used to use.

Forty meters in length and five meters in width, it had enough room for two people and fifty kilograms of cargo, if necessary. The wings were swept back affairs, and they automatically unfolded to thirty-three meters upon takeoff.

"It is an impressive vessel," Lynni said as I went through the pre-flight checklist.

Darn right it was impressive. I'd kept up the maintenance of the craft every two days or so. Since Lynni had arrived, I'd let things slide, but since she was now part of the crew, I had to make good on my concept of acting like a captain.

"Thanks. It is."

After I ran through the checklist, I popped the hatch and we climbed in. "Okay, we're ready," I said as I got into the pilot's seat. "I used to fly this a lot. Recently, no."

"Why did you not tell me you had this craft on board your vessel?" Lynni asked from behind me. She sounded annoyed. "I could have used it to rejoin my people."

Was there some universal law that obligated me to tell her everything? Rhetorical—there wasn't. Still, she didn't sound angry, merely confused. I clicked on the start-up switches.

"The Darter has limited range, about a quarter of a parsec at most. Its interstellar radio's range is limited to that distance, and it only has enough oxygen for about sixteen hours. If your world is farther away than the distance I said, you'd drift until you ran out of oxygen, and that's no way to go."

She humphed her disappointment and settled back in her seat. "Buckle up," I said and sent a signal to open to the bay doors. After the engines came online, we took off and jetted out of the bay.

To be honest, it was sheer joy to handle this ship. I'd trained on it during my days on Earth as well as my early days on the ship and found that it handled smoothly. My flight instructor back in Utah—a hard-faced, grizzled veteran of the air wars named Victor

Morton—had told me I was one of the best young pilots he'd ever trained.

"You know more about this ship than most of the ten-year guys do. I can teach you a lot — I already have — but you seem to have that special instinct in flying it. If you ever want to captain a star fighter, I'll put in a good word for you."

Me, a captain? It had never occurred to me, although I'd enjoyed flying. My father had taken me aside a few days later after I'd landed from a solo flight and said that Morton had spoken to him. He'd been incredibly upbeat and had worn a smile a mile wide. *"I'll agree with Morton. You're a natural pilot. I don't have to teach you a thing!"*

High praise—he had very rarely praised me on anything. But, after thinking it over, I'd realized that he really didn't know how many times I'd thrown up after a practice run—or how much I'd sweated during the flights, both within the Earth's atmosphere as well as outside it, or how many hours I'd devoted to learning in the virtual simulator my holo-puter put up for my benefit.

However, that had been then, and this was now. Once I flew out of the landing bay, the Darter handled as beautifully as ever under my control. As we cruised through space, Lynni gasped and began to make a series of dry heaving sounds. I didn't bother turning my head. She had space sickness. I'd had the same reaction the first couple of times I'd flown with my instructor.

"Bags should be in a small pocket in front of you," I said. "On the back of my seat, I mean."

Her voice came out breathlessly. "I see them."

A moment later, the rustle of bags sounded, followed by the most godawful barfing sounds I'd ever heard…and the smell was horrible! The sounds of throwing up continued, so I focused my attention on the monitor. We flew over a landmass that the Darter's computer said was roughly the size of the US, so I'd aimed the ship there.

Flames lit up on the surface of the Darter as we entered the atmosphere. Reentry was rough, what with the ship shaking and Lynni heaving. I breathed through my mouth until we touched down to the surface of the planet twenty minutes later.

Once there, I immediately cracked the hatch. Oh, yes, sweet relief! Warm, fresh air flowed around me, and it was a thousand times better than the recycled air on the ship.

As for Lynni, she got out holding the barf-bags — five of them — and she deposited them near the ship's stern. "I am sorry," she muttered then spat out a mouthful of yellow bile. "I am not used to…space travel."

Uh-huh, and she'd wanted to fly the ship? Not likely. "Feeling better now?"

Her skin had turned a bright shade of blue, but her normal color soon flooded back. "I will be…fine. Where are we?"

Good question. It was hot out — and immediately, I started to sweat. It had to be around twenty-seven degrees Celsius, but I could deal with it. Being on a planet and having earth beneath my feet helped put me in a more positive mindset. I could actually live here. Yeah — this place would do nicely.

We'd landed in a field near a forest of bluish-purple trees. Yellowish-green grass surrounded us. It was waist high, and it felt surprisingly soft to the touch. The smell of the air was pure and sweet, untouched by any civilization. There was no buzz of electrical poles or wires, no insects…in fact, there was nothing near us, save the trees.

And they were something else! Outside of their color, they were tall, in the realm of a hundred-and-fifty meters and perhaps more, with wide, pancake-shaped leaves, and they seemed to blot out the sun. "Do we enter?" Lynni asked, while pointing at the forest.

I didn't get any bad vibes from the trees, and they didn't emit any unusual odor. "Yeah, why not?"

Lynni took my arm as we slowly approached the forest, our feet scrunching the soft earth. Her touch, light and yet with a hint of great strength, sent a thrill through me. It was like being on a date — sort of.

I noticed that while there was no pathway, the space between the trees was wide enough, and the forest floor was relatively flat and even. A smell, something like freshly cut hay, wafted over, and once more, the feeling of home hit me.

"This is beautiful," Lynni said as we walked along, keeping an eye out for any suspicious movement. However, there was none. "We have forests on our world, but nothing like this!"

"No?"

She shook her head. "No. Ours are far fewer in number. They are also smaller, perhaps four meters in height at the most and green, with tiny leaves. These are giants."

Giants and gigantic, yes. They practically covered the surrounding area. I remembered my lessons about the old-time pioneers on Earth around four hundred years before. They'd built log cabins and other primitive buildings, tamed the land and forged a new society.

Our sojourn continued, with the foliage around the trees becoming denser. I pushed it aside, feeling the roughness of it against my skin. It didn't feel much different from the bushes and grass back on Earth from what I remembered, and the longing for a home intensified.

"You are thinking of something," Lynni said. "Your brow is furrowed in concentration. What is it—a place to live?"

She must have been a mind-reader, and had I been that obvious? Probably. "Well, yeah. And I told you about it on the ship, right?"

Lynni glanced at me. "You would live alone?"

Oh, was this leading where I thought it was? "Uh, if I had someone to spend time with, that would be better."

She remained silent, but a shy, almost embarrassed smile came to her face. "That would be interesting."

Silence then descended, and after a few more minutes of tramping around, the question of personal relationships arose, with me doing the asking. Lynni laughed softly when I mentioned her having a boyfriend.

"If, by that, you mean a mate, the answer is no. While we are promised to each other around the age of twelve, the interest—the physical interest—does not begin until we are sixteen. When I reached my sixteenth year, the way you judge years, that was when many boys became interested—at least, at first. On our world, we have a saying—many attempt, but few succeed."

From the way she phrased her answer, it sounded like a contest. "It can be considered such," she replied after I'd brought up the concept of competition. "Men and women are expected to vie for one another's affections, either through accomplishments in the arts or sciences."

Sadness coated her next words. "In my case, though, my fangs...my claws...and the fact that my stomach is transparent. Once the males on my world saw what I was and what set me apart, they wanted nothing to do with me. I mentioned that other boy who kissed me, did I not?"

"Well, yeah, but—"

"But what?" She faced me with an innocent expression, her lips parted just so and her eyes, glowing.

My stomach lurched and my heart skipped a few beats. "But, uh, well, if I asked you out, would you say yes?"

By now, we'd entered a deeper part of the forest and it was getting dimmer as well as harder to move around. "Well? If you don't want to go out..."

Lynni suddenly stopped and reached over to grip my hand. "It is an idea that I am in favor of, although I do not want to be asked out of pity."

I turned to her. "It's not pity."

An odd smile came to her face. "What is it, then?"

Okay, here came the explanation, but her jaw abruptly sagged. She wasn't focused on my clumsy attempt to say that I liked her. She was thinking of — and looking at — something else.

A second later, she clamped her mouth shut and pointed at one of the trees that lay dead ahead. "Over there."

I followed her finger. "Uh, yeah. What's going on?"

"Look."

She'd pointed at a particular tree, one that was much larger than the rest. It had a scarred trunk and grayish bark instead of the usual blue-purple combination. "Okay, what am I looking for?"

"That tree...the big one...it moved."

Lynni had to be joking. Trees didn't move. They were living organisms, yes, but they had roots and stayed where they were. "Moved?"

She turned to me, her eyes wide, and I could tell she wasn't kidding. "Yes, it moved. The branches moved, as if they wanted to swat something aside."

Maybe there was something in the air, after all. I didn't smell anything like a drug, though. "Don't be dumb, Lynni. Trees are trees. If they moved, it's because of the wind or something."

Now, her eyes narrowed, and she let go of my hand to plant both of hers on her hips. "Is there any wind here?"

Good point. Since we'd entered the forest, the wind had died away. "No."

"There is your answer," she said sharply. "My people are not ones for fabricating stories. I saw what I saw."

Indignation, thy name is Lynni, so I felt it was best to say nothing. We continued walking, but now, my senses were on high alert. The pleasant smell had faded. Instead, a smell unlike rotting food replaced it, and...

"Oh, holy crap!"

That exclamation burst out of me, and it caused Lynni to clutch my arm—painfully. "What is it?"

"You were right."

She would have to be right. A rustling sound from the tree confirmed that its branches had moved—and they were moving now, going lower, as if to block our way. "That tree...is alive," she said, her voice suddenly fearful.

This couldn't be happening, but it was. "Uh, Lynni, it's time to leave," I murmured, and we turned around to retrace our steps out of the forest.

It was then that the biggest tree rolled forward on tube-like roots. "Oh, this is not good," Lynni whispered in a little girl's voice. "This is *not* good!"

Fright hit me between the eyes and my body began to shake. The forest—if not the entire planet—was alive! "Tell me about it."

My case of drop-a-load got worse when the largest tree rolled straight in front of us, its branches crossed in front of its massive trunk. It quivered all over, its branches agitated now, and a sound emanated from deep inside it, a sound like a saw cutting wood, only I had the feeling we were the wood and it was the saw.

My suspicions were confirmed when a split in the trunk began at its base and rapidly worked its way upward. It wasn't a straight split, either—more like a jagged line—and it made a horrid cracking noise that made my spine practically seize up.

"Is that...?" Lynni asked in a tiny voice before falling silent.

Oh, hell, it was! A mouth formed on the tree, one with sharp, irregularly shaped wooden teeth that moved rhythmically, horizontally, and with purpose and power. The other trees didn't have mouths, and neither did they shift their position, but they put their branches down as if to ward off any attempt at escape.

As for the leader, it was larger than the rest, and it advanced on us, its mouth growing ever longer and wider and moving ever faster. The sawing sound, a harsh rasp, grew louder and my nerves got more and more frayed.

"What do we do?" my partner asked.

Leaving would have been the best idea, but just as I summoned up the ballpower to do something and got my nerves to function, a branch from the leader tree whizzed past my head. That was novel.

Another branch then another buzzed over our heads and smacked into the trees behind us. That wasn't a warning. It was simply nailing down its aim at its targets—us. As the assault continued, a sudden stab of pain threw me to the ground and a gasp of agony erupted from my lungs. "Aw, crap!"

One of the branches had gotten through, slamming into my right shoulder. Lynni immediately threw her body over mine. "Is it bad?" I asked.

Getting injured was never a good thing, and the branches continued to whiz over our heads. "Bad enough," she said, and in a quick move, she yanked it out.

What else could I do but yell in pain? "Ow, damn it!"

Comparing aches and pains seemed pointless, but when I remembered banging my knee a few months ago against a drainage pipe and compared it to the pain of a wooden spear entering my body, it wasn't overly difficult to figure out which was worse. In a quick motion, Lynni tore off a piece of her bodysuit and stuffed the patch against my shoulder. "Wait here."

Right, where else was I going to go? "Lynni, don't…"

Too late. She charged the main tree, her claws out, and she proceeded to deflect every branch it fired at her. Her hands moved like lightning, and her claws slashed each thick branch to splinters.

"Get away from him," she yelled. "Try me!"

Oh, she was fierce! Moving quickly, she attacked the leader tree, her claws raking its massive trunk, and it emitted a sound akin to a scream. Good... Even though it couldn't communicate, it could feel pain. Her arms moved faster, and the slashes grew deeper. "Try me!"

Fury was fine, but it wasn't enough as the leader tree advanced on us and smacked her across the face, sending her staggering back to my side. Lynni shook her head to clear it, muttering, "It is too tough. What can we do now?"

Good question. We couldn't go around. The other trees were blocking off our escape. They must have been taking orders from the biggest of the big...telepathy, maybe. Maybe their roots sent signals. I didn't know and didn't care.

As the large tree drew nearer, I wondered how to get out of here. What had Nerfer said...last-ditch resort?

Yes!

"Lynni, can you throw something?"

She blinked. "Throw what?"

With an effort, I pulled the guller from my pocket. "This...this rock. My right shoulder—I'm right-handed. I can't do it."

After giving it to her, she asked, "What is this?"

"Nerfer...he told me...said it was a last chance. When that thing opens its mouth, throw it in."

"Understood."

The tree grew closer, its mouth moving ever faster, and the chop-chop sound of its teeth grew louder. "Now," I said. "Now!"

Lynni threw the guller straight and true at the oncoming tree. It went into the mouth. The tree gave an audible gulp, then it began to bulge in twenty different directions. Had it possessed eyes, they would have shown surprise, but no other features save the mouth moved.

It then gave a horrible groan, as if it realized that it had just eaten a particularly indigestible morsel. *Uh-oh...*

"Lynni, time to leave!"

Heedless of the pain in my shoulder, I got up and we started to weave our way among the branches to freedom. Just as we reached the exit point, an enormous bang sounded, white light filled my vision and I found myself on my stomach. We were out of the forest, maybe twenty meters from our previous position. When I turned around to view the forest, only smashed trees remained.

"Can you get off?" a muffled voice asked.

Someone's hands pushed at my chest, and the voice came again. "Please, get off."

Lynni! "Uh, sorry."

With an effort, I rolled over, a hand to my injured shoulder. She got up, shaking her head. "What was that?"

"Bomb blast," I said, hearing my voice echo. My ears still rang from the explosion, and a sharp pain filled my right side. Oh, wonderful, first my shoulder and now, this. The pain came from a spot just beneath the short ribs. A branch had speared me, and blood was leaking out, although not excessively.

Lynni didn't wait to ask me if I needed help. She simply pulled the branch out in one smooth motion. I was worried that the branch might have poison on it or in it. Bleeding to death wasn't on the menu, but being poisoned wasn't, either.

"Gah!"

If anything, this one hurt worse than the branch that had gone through my shoulder, and a cry of pain erupted from my lungs. A spurt of blood from the wound followed. Lynni, though, refused to let me suffer as she quickly tore more of her suit apart and fashioned a crude bandage. She then slapped it against the injured area and told me to put pressure on it. It wasn't perfect, but it stopped most of the bleeding.

"Get up," she said as she helped me to my feet.

The blood loss wasn't that bad — yet — but we had to get back to the ship. Although our scout vessel lay only a few meters away, it might as well have been a kilometer, and that would have meant my death.

Lynni, though, wasn't prepared to let me expire. She helped me over to the Darter and practically threw me inside. She was a lot stronger than she looked. Once I was seated, on went the com-link. "Nerfer, you there?"

His voice crackled over the airwaves. "Yeah, kid. What's wrong?"

"Got stabbed by a tree. Get the med kit ready."

Silence. Then, "You got stabbed by a tree? What'd you do, pick some of its fruit?"

"Not funny. Just get ready!"

"I'll be waiting."

With an effort, I started up the engine and punched in the coordinates. "I cannot fly this craft," Lynni said. She sounded on the verge of panic, but she hadn't been injured. I had.

"You won't have to. I put it on automatic pilot. Hang on. The hatch is closing."

Good thing, too, as the trees that had survived the blast came after us, rolling on their roots and emitting horrible screeching noises. Their branches slashed at the hull, but the Darter began to move forward faster and faster, then we blasted off.

Exactly twenty-five minutes later, we arrived back at the landing bay. Fortunately, Lynni didn't have a recurrence of her space sickness. She merely kept her hand on my good shoulder and told me to stay awake.

I was in too much pain to sleep. Once we landed, Nerfer met us in the bay, holding a small box the size of a paperback novel. Lynni helped me out and he went to work right away, examining me with another device, a fist-sized body scanner that could check out everything from internal organs to blood vessels.

He played the machine up and down my body, and the device beeped. "You're bleeding badly, and you've got internal damage."

Tell me something I don't know. "Can you do something?"

Nerfer hefted the first device. "The Hifu Ray should help."

Ah, yes, the Hifu Ray. It had been a gift from a grateful traveler whose ship had broken down two years before. My father had sheltered him for a few days while he'd repaired his ship, and as a present, the alien—a little toad-like man—had given us this gift. He'd said that it would heal small damage in our inner selves.

He'd sure had an odd way of speaking, but whatever. The ray had worked on a deep gash to my father's thigh. He'd gotten it while repairing something in the engine room. The machine's rays had closed the wound in a matter of seconds.

Nerfer used the ray to do the same thing to my torso wound. Agony flashed through my body, and I cried out in pain. The pain continued when he turned it on my shoulder. Within seconds, though, right before my eyes, my wounds largely disappeared.

His pseudopods patted his containment suit, and he pulled a needle and some bandages from a pocket. On went the bandages, and he stabbed me in the shoulder with the needle. "It's a combo antibiotic-painkiller shot," he said. "Maybe you won't die."

Some bedside manner he had. "Thanks a lot."

A faint chuckle came from him. "Curse me out if you want. You'll live. I can't have the best cook on this ship die on me. Bad for my reputation."

Well, well, a compliment. I'd take it. He and Lynni helped me back to my parents' room. Once there, they laid me on the bed. Nerfer said something about piloting the ship, while Lynni stayed by my side and murmured, "How are you feeling?"

"Still in a lot of pain, to be honest." The shot hadn't helped that much.

I tried to shift my position, but I didn't get anywhere until Lynni gently grabbed my uninjured shoulder and my waist to hoist me into a more comfortable one. "Thanks. You were, uh, pretty spectacular out there."

Her eyes widened. "I was?"

"Yeah, with the claws, deflecting those branches. And, uh, thanks for saving my life. I mean, putting those bandages on me and all that."

Suddenly tired, I lay back, feeling the softness of the mattress against my skin. Lynni didn't respond at first. Then she muttered something about never leaving anyone behind.

"What's that?" I asked.

A tiny smile emerged. "In our culture, we are taught that one should never leave an injured friend behind. If they can be saved, then we must try to help them."

It was a noble sentiment. "I'm not from your world."

In a slow move, she traced her hand down the side of my face. A gentle, caressing movement, it made me feel as though she cared. "It does not matter. You and Nerfer saved me as well. Do you not remember?"

I did, then the ship began to shudder. "Shift occurring, shift occurring," the computer intoned.

We were leaving. Lynni hung onto my bed for support and asked, "Are you glad to be leaving that world?"

More than ever. "You know, I'm never going to look at a tree the same way again."

Chapter Eight

"Breeto."

Dreams — everyone experienced them at one point or another. Most of mine consisted of variations on the last serious talk I'd ever had with my father. It had started out as a discussion, but what it came down to in the end — at least, when a teenager and an adult were concerned — was an argument.

Had we been on Earth, it probably would have been over something silly, really, such as hanging out at a party where the other kids drank or did something harder, although I'd never been interested in drugs.

But since we weren't on Earth anymore, the sore point in my relationship with my parents wasn't drugs. It was their dreams versus mine. They dreamed of staying in space. I hoped to return to launch point Earth, for the simple reason of feeling terra firma under me. The more firma, the less terra, as the old joke went.

It was a very old joke.

And while I'd mentioned it to my parents after our first year in space had finished, and while we'd had discussions — meaning, they soon descended into arguments—my parents had listened to me then promptly gone back to their experiments and the day-to-day minutia of operating this ship. Yeah, like my opinion had mattered for anything. Rhetorical—it hadn't.

I'd thought we'd turn around after a year had gone and go home. I should have known better.

"Rick, this is our life here," my mother had said, favoring me with an indulgent smile, which meant she hadn't really been concerned with my problems. *"Please understand. We have a mission to complete. We didn't want to leave you behind on Earth."*

Then she was gone, and I'd kicked the wall in frustration. I loved my mother. She was kind and wise and she'd always been there for me—until the day she wasn't. There'd always been that link then suddenly, like a shooting star, it was gone.

My recollections of the good ole days then shifted to the last real conversation I'd had with my father, three months and six days before. Nerfer had already come on board and had filled in most capably and faithfully at the helm and in the kitchen.

On that day, we'd had a guest, a cyclops-like plant creature that had stood less than a meter in height. It said that it was neither male nor female, and although I'd never seen such an odd creature before, it had been friendly, full of stories of other galaxies and strangely shaped beings. My father had listened with rapt attention as we'd eaten lunch in the diner.

Even though the guest had come across as being genuine, hearing them talk about space and methods of propulsion and everything non-terrestrial had turned me off. I'd gotten up, inadvertently knocking my plate off the table. It had subsequently shattered as it hit the floor. *"Sorry,"* I'd said. *"My fault. I'll clean it up."*

To his credit, the alien visitor hadn't gotten angry. It had merely looked surprised, its gray eye blinking a few times. It had then nodded and spread its branch-like arms, arms that resembled plastic straws dyed a bright green, and it had offered to help me. *"No, that's okay,"* I'd said. *"Please, um, finish talking."*

I'd hastily picked up the pieces and come back with a rag to wipe everything up, cursing myself for my clumsiness. Mess cleaned up, I'd dumped the shards of the plate in the sink, along with the rag. I'd finish the job later.

Lunch had resumed, but the mood of bonhomie had been broken, and the guest had quietly suggested that it should be going. My father had looked embarrassed to no end but had graciously gotten up to usher our guest through the door.

"Thanks for dropping by," I'd said, summoning up the cheeriest tone possible. It hadn't sounded convincing, but our guest had bowed and taken its leave.

Once he'd departed, I'd started washing the dishes and hadn't looked up, even though I'd heard the slap of my father's shoes on the metal. Silence had ruled. I hadn't been much of a talker to begin with, but this...something had to be said, and my father had broken the ice by asking, *"Something wrong, son? After that little mishap with our guest — "*

"Sorry, Dad."

He'd reached over to shut off the water. *"Something is wrong. C'mon. This is your father speaking. Tell me."*

If he hadn't been able to figure it out...never mind. *"Why are you asking?"*

He'd pointed at the sink. *"You're running the water over the garbage and you're pouring soap all over the dishes."*

Oh, crap. I'd zoned out. *"If you want me to tell you the truth, it's about Mom."*

"Rick, your mother is gone."

His voice had rung with immeasurable pain, but even though it had hurt me to tell him, I'd had no choice. He'd asked me, and he'd deserved to know the truth. *"I know that, so, isn't it time to go home?"*

My father had cast his eyes to the floor. He seemed to have some trouble breathing, as he'd coughed and cleared his throat noisily before taking in a few deep breaths. *"Rick, I promised your mother we'd finish our mission. It was my promise to her.* Mine.*"*

We'd had this conversation before. It had always ended the same way. I'd shut the water off and turned to him. *"Dad, what about* my *mission? What about* my *life?"*

My question had come out plaintively, almost begging him, and what had I gotten in return? A somewhat lame shrug. *"We thought you'd be happy up here. We're a family. That was our plan all along."*

Their plan — now *his* plan — and what part had I been to play? Accomplice? Add-on? No, more like unwilling passenger. *"All right, Dad, look at me."*

When he'd picked his head up, I'd added, *"Where do I fit into this?"*

"It's your ship — "

"No, it's not *my ship!"*

We'd gone through this, too, and now, out it had come. All the resentment, all the loneliness and all the anger, everything I'd kept bottled up inside, it had bubbled to the surface. I'd smacked the grill for emphasis. Good thing it had been off.

"It's not. You and Mom refurbished this ship. You upgraded the computer system. You reinforced the hull and all that. You did – not me.

"Then Nerfer came along, and you let him stay here after Mom died. He handles the ship maybe half the time. You handle it the other half, and if you're feeling generous, you let me sit in the captain's chair for a few minutes. I'm just here to clean stuff up. That's all."

He'd looked up at me, his right eye twitching, and a spasm had rippled over his features. He'd swallowed hard before saying, "Son, even if I let you take over the captain's duties, we can't go home, yet."

What in the hell? "Why not?"

My father had started to answer me, but without warning, he'd pitched onto his face and had started to vomit. Convulsions had shaken his body, and when he'd groaned and turned over, he'd opened his mouth in a soundless scream. I'd flinched. His tongue had swollen to alarming proportions. "Nerfer! Get in here!"

My cries had caught the attention of our pink passenger. He'd emerged from the storage room behind the main counter and had oozed his way in to examine my father with a dispassionate air. "I've seen this before. The tongue is a giveaway. If the species doesn't have a tongue, then the eyes bulge out. I'm pretty sure that he's got Bridorran Fever. Get him up."

While I'd had no idea what that was, I'd laboriously heaved my father over my shoulder in a fireman's carry. On the way to the infirmary, Nerfer had told me about Bridorran Fever. It had acted much like the Black Plague of old on Earth, except that the earthly version had been carried by rats. No rodents had been here. Bridorran Fever had been viral, and on most species, it had hit the unsuspecting victim's body and started a reaction within a few minutes.

The results hadn't been pretty. Once we'd gotten my father, now ranting and raving, to the infirmary, we'd strapped him down to stop him from hitting us as well as inadvertently injuring himself. I had been frantic. *"What is it?"* I'd wanted to know. *"What's going on?"*

"Going to run some tests," Nerfer had replied as he'd taken a needle to draw some blood from my father and had run it through a small analyzer.

I'd waited, watching my father writhe in agony, and finally, after a few minutes, Nerfer had grunted. *"Yeah, it's Bridorran Fever. The tree guy must have been a carrier."*

Rage had immediately filled me at the possibility of the cyclops tree delivering deadliness, and while I'd wanted to hunt it down and turn it into salad, Nerfer had set me straight. *"Bridorran Fever is incredibly fast-acting. That's bad enough, but a lot of people, not to mention aliens, are either asymptomatic or immune. On the other hand, some of them are carriers."*

"So?"

He'd answered me with a great deal of patience. *"So, our visitor may not have known that it had it. I don't know about Earthers that much, but these tests don't lie. If you don't get sick in the next few minutes, that means you're immune. I'm just hoping that your father will pull through…maybe."*

He'd uttered that word with a horrible sense of finality. In my case, I'd never exhibited any symptoms, so immunity had become my middle name. My father hadn't been so fortunate. 'Maybe' was a five-letter word. His condition had then become an eight-letter word—'hopeless'.

It had taken only forty-eight hours. His face had swelled even more terribly than his tongue, his fever had climbed to almost forty-two degrees centigrade, and he'd sunk into a coma. After he'd taken in one final, rattling breath, he'd died.

Then there was the flight to yet another galaxy and new aliens to meet and rescuing Lynni for the first time then the attack of the trees, and I was…

"How are you feeling?"

Lynni's voice woke me from my nightmarish trip down memory lane. How long I'd been out, I had no idea, but I opened my eyes a crack and caught a glimpse of the tiny clock on my parents' night table. It read four-thirty p.m.

After wiping sweat from my forehead, I shut my eyes again, hoping to return to the land of the stars, but that wouldn't happen. Not today. Still, I'd been fortunate, not only to have survived but also to have been able to pass out and not dream about something truly horrid.

Well, if witnessing a parent's death wasn't horrid, then what was? The attack of the trees had been traumatic enough, but it was the memory of losing my parents that really messed me up. Perhaps Lynni understood what I was going through…perhaps not. But the most important thing was that she was here.

She gently touched my shoulder — my bad one — and I winced. She would have to do the probing thing. The healing ray had worked, but some residual soreness remained. "How are you feeling?" she repeated.

Now, full consciousness hit, and I sat up with a groan. My body hurt, and it became a journey to find a place where it didn't, so soon, I gave up. A quick examination showed I was still wearing my old uniform. She'd donned a new one. Pain or not, I forced out a grin and the answer of, "I'll live. You?"

"I am well."

"Glad to hear it. Where's Nerfer?"

She pointed in the general direction of the bridge. "The captain is guiding this ship, as usual. He found an extra uniform for me."

Oh, the captain thing again? Whatever. There was no point in correcting her. "Um, did he send you here to check up on me?"

A look of indignation mixed with concern shone from her eyes. "No, he did not. I came of my own accord. I wished to thank you for what you did on the planet."

What had I done, except get stabbed? Oh, wait, I was also the one who'd wanted to go there in the first place. While I hadn't known about the danger that planet posed, it was still my fault. Me and my dreams of finding terra firma…

"Well, you used your claws to stop that tree. And you threw that rock, so you saved me."

Her expression switched to one of gratitude. "That is partially true, but remember, you gave the rock to me. You knew what to do, and that is something I was not sure of. You are also a great pilot. I…I thank you."

Let's call it even. "Okay, since we're a mutual admiration society of two, what do you want to do later on?"

Lynni's look of gratitude segued into one of surprise. "Do? Are you capable of walking?"

In answer, I got up and swung my legs off the bed. After hopping to the floor, a moment of dizziness accompanied my dismount, followed by a brief staggering-around period. "I'll make it."

Healing was something that only time could do, rays aside. Being young and strong also helped. Lynni's expression of surprise turned to skepticism, then it moved into acceptance and relief, indicated by a small sigh. "Then, I wish to do something with you."

If that wasn't a loaded question, I didn't know what was. *Choose something neutral.* "How about dinner? I'll cook, and you can tell me if my cooking is better than Nerfer's. Let's say, in about three hours?"

That would make it seven-thirty p.m. I still went on biorhythms and time as we measured it on Earth. Some habits were hard to break.

A smile came my way. "I shall look forward to it." Her smile then faded. "Is what I am wearing sufficient?"

Oh, good question. This was a date, after all. "Uh, hang on."

I went to the dresser where my parents had stored their clothes, rooted around in one of the drawers and came out with a blue dress with frills on its sleeves and around the neck. It was old-fashioned in its appearance, a family heirloom. My mother had gotten it from her mother, who in turn had gotten it from her mother.

Ancient or not, it deserved to be worn. "This was my mother's. I guess it should fit you, even though you're taller than my mother was."

Lynni accepted it hesitatingly. "If you are sure. I do not wish to take that which is not mine, but—"

"That's okay." I put my hand on her shoulder as a gesture of friendship. "She'd probably say it would look great on you."

My date turned on a million-watt smile. "I am thankful for this. I will wear it."

She practically skipped out. Once she'd gone, I inhaled deeply, which wasn't too smart, as it hurt my ribs and it made me cough, which also hurt like hell. Once I'd finished my hacking fit, a rank smell came through to me—my body odor.

In the shower room, I shucked my suit and gently peeled off the bandages that Nerfer had slapped onto my body. The antibiotics as well as the painkiller were working. My bruises had largely faded, and the cuts had mostly healed. A hot shower got rid of the stench and most of the soreness, then I went back to bed to lie down again.

While counting the holes in the corrugated ceiling, another memory floated back to me. Sarah Mullins. Sarah...I hadn't thought about her in a long time. My first crush.

We'd met on the army base when my parents had been transferred to Salt Lake City. We'd been almost fifteen at the time. Her parents had been top-flight engineers, the same as my parents. We'd gravitated toward each other, even though I hadn't been able to tell her how I felt, not right away.

"You like me, don't you?" she'd asked.

We'd sat in my room, me studying some geometrical equations on my holo-puter, while she'd busied herself with one of the few remaining paperbacks around. It had been an old story by one of the most famous writers in the early two-thousands. Something about a cat-girl and her boyfriend—it had been a fine read. I'd looked up from my studies. *"Yeah, sure, I like you. Why?"*

She would have had to ask. My friendship with Todd had finished—punching him in the face repeatedly had done that. Sarah had known about it, and while she'd felt bad about my one-sided fight with him, she'd known that I'd done it because I cared about her, even if I hadn't been overly articulate in saying so.

Sarah had put the book down. *"Because I like you, too...a lot. I thought that we'd, you know, continue to go out and be with each other. That kind of thing."*

Oh. I'd been slow on the uptake. With a sense of gratitude, I'd said, *"Cool, I mean, sure. That would be great."*

Pithiness had not been part of my character. Sarah had been cool, but because I'd been in the adolescent awkward stage, not to mention having had zero experience with women, I hadn't been the best candidate for a steady relationship.

All crushes had been weird, anyway, failures waiting to happen. For me, it had been a kind of a secret just waiting to bust out. It hadn't mattered who you developed feelings for. It hadn't even mattered why. It had just happened, that deep and yearning desire that could either fulfill one's desires or smash them for all time.

In my case, it had come down to keeping my mouth shut, at least around Sarah. The other guys had asked her out, but not me. Even so, she'd turned them down, one after another, and now she had been there and I'd never known what to say.

Still, lack of verbal dexterity or not, we'd been in tune with one another. Blonde and green-eyed, slender and yet toned, she had been the first girl I'd ever liked. She had also been the first girl I'd ever kissed, awkward as it had been when we'd first done it.

"I guess we'll get better with practice, won't we?" she'd whispered when we broke the clinch.

"I guess we will."

Our time together had been marked by long walks, study periods and kisses here and there. During our time together, I'd thought that our relationship would last forever. First-time lovers always thought that way.

One year later, she'd become the first girl I'd ever said goodbye to when my parents and I had blasted off in our cargo ship for parts of space unknown.

"I'll miss you," she'd said shortly before I boarded the ship. She'd wiped a few tears away with the back of her hand and had sniffled. *"You know I will."*

"I'll miss you, too," I'd replied, knowing that her life would go on without me and feeling my heart break just the same.

We'd clung to each other for moment, then she'd released me and turned away. I'd boarded the ship, the hatch closed, and...that had been that. Perhaps my parents had known how much it had hurt me...perhaps they hadn't. They'd never mentioned it, and my life had continued—until Lynni showed up, and now I was older and still inexperienced, and who could I talk to about all this?

Well, there was one person. I got dressed in a uniform and made my way to the bridge. Nerfer was in the kitchen area, cleaning the grill. I knocked on the door and he looked up. "You feeling better?"

"Yeah, thanks for fixing me up."

He observed me closely then grunted, "You want something?"

"Advice."

He swung around and put down the rag he'd been holding. "About what?"

Suddenly, my throat decided to seize up. "Uh, well, it's about Lynni."

A chuckle came my way. "You have something going on with her?"

Gliddods were very perceptive — or maybe my face had given it away. Who knew? "I don't know much about her. She's nice. She likes me — I think — and you know that I want to go back to Earth."

Bob-bob went his body. "Yeah, you never kept that a secret. So?"

Didn't he get it? "So, in the future there's the Earth thing to consider. There's the ship thing to consider...lots of things to consider."

Nerfer made a dismissive gesture, forming three pseudopods and making a gesture of someone tossing the garbage out. "You're thinking of the big picture, kid. Don't. It's a mistake, but a natural one for someone your age, I guess."

Uh-huh, act like a big brother, why don't you? "Well, what's wrong with having a plan?"

He squished his way to his feet. The computer was running the ship on a straight course, so I leaned against the counter and repeated my question.

"Nothing," he replied. "But you're forgetting one thing. You can't control this ship. Regular propulsion, yes, but still, you're a long way from home and there's no way to turn it around."

"Well, yeah, but —"

"And you can't control the shift. Me, either. I don't know why it happens, but it does. So, since you're asking for advice, here it is."

Great, now he was going all fatherly on me. Then, again, I'd asked him. "What do I do?"

Nerfer shrugged what passed for shoulders. "Kid, it ain't all about where you're going. It's where you are right now that counts. No one can see their future. No one, and I been around. I can tell you, though, that Lynni likes you. A blind person could see that."

"Okay, so—"

"So, treat her nicely, have fun and no, I'm not going to wait up for you or bother you unless there's an emergency. You're seventeen, and while you're not quite an adult, you're going to hit that magic eighteen mark faster than you think. That means you're almost an adult, so act like one. See you later."

He oozed his way over to the storage room, while I walked back to my cabin thinking about what he'd said—and also thinking about what to wear, say and do, in that order. Wear? Jeans and a T-shirt? It was always a comfortable twenty-two degrees Celsius here, anyway.

No, if Lynni were going to wear a semi-formal dress, then I couldn't go casual. Fortunately, I'd packed a suit before leaving Earth, and while it was sort of old, it still fit—at least the pants did. The jacket was too small. Still, it was formal looking, a nice dove gray, and I had a white dress shirt and gray tie, so my wardrobe for the evening was set.

As for the saying and doing concept, I had no idea what Lynni liked, outside of food, but that gave me an idea. How had people gone on dates a century ago? After sifting through a ton of information, it seemed as though they had often lit candles and had a romantic song or classical music playing in the background.

Seven p.m. ship-time saw me on the bridge and fussing about in the kitchen with a full-length smock over top of my clothes to protect them from potential spattering of the food. Veal alfresco, fettuccini and a Caesar salad were on the menu. We had no wine—and

I'd never cared for it, anyway — so water would have to do...

"Rick?"

I looked up to find Lynni in the doorway. She'd put on my mother's dress, and while it was somewhat short on her, she looked incredible, the frills giving her a Victorian look the way I remembered it from the history vids. She ducked her head shyly. "I am early, I know. I am also not sure if this is the correct way to wear it," she said, gently pulling on the sleeves. "Do I look presentable?"

Yes, she most certainly did. "Uh, yeah. You're fine. I mean, come in. Dinner's almost ready."

She bowed her head. "Your manner of dress is formal. You look good."

I pulled off the smock. "Thanks. It's, well, it's a special occasion."

"Can I help?"

"Have a seat. I'll serve."

Dinner was a quiet affair. I'd forgotten about the candles, but the computer had chosen a so-called romantic song from almost one-hundred-and-seventy years ago, something about smoke getting in a person's eyes.

Lynni didn't complain. She listened attentively to the music and more selections, noted their pleasant sound, and after that, not more than twenty words passed between us. In fact, outside of the music, we spent most of the time looking out of the window at the inky blackness of space. As we ate, I tried to think of something pithy to say. Nothing came to mind.

Lynni was also quite reticent, but she did compliment me on the dishes I'd prepared. "It is quite good," she said as she sampled everything. "I am developing a fondness for Earth food."

"It likes you, too," I replied. "Food always makes things better." Or so I hoped.

That got a giggle from her, and from that point on, she began to open up. We talked of her early life—there wasn't much to tell, outside of her days at school, studying with the other girls and boys who didn't care for her enhancements—the times she spent with her father and her city of Nelvok, the capital of Kagekia.

"I was happiest when I was at home," she said between bites of her veal. "The other children were unkind, and I never felt like one of them—never. My father was the only one who understood me."

Her world was modern, she said, full of metal and chrome and glass, something far advanced from what Earth had. "But, outside of my father, it did not mean much to me."

"Why not?"

Lynni bit her lip. "Because I was always alone. I was different. I knew that then. I know that now."

Confidence didn't seem to be part of her psyche, unlike before. How could I tell her that it didn't matter? "Uh, I wasn't part of anything, either, and we're here and I like you and it doesn't matter to me. I said so before, and I meant it."

She looked at me, a hint of tears forming in her eyes. "You are being honest?"

"Yeah."

I put my hand out. "What are you doing?" she asked.

"I'm asking you to hold it."

Lynni brushed her tears away. "We have held hands before."

Yes, we had, in the forest. But that was a different time with a different set of feelings. At first, she hesitated, then she took my hand in hers, entwining her slender fingers with mine. "Thank you."

"No problem. Eat up. Cold veal doesn't taste that great."

Another tiny giggle came from her, and she finished off her meal in record time. After that, we washed the dishes together. It was a quiet time, one of bonding, and when they were clean, she suddenly put her arms around my neck and kissed me. "I know that I am being forward, but that is how Earth people do it, is it not?"

"Uh, yeah, but how did you know?"

"There was a book in your room. I read it. It was a nice story about a boy and a cat-girl."

Oh...yeah. "Well, that's what we do. Um, do your people do things differently?"

Lynni released her hold on me and twirled her hair, a move that combined diffidence with coyness. "I do not know. I have had only one kiss and that was with someone I detested. Other than that, I have no experience in such matters."

"Well, you just kissed me."

Now, a distinctly coy smile adorned her lips. "I did, and I enjoyed it. As for what our people do differently, I have heard that if a couple likes each other, then the male rubs the female's stomach as a sign of affection."

"Oh." I could get into that — but her permission had to come first. "If it's okay?"

Her eyes widened. "Are you sure?"

"Yes."

Back at my cabin, she slipped inside the bed and lay down, her eyes regarding me calmly. "I shall guide you," she said.

Guide me? Like I knew what to do. "Um, sure."

"Get in beside me," she instructed. "Put your hand on my stomach."

For someone who said they had no experience, she was rather forward, but...fine, go with it. Perhaps her people were like that. "You may touch me," she whispered. "I am ready."

My hand slowly strayed to her belly, and I felt the galaxy inside her move when I rubbed her tummy. Then I stopped. She'd been purring like a cat, but my hand encountered three distinct depressions — the belly buttons. She stopped purring. "Yes, I have three of them. You saw them before, did you not?"

I had. "I've, uh, never known anyone with three belly buttons."

"Do you not have three as well?"

How to respond? "Uh, no. Humans have only one."

Her hand explored my stomach, and she murmured something that sounded like "I care for you." A moment later, she stopped. "I must tell you something."

Uh-oh, had I done something wrong? Or was she going to say she wasn't interested? If so, that would have been the ultimate in getting rejected. Hoping against all hope, I asked, "What?"

She turned to me, her eyes wide and without guile. "We must stop."

Oh, great, friend zoned. I withdrew my hand. "Uh, is it something I did?"

"No." She snuggled closer to me, but I caught the embarrassed expression on her face. "I can feel the galaxy within me shift. If it is dislodged by any...violent movement, it may expand."

Violent movement? She means…oh. Like I have any experience – not. "I, uh, yeah, okay."

At that moment, my desire to do anything deflated, and not even the gentle touch of her caress upon my face improved things.

Still, she wanted to be with me, and we were together, so, go with it. "I…I wished to be with you before," Lynni said. "I am in my eighteenth year, and I wish to be with you now. I have not changed my mind. This is a feeling I have that I cannot deny and do not wish to."

Denying her feelings was one thing, but all the same, since we couldn't do anything – aw, hell, forget it. "You are disappointed?" she asked.

Of course, yes. "Yeah, but I understand."

Before I could say anything else, she drew me close and kissed me. Although she spoke in a whisper, it was still filled with passion. "Our people kiss, too. What I asked you before – that was a sign of trust as well as affection. I wanted to know whether you were trustworthy or not."

"And now?"

Her eyes told me that she trusted me. "Until my father can somehow extract that which is within me, we shall have to limit ourselves."

A long time ago, people would have called this moment a downer. In my case, it was a literal downer, but I saw her point. "Guess we'll wait, then."

Lynni's voice was soft. "Have you had a lot of experience in this act?"

She would have to ask. *Be honest.* "Uh, not, no. None, in fact."

"I have not, either. But I shall look forward to it once I am rid of that which is within me."

Waiting was okay. At least, she cared for me — and that would have to be enough. Lynni decided to go back to her room, but at the door, she said, "In our culture, we have a word that describes two people who have identical feelings and who care for each other. We say, *breeto*."

My universal translator gave me the proper meaning. It meant 'us'.

Chapter Nine

Problems

For the next forty-eight hours, no visitors came our way, our interstellar com-link remained quiet and Lynni and I spent most of the time getting to know each other better.

Holding her, being with someone who cared for me and made me feel as though my life had a purpose instead of simply drifting upon the interstellar tides — that was the difference between night and day, even if eternal night lay only a few meters away through the unbreakable glass.

Naturally, culture played into things, and it was a revelation to learn about Lynni's world. Her language was complex, but I managed to nail down a few expressions. It was a nice way to get to know someone.

In turn, she monopolized my holo-computer to learn about Earth life and its culture, specifically, that of the United States. It had been central to my upbringing, so she studied it. Language, customs and other things as mundane as flags fascinated her.

"I did not know your people prized flags so much," she said. "To wave them at sports matches, to use them in politics — it is all so different."

Ancient history, but, yes, we'd done that. "Your people don't?"

She shook her head. "We do not. Our culture is one, although I am somewhat outside that culture."

Fangs and claws — Lynni was talking about them. "Well, you've got a place here," I replied, which caused her to melt into my arms, and our love began anew…almost.

"You have someone special in your life," Nerfer said to me on the bridge when I went up to relieve him. "I don't mind handling the helm for a while. Ship's on automatic most of the time, anyway, and if a message comes in, I can answer it."

I didn't know what to say at first. He'd never been that generous before, and his comment made me see him in a new light. It also made me realize how much of a selfish asshat I'd been. "Uh, Nerfer, you don't have to. I mean, being a captain means being on the bridge, just in case — "

"If there's an emergency, I'll call you. Rick, go spend time with your girl. I'm fine here."

What else could I say except thank you? He waved me off with a gruff, "You're young only once. Have fun."

Fun meant a lot of things, but practicality ruled and living accommodations came first. "This is your parents' room, is it not?" Lynni enquired as she examined my room. "You should honor them by keeping it clean."

One look at the rumpled clothes and messed-up sheets showed that she was right. Lynni didn't wait for my approval. She simply set about cleaning up the place. As she placed everything just so, her gaze lingered over a picture that sat on the nightstand. She picked it up. It was a picture of my parents — their wedding picture.

My mother wore a white wedding dress, my father, a tuxedo. It was the only time I'd ever seen them wear those clothes. Their usual garb was an army uniform, a drab grayish-green affair that hung loosely from their frames. Everyone on the research base wore the same kind of outfit.

However, on that day, my parents had worn those clothes to celebrate the fact that they had entered a union. Lynni turned around to hand me the picture. "Are all people on your world joined in this fashion?"

It was difficult to answer. Since the virus had almost wiped Earth out, many customs considered old-fashioned by society had disappeared. One of them was marriage ceremonies. With the impermanence of life — so I'd read — people tended to forgo the elaborate rites and passages of old. They simply chose to live together.

But my parents had wanted something more, something auspicious to mark that day. It was the only picture I had of them, and it remained where I could see it daily. It was how I chose to remember them.

"My parents wanted to look special, I guess. It was their day."

Lynni nodded and flipped her hair over her shoulder in an absent-minded gesture. "On our world, we do not have such a custom. I think that I told you that our people are promised to each other at a young age, perhaps twelve of your years, as you would measure them."

She'd told me, and it still came as a surprise. At twelve, I'd barely thought about girls. But now... different story. "That young?"

"It is our way."

She went on to tell me that neither the boy nor the girl would know the other to any degree until their wedding day. That was kept secret. Only their families knew. It was based on mutual compatibility of the families and their names, not what their children wanted.

"Perhaps you would call it duty," she said. "Perhaps something different. I do not know. I was...I was never promised to anyone. That boy I told you about before — that match for me — was the only man I'd ever met, up until now."

A sense of sadness pervaded her words. As an outsider, she could never fit in. I put the picture back on the nightstand. "Well, for what it's worth, like you said, there's someone here."

In a flash, she was in my arms, yet she held back, as if she was giving — or had already given — away too much of herself. Shyness, coyness...something else, maybe, or maybe she was asking for a commitment. "Is that a promise, or are they only words?"

At her question, my heart skipped a beat and maybe three or more. Right then, there was no one else who could have changed my mind. "Both. They're words — and they're my promise to you."

Lynni's lips met mine. "I shall hold you to your promise."

After the kiss, though, she said, "I think we should visit Nerfer."

"Why?"

"I am hungry, and he is alone. He is a friend to you, is he not?"

Alone—yes, she was right—and he was also a friend. Even though he was most capable of commanding the bridge, leaving him alone wasn't right. I'd been alone, too, but at the very least, my world still existed. His was gone forever...

A sudden shudder caused me to snap back to reality. Lynni's look of affection turned to one of concern. "Rick, what is happening?"

Like I knew? Another series of shudders hurled me over the bed. A series of clanging sounds began, like heavy stones or something worse hitting the hull of our ship. As we exited my room, the clanging continued and the alarm went off. Then the ship's engines stopped, and that was the most disconcerting thing of all. "What is it?" Lynni asked.

"I don't know. Wait here."

I ran to the bridge where Nerfer was in the process of checking things via the computer. The clanging had stopped, but the alarm continued to sound. "What's going on?"

In answer to my question, he pressed a button on the console and a three-dimensional hologram leaped up. "We just passed through a meteor shower," he said. "Computer's showing damage—holes. The bridge viewing screen is intact, and the ship has some self-sealing capability...but not everywhere."

His pseudopod shot out to indicate a hole that was approximately fifty centimeters across in the aft section. That was near our central control system console, which included our life-support system, and a second later, a light on the computer console began to blink.

"Does that mean what I think it means?" I asked.

Nerfer received my question with a bobbing motion of his body and the reply of, "Yup, that's the life-support system. It's been compromised — probably by one of those meteorites."

He tapped a few buttons and an image of a timer leaped up. *Forty-three minutes*. He shut off the image and said grimly, "That's how long we've got, oxygen-wise, unless we plug those holes."

"Can't you close off the room?"

"Yeah, I can, but the machinery's been damaged. It has to be fixed. So does the hull."

His last four words sent a shiver of fear up and down my spine. "Uh, and how are we going to fix things?" I asked carefully.

"One of us has to go outside and patch the holes. I can do some of the holes from inside, but not all of them."

"One of us," I echoed, dreading the outcome of this conversation.

He pointed at the ventilation panel and its surrounding support systems. "Can you repair that?"

"No."

I hated to admit it, but in all the time I'd been on this ship, I'd failed to learn how to repair some of the systems. They'd always functioned perfectly before, so I hadn't bothered. It was a stupid lack of foresight on my part. Then again, I'd never thought about my parents dying, either.

The answer was clear. "I'll tell Lynni then I'll meet you at the airlock."

"Hurry. I have my containment suit on. All I need is a helmet and an oxygen tank."

Inside my parents' cabin, Lynni had gotten dressed and was sitting on the bed. She looked at me with concern when I entered. "What is wrong?"

How to tell her that things were bad? "Uh, I have to go outside. Damage to the hull. I'll be back soon." I said that with all the confidence of someone who was scared out of his mind over what might happen.

"I shall go with you."

Oh, no, you won't! "Lynni, there are only two space suits, and you don't know how to repair things. I need one, and Nerfer needs the other. He has to fix the life-support system in the engineering section. The best thing for you to do is to stay here."

Her gaze fell to the floor. "It is dangerous, is it not?"

Tell her the truth. "Yeah, it is. Look... It's not about me being the guy in this relationship and telling you what to do. It's just that—"

She lifted her head. "That you do not want to see me injured."

All right, she got it, after all. "Yes."

Lynni bit her lip and tucked her chin into her chest while turning away. It was a childlike and somewhat childish gesture, but at that moment, I realized that she genuinely cared for me. "I want to help, but as I am not a specialist, I will wait for you."

"Hey, you don't have to..."

By that time, she'd already clammed up, spiraling into herself. I touched her on the shoulder, hoping she wouldn't shrug it off. She didn't. Instead, she grabbed my fingers gently and squeezed. "Come back to me," she whispered as she let go of my hand.

"Count on it."

I ran to the airlock where Nerfer was waiting. He already had his helmet on, and he held a space suit in one hand, a metal plate in another and a laser pistol in a third. A fourth hand clutched a small sealant gun. I got dressed with his help. Once inside the airlock, my helmet on, he pressed a button on the side of the suit and the oxygen started flowing.

I gave him the thumbs up, even though my insides were quivering, and he handed over the repair materials. "Get the big hole patched before hitting the smaller holes," he said before leaving. "I'll get to the smaller ones after I finish repairs on the life-support system."

"On it."

I strived to impart a sense of confidence and can-do attitude. This was what I'd trained for, in part. I'd practiced this safety protocol in a virtual environment as well as in a training room on Earth, and I'd also been outside on space walks to inspect the fittings and clamps and docking instruments.

But my father had always had my back in the past. Not now. And the danger of meteors was still present.

Screw it – just get the job done.

My suit was equipped with a safety line which I immediately clamped onto a hook inside the airlock. It was also equipped with an oxygen tank that had enough breathable air in it for three hours. Add in magnetic boots to keep a grip on things, plus a mini jetpack that could get me from point A to point B if both were about three hundred meters apart. I was ready, so I opened the door to meet the universe.

Slowly, carefully, my nerves on edge, I edged my way outside by grabbing onto the handholds on the walls. A ladder just outside the door to my right took me to the top of the ship, and I climbed slowly but steadily to the top. My target lay around far down the ship, near the aft section. Even though Nerfer had stopped the engines, the ship still drifted.

Interstellar winds didn't bother me. As for solar radiation, my suit would keep it out—hopefully. Once I climbed to the top, I couldn't help but gasp. This was the unending, the infinite, the endless void, and it was wrapped around me. The concept of being surrounded by this ebony blanket made me gaze out at the stars, and they were beautiful. It seemed as though I could reach out and touch them.

Only when I heard my breath rasp inside my helmet did I understand how close to eternity I truly was.

"How's it going, kid?"

Nerfer's voice crackled from my suit's com-link and jerked me back to the task at hand. Our ship was losing air and I had to work fast. "Halfway to the damaged area. I'll contact you once I get there."

Fortunately, my father had installed guard rails on our ship, so that gave me more support and something I could pull myself along with. The rope trailed behind me, and I shook it out occasionally to make sure it wouldn't snag on a protruding shaft of metal.

Soon, I reached my target and signaled Nerfer. "I'm here."

"Good for you, kid. Get going. I'm starting the repairs now."

A faint click signaled that he'd closed the communications for the time being, so I got to work. The plate I held in my hand covered the hole and seemed to provide a comfortable patch. Fitting it and sealing it took no more than fifteen minutes.

The bright light of the laser caused the odd comfort of the eternal night to slip away, and even though I'd felt scared in the past, at that moment in time, my fear left me.

Well, no, the fear never really left. Something else replaced it—concentration. Focus. Narrowing my mindset and skillset down to the task at hand. Concentration here was key. My father had always told me to let other thoughts leave and allow only thoughts of the job to stay. *"You're outside, in a vacuum, and you can't allow anything to distract you,"* he'd said. *"Work hard, work fast or suffer the consequences."*

Wise words. Get it done. Patch...down. Laser...burning. Seal...completed. Once I finished the job, I checked out a few other holes. There were about twenty, so I kneeled at the damaged sites and carefully fired the sealant gun, patching them. After doing that, I contacted Nerfer. "I'm all done. How are you doing?"

"Same," he answered. "The life-support system is functioning. All is well. Better hurry, though."

Okay. "Uh, why?"

"Sensors detected a micro-meteor shower coming our way."

We'd just been through a major one, and now, the midgets must have decided to get in on the action. His warning got me moving faster. "See you soon."

He clicked off and I started back. Well, that seemed simple enough. Halfway home, though, my concept of simplicity went out of the window. Oh, wait, there was no window. I kept slogging along, and wouldn't you know it, my right foot caught on something.

What in the hell? I reached down. My foot had gotten lodged in a tiny dent in the metal, a dent caused by the meteor barrage or by earlier contacts with objects from space. As I gently worked the material free, my right wrist snagged on a piece of the metal and the fabric tore.

"Oh, shit."

Disbelief coupled with fear fueled my journey back to the airlock. Any hole in a suit, no matter how small, was potentially fatal, and the air began to rush out.

Fortunately, the suit had self-sealing capability, but I still gripped the tear and covered it out of instinct. Then I began walking back to the airlock as fast as humanly possible, awkwardly hanging onto the rope.

My suit also had a built-in minicomputer in its visor that gave a readout on my vitals. It showed that I'd lost more than ten percent of my air supply in less than three seconds. How could that be, unless…yeah, it had happened. Another message flashed across my visor. *Oxygen tank — damaged. Air leak.*

Marvelous. A meteorite had damaged my oxygen tank. Damn, damn! My breath rasped in my ears.

Walk faster — faster! My visor flashed another warning — forty percent of my oxygen was gone, and the carbon dioxide level was climbing rapidly. My legs felt leaden, and my chest began to constrict. This situation had already gone south in a hurry, and it was getting worse. Move faster…move faster! "Nerfer, get the airlock ready!"

A moment of silence, then his raspy voice came through. "What's wrong? You sound out of breath, kid."

Very perceptive, wasn't he? "I *am* out of breath. My air-tank's damaged and I tore my suit!"

When he came back online, he sounded concerned. "What's the readout on your suit's computer?"

I was down to fifty percent. "Half gone."

Nerfer sounded confident. "You've got enough oxygen to make it. Breathe shallowly. Pace yourself. You can do it."

I had no other choice, and Lynni's face flashed in front of my eyes. Yes, she was important, too. In fact, she was my main reason for wanting to make it. I kept hustling, breathing shallowly but regularly.

Something stung me. A jagged hole appeared in the left sleeve of my suit. Another micro-meteor had decided to get me. *Wonderful*. My suit sealed itself once again, but time was running out. In a desperate effort to stave off death, I fought my way back, step by step and meter by meter.

Tiny rocks bounced off the hull. Vacuum of space or not, in my imagination, they made a metallic sound. My breathing sounded in my ears, heavy and rapid. I strived to keep calm.

More micro-meteors flew around me, two of them pinging off my helmet. Despite my best efforts and modern space tech, I was still losing oxygen. Forty-five percent...forty percent...the numbers fell slowly and inexorably.

When all seemed lost, glory be, the sight of the ladder swam into view as black spots began to swim before my eyes. More pinging, then the swarm of tiny, impersonal, stinging rocks went elsewhere to seek a new victim.

Twenty percent.

My lungs were on fire. They needed air. It wasn't coming. Massive cramps hit my legs as well as my back, and, at the same time, a great sense of lassitude hit. It would have been nice to simply sit and observe the heavens. What a weird-ass thought, and why not? I was in the perfect position to do so...

No! If I sat down, I'd die. Movement was key. Movement was life! *Breathe shallowly... You got this...You got this...*

At the ladder, I swung my legs over to the top step. They'd already locked up, and in desperation, I slid down. My left leg caught on another snag and more fabric tore. "Ah, screw it," I muttered.

Bottom — my feet hit bottom — and my mind barely registered the impact. The visor gave me the readout — three percent. In a last-ditch effort, I hauled myself into the airlock and punched the button to close the door. It slowly slid shut, and the decontamination procedure started.

The sound of air rushing in filled the small space, and my hands fumbled with my helmet. *Get it off. Get it off!*

A click sounded and the helmet came loose. I pulled it off and let it drop while falling to my knees and inhaling deeply. My lungs couldn't take everything in, not immediately, and I coughed and heaved out bile.

Damn, that had been close! My heart raced almost out of control, and I fell on my side, holding on to my chest and praying that I wouldn't die. After a couple of minutes, my ticker slowed to a steady thump-thumping.

At least we had air, now. Once I felt ready to get up, I shucked my suit, exited the airlock and ran to my cabin to see if Lynni was there.

She wasn't. Maybe she'd gone to my parents' cabin. I checked. No one was there. The bridge was my next target, and she wasn't there. "Lynni?"

My voice echoed off the metal walls, but there was no reply. Now, I was starting to get unnerved. "Lynni!"

"Hey."

I whirled around at the sound of the voice. Nerfer had come in. "Did you see Lynni?" I asked.

He swayed from side to side, meaning no. "I was in the machine room, checking the ventilation and life-support systems. I just got back."

Nerfer sniffed the air and turned to me, his faceless form morphing into a visage filled with worry. "Someone's been here."

I nose-tasted the air. A heavy smell, gamey, redolent with body odor and old food and more—Nerfer was right. Someone had been here. Lynni wasn't around, anymore. She'd been kidnapped.

As if on cue, the interstellar com-link crackled to life. I pressed the button to let the call in, and the messenger's voice, something extremely nasal, as though the speaker's tonsils had never been removed, filled the bridge. "Earth vessel, do you recognize this voice?"

A chill ran down my spine. Whoever it was, he'd had something to do with Lynni being gone. "No. Identify yourself."

"My name is Zitik, the new leader of the Yelten people."

Yeltens—oh, hell, they were compatriots of the yak-guys who'd been vaporized by Kulida and his buddies a few days ago. This Zitik dude was either out for revenge or profit or both. "What do you want?"

"We have your female companion. If you do not wish her death to be slow and painful, you will give us what we want."

Lynni—they'd taken her! Stall for time. "And what is that?"

"The means to take that which is inside her out. If you provide us with the tools, we can trade. The girl has told us that what is inside her can be extracted with a minimum of pain and a maximum of efficiency.

"So, therefore, I put it to you in simple terms — the life of the girl for the contents of what her body carries. You have five seconds in which to decide."

Chapter Ten

Trade

It took no longer than half a second for me to decide. "Okay, stop! I agree, but I want to speak to Lynni first."

Zitik sounded peeved-plus, and his nasal tone grew deeper and more annoying. "You are in no position to demand anything. We are the ones who hold the reins of power in this transaction. If we wish, we can simply dispose of the girl."

I heard Lynni yell, "Cut me open, and what is inside of me will expand to dimensions your tiny minds cannot conceive of! Kill me, and the same result will happen. Use what little gray matter you have and come to the right decision."

Other angry voices told Lynni to shut up. That was followed by a cry of pain, as if she'd ripped one of the henchmen's eyes out. She bellowed, "Try fathering children now!"

Her withering retort to Zitik almost made me laugh—almost. Nerfer snorted with derision, then, yes, I laughed. I couldn't help it.

All the same, this was a deadly serious affair, and Lynni's life was on the line, which demanded a serious approach. "I guess you have your answer, Zitik. Put my girlfriend on. *Now*."

Another rustling sound in the background, then Lynni's voice came over the airwaves. "They are allowing me to speak. Be careful, Rick. I do not wish to lose you."

"I don't want to lose me, either…or you. We'll make it. You'll see."

Mr. Uber-Yelten cut in at that point, ordering someone to take her away. I heard more yelling and cursing as Lynni was dragged away, threatening to disembowel herself right then and there and end it all.

Once things quieted down, the yak-man said, "Your companion has quite the temper. This is troublesome for all of us, and we only wish to conclude this business as soon as possible."

I did as well, preferably with my life and my girlfriend's life intact. "Where do we meet?"

He proceeded to name a place in this galaxy — Nerridon. "You may not be familiar with it, Earth-trash, but that pink mold with you might know."

The message cut off after that. With a snarl of barely contained rage, I started smashing the dishes that were next to the sink, and once I'd finished with them, I walked over to the console and started kicking it. "Those…bastards. Those rotten bastards! I'll—"

"Stop kicking the computer console and get your head in the game," Nerfer cut in. "I know you're angry but trying to ruin the ship without making a plan gets us nowhere."

"Wouldn't you be angry?"

Another kick dented the side of the console, and at that moment, I didn't care if it damaged the computer or not. Sure, it was childish, but at the same time I felt helpless and powerless and a lot of other 'esses'.

Nerfer oozed a pseudopod from his body and placed the newly formed hand on my shoulder. "Hey, I just got called 'mold'. How do you think that makes me feel? I'll answer that. It makes me feel like kicking someone's butt from here to Alpha Centauri. But getting angry is exactly what they want."

Perhaps he was trying to assuage my anger as well as my guilt for losing someone who meant everything to me. It didn't have much of an effect, as I continued kicking the console. The next kick caused me to howl in pain and I hopped around, cursing. "What is it?" Nerfer asked.

"I think I broke my toe."

After unzipping the ankle zipper on my uniform, I slipped my foot out to examine the injured digit. No, not broken, just bruised. I slipped the suit over my foot again and zipped up. "All right, no more kicking. You know that place...Nerridon?"

"Sort of. I've never been there, but I've heard about it. And the sooner we get there and the sooner we get out of there with your girlfriend, then the sooner we'll all be safer. That's my take on it."

Merely the mention of Lynni caused me to reflect on my former course of action. The feeling of helplessness flowed through me even more strongly. "What would you do?"

A pseudopod shot out of his body, and he pulled me down to face him. His usually formless visage took on a new appearance — mine. In a stern tone, he stated, "You're the captain. Act like one."

Crunch time — that's what the old-timers used to say. In his usual direct manner, Nerfer had simply reminded me that it was time for me to step up. All right, act like someone in charge, and I turned to the computer. "Computer, show me where the planet Nerridon is in relation to our position and set a course for there."

Immediately, a three-dimensional holograph leaped up and its tinny voice provided the information. "Setting course. We are approximately twenty minutes away from that destination. However, Nerridon is not a planet but a manmade construct."

"Define 'construct'."

According to the information, the place we were looking for was a space port, one used by the Yeltens to conduct their business. They were salvage experts, raiders, commercial traders, and like all rogue elements, they needed a safe place to hang out.

Sneaking in was impossible. Not only did they know we were coming, but they also had the advantage with their portal gizmos that could beam them anywhere.

"Not everywhere, though," Nerfer said. "In my experience, those portal devices have limited range, about a thousand kilometers at most. They're not limitless. My guess is that while we were fixing the ship, they pulled their space craft within range, walked through their gates onto this ship and they kidnapped Lynni. That's how they knew what I looked like. They probably saw me in the engine room and figured out what was what. Either that or Cradd had told them what I looked like."

It all made sense. "So, how are we going to get her back?"

He faced me squarely. "Like I said, you're the captain. You tell me. I'll back you up, all the way."

Think fast! "Well, since we can't cloak ourselves and since they're expecting us, the first thing we do when we're within range is to get some numbers."

Getting numbers was what it was all about. We cruised through the darkness that was space, and once we were within range, the computer's sensors told us that the space port—it was on a large, artificially constructed asteroid—was severely undermanned.

"Sensors read only five individuals on that site," the computer said. "Heat signatures indicate that four of them are in line with the physiologies of the Yelten race. The fifth has a higher core temperature. It is that of another race."

"Lynni," I breathed out.

With the mention of her name, resolve took over. I wondered aloud why so few of the enemy were around. Nerfer mused on my question, multiple arms under the blobby vicinity of his chin. "My guess is that they're probably out doing other jobs. They're hard workers, I'll give them that. If there's money or cargo or something that's valuable, then those beast guys will go get it." A huff came from him. "So, you got a plan?"

Only four guys...that gave me an idea. "Yeah, get out of your suit."

He uttered a squawk of surprise. "You want me to *what*?"

"I'll explain."

* * * *

Twenty minutes later

The Darter, as always, handled beautifully. On the way down to the asteroid, the interstellar radio on board crackled. "Unidentified vessel. State your purpose or be destroyed."

Impatient maggots. "This is Captain Rick Granger. You have my girlfriend, and I want her back. You requested my presence here. We have a deal, remember?"

Whoever had hailed me gave way, and I heard a very nasal voice. It sounded like Zitik, but it wasn't. "Ah, yes, the Earth slime approaches. My name is Bikor. We have you in our sights. I am sending you the proper coordinates. It is to a protective dome we have constructed. You will land there."

A series of numbers flashed on the screen then disappeared. With grim determination, I continued, and soon, I realized the full scale of what the computer on Port Anywhere had been talking about. Up close, this place got more and more impressive, which meant it also became more and more dangerous.

Nerridon had been constructed on a large asteroid, two square kilometers, according to the computer readout. It was a place of operation hewn from the rock and reinforced with manmade materials. A hangar had been built into the rock and the doors were open. One of the yak-men was outside the hangar. He wore a black space suit and waved a bright red glow-stick to guide me in.

"Here we go," I murmured as I landed on the strip there and taxied inside. Once past the gates, I slammed on the brakes, came to a halt, then cut the engines. I turned around to see the man who'd waved me in press something on his suit. The hangar doors slowly closed.

A moment later, the interstellar radio came to life. "This is Bikor," the voice said. "I am the one who guided you in. Wait until I give the order to leave your vessel. The hangar deck is pressurizing."

I waited, hoping against all hope that my hosts would do exactly as I thought they would. While waiting, I patted the extra uniform I carried under my suit as well as a hand-laser. Two minutes later, Bikor's voice came again. "There is oxygen for you to breathe. Exit your space vessel."

Not much choice there. I got out and jumped onto the hard ground. Bikor took off his helmet, revealing a hairy head and an ugly visage. The vacuum of space as well as his suit had contained his stink before, but with the helmet off, it drifted over and made my nose beg for mercy. I'd get no mercy here.

"Raise your hands," he ordered in a no-BS tone.

I did so, and in a smooth move, he produced a gun from the folds of his suit with his right hand. Around his wrist was a small silver band—his translator, no doubt. He kept the gun trained on me as he checked inside my ship. Once he got to the back seat, he wrinkled his nose and turned around with an aggrieved expression. "What is that yellow puddle you have in your ship?"

"Oh, I should have gone to the bathroom before I left. Sorry."

"Savage."

If you say so.

He waved his weapon to indicate I should start walking. "You may put your hands down. Move ahead. There is a door in front of you. Go through it. You will find your friend there."

Not much choice there, either. I went through the door, only to find three other yak-men sitting around a wooden table on what passed for crude chairs. Lynni sat on the floor a couple of meters away. She wasn't bound and looked healthy enough.

The room was filled with crates, probably full of stuff the Yeltens had either traded for or stolen. A stink of body odor filled the room, and I wondered if the word hygiene figured into their vocabulary or culture. Soap probably wasn't a word they were familiar with.

"Lynni, you okay?"

She nodded and shot her captors a look of rage. "I will be fine, once I am free of these people."

I started for her, but I got only one step when something hard hit me from behind. Bikor—what a jerk!

The blow caused me to stagger, but I righted myself and got into a fighting stance. Another yak-man, larger than the rest, got up. Yeah, that had to be the leader, and I gestured him to move forward. "C'mon!"

He obliged me by charging in. This man was big, but nowhere near as large as the battle droids I'd trained against. When he swung, his punch floated over in slow-motion, which gave me plenty of time to duck then leap up to throw a punch to the side of his face.

It gratified me when he went down. My sense of elation faded when the rest of the scum piled in on me. One against one, I could hold my own—maybe. All of them against me was a mismatch. Punches and kicks rained on my body and head, and I couldn't keep them off.

As the lights flashed, the room spun, Lynni's screams echoed all around and darkness settled in.

Damn.

* * * *

I'd been knocked out before, but not by human or humanoid hands. No, my bout of unconsciousness had come at the metallic claws of my sparring droids. That had been...a little over a year, shortly before my mother had gotten sick. The place—aboard our ship, naturally, in one of the cargo holds. It was big enough for a place to practice, and I wouldn't bang into anything.

My father had continually counseled me to keep my hands up. I'd been facing off against Dewey, one of my mechanical trainers. Huey was the other. They were both of identical size—two meters in height and around two hundred kilograms in weight—but Huey had a red dot on his chest and Dewey had a blue one.

They'd been programmed to offer a variety of self-defense moves as well as offensive moves in boxing, karate, judo and kung-fu, among others. Built like people but infinitely stronger, they outmatched me in terms of strength.

"Keep your hands up," my father had repeated. *"They can adapt to your moves. They've been programmed to adapt and counter. You have to do the same."*

Dewey had gotten in a quick jab to my face. It had stung, but I'd shaken it off and circled out of range. *"Dad, it's not like they're my height or weight or whatever."*

As I'd moved and sidestepped Dewey's punches, I'd made sure to keep out of range of Dewey's left hook. He'd been in boxing mode, and that had been his special move of the day. Other days, I'd practice wrestling or judo or karate with either one of them or sometimes, both, but today had been the ancient form of fisticuffs.

Then, I'd seen my opening and had tagged the droid with a straight right. While I hadn't been able to knock them down, I had been able to score points. The first one to ten points had gotten a break. Dewey hadn't needed to rest. This human had.

"Good shot," my father had said. *"Keep your guard up, though."*

"Yeah, sure…"

It had been a stupid thing to say. Mistake number one had come when I'd turned my head to look at my father. Mistake number two had been not ducking, just in case.

I'd never seen the right cross coming and had woken up in the infirmary with my mother glaring at my father and her eyes flashing with rage. She'd probably been yelling at him for pitting me against a droid that could have torn my head off.

"How do you feel, Rick?" she'd asked after swiveling her laser-like stare from my father to a softer, more sympathetic look to me.

My jaw had hurt where the robot had tagged me, but after moving it around, none of my teeth had been loose, and the healing rays had already helped. *"I'll make it, Mom."*

"Good."

The matches had continued, then the death of my mother had come, followed by Nerfer's arrival, the passage of my father then suddenly we had company of the Kulida kind and they'd left their cargo on my ship and her name was Lynni and I was…

* * * *

"Uh…"

Minutes or hours later, consciousness returned. I felt like the back of my skull had been shattered, put my hand to the sore spot and it came away smeared with blood. The rest of my body hurt, but the suit inside had largely protected my ribs, so that was something to be grateful for.

My laser, though, was gone. After my vision cleared, I took a furtive look around. I was in the same room as before. Four yak-men sat in a semi-circle three meters in front of me. They all had translators on, and the biggest of them all—the one I'd tagged—had his ass parked on a chair and was staring at me with hatred. Up close and personal, it was easy to see his swollen cheekbone.

He leaned over to breathe foul air in my direction. It covered my face like a smelly blanket. "I am Zitik. We are here to conduct a business affair and nothing more. I should kill you, not only for the insult of your touch upon my person but also for your part in my compatriots' murders. However, I will not."

Okay, it had to be said. "Hey, moron, your guys jumped me first. I'd call hitting you a case of self-defense. As for your men getting killed, I had nothing to do with it."

Anger radiated from his ugly visage. "I dislike liars. Have you forgotten that the leader of our empire was recently slain by a Rattanian, one who was on your vessel? We were not that far away, listening to the transaction in our ship. That is how we knew what had happened."

Paranoid—they were paranoid to the nth degree—and it was impossible to keep the sarcasm from my answer. "Well, if you were listening in, then you know that our ship isn't armed and that we offered the place as a neutral area so you and Kulida's gang could do your business. We don't take sides, and your men got the equivalent of fifteen family-style meals. I got a card as payment. You owe me."

"We owe you nothing," he snarled.

"No? I repeat…we're a neutral vessel."

Right, like he was really going to believe me. He didn't, as he got off his chair to shove his face within a few inches of mine. His stench spread out like a fisherman's net upon the waters. Had I been a fish, I would have suffocated, as his smell practically sucked out all the oxygen in the room.

"Your words of neutrality hold no meaning here. The fact that you allowed the initial deal to transpire makes you an accomplice. Therefore, you are just as guilty in my eyes as the Rattanian scum is. The fact that you fled that area of space makes you doubly guilty."

Call this a seriously warped view of what justice really was. Was it worthwhile telling him about my ship's galaxy-shifting capabilities? No, it wasn't. He probably wouldn't have believed me.

Zitik continued his tale of victimhood, grinding his teeth as he did so. "After our leader's murder, we decided to return home. Our world is not far from this place, and it is by good fortune that your ship landed here."

Yes, our good fortune. Sometimes I hated randomness. "I don't suppose the card that Kulida gave me will work here?" I slowly took it out of my pocket and held it up.

A mirthless laugh escaped his lips. "No. You are here for the girl. I do not wish her presence here anymore than I wish yours. I only wish what is inside her. After I receive my prize, I shall spare your lives and let you go."

That seemed like an equitable tradeoff, even though it was a given that he wanted to kill us. "All right, let me look at her."

Zitik turned to one of his men and said, "Bring the girl."

His minion obediently replied that he'd get her. With numerous scratches on his face that still oozed greenish-gray blood, he got up slowly, wincing in pain, and he exited the room, groaning softly. My girlfriend really had fast hands and feet.

A minute later, Lynni walked in at gunpoint. The weapon had been shoved at the small of her back, and she whirled around to smack it out of the man's fingers. It skittered over to the wall while he stared at her with muted rage. "You cannot even cover a prisoner properly. I kicked you in your manhood before, and now I have taken away your other gun. You are beyond pathetic!"

Zitik and his men roared with laughter. As vicious as she was, though, the opposition was armed, and she couldn't outrun a laser blast or whatever charge those weapons carried. The Yelten leader continued to chuckle in an obvious good humor. "Girl, you have more courage than many of the warriors who battle under me! I respect that."

Lynni said nothing. She sat on the table, glaring daggers and missiles at him. Speaking of warriors, though... "Where's the rest of your crew?" I asked.

Zitik lost his sense of jollity in a nanosecond. "They are on missions. Perhaps you have heard that we are a trading people. That much is true. But we are also salvagers."

"Salvagers," I echoed, inwardly seething. "You kidnapped my girlfriend, and you call that business?"

He smirked, scratched the side of his nose and offered an incongruously gracious smile. "No, we call that entrepreneurship. Semantics is not my strongest point, I must admit. We are here to make a deal, as are you. Therefore, if you wish to live, if you wish your lady companion—your girlfriend, as you put it—to live, you will give me what I ask for."

"I had a surgical laser with me. Hand it over." It wasn't a surgical implement, but he didn't have to know that.

Another mean smile wreathed Zitik's face. In a slow, almost insolent move, he took it out of his pocket and handed it over with the admonition of, "Use it wisely, Earth-trash."

Sure thing, Commander. With a quick wink, I instructed Lynni to lie on the table. Did Kagekians understand the concept of winking? From her brief study of Earth's culture, I hoped that she'd picked up on it, although her face remained blank. Zitik and his men stood nearby, their guns drawn but hanging at their sides.

I flicked on the tiny laser, narrowed its beam and asked the men to hold Lynni down. "One of you, grab her legs. Bikor, grab her arms. I'll have to open her suit to perform the operation."

Bikor put down his gun and took control of Lynni's arms. His compatriot took hold of her legs, and they stretched her body taut. Of course, they leaned over, their eyes gleaming. God, this was so perverted! I zipped her suit down a few centimeters with my left hand while lifting the scalpel in my right.

My girlfriend's expression changed from bland to terrified, so I quickly mouthed, "You'll be okay," and she relaxed.

Timing was everything. When Bikor and the other unnamed man leaned in closer to get a glimpse of my girlfriend's body, I sliced Bikor's throat open. Blood fountained into the air and over everyone, including me and Lynni.

As she screamed her protest, Bikor fell, gasping for breath and finding none, his hands scrabbling at the slashed area in a futile attempt to staunch the flow of his life's essence.

Gorge rose in my throat. While committing such an act horrified me, if it was a question of Lynni's life as well as mine, then I'd choose us. I whirled around to attack the man holding Lynni's legs. He got the same treatment, but he instinctively ducked his head and received only a slash to his temple. The slash, though, bled profusely, dripping into his eyes, and while he was trying to wipe the blood away, I carved open his throat. He joined Bikor in hell.

While all this was going on, Lynni zipped up her suit and jumped on the third man, tearing his throat open with her claws. He went down, and Zitik bellowed something incomprehensible in rage. "You are next," she said, and she leaped at him, her claws going for his face.

Her initial attack stunned him, but he soon recovered and easily tossed her to the far wall. She hit hard and slid down, half out of it. I only hoped it wouldn't dislodge the mini universe inside her, but since nothing happened, maybe we were safe—for now.

Zitik pulled out a small handgun from his suit and fired a shot into the nearest corner, vaporizing a small crate with a blast of blue plasma. "Enough!"

That got my attention. With a shaky arm, he brandished his pistol in my face and I looked at death. "You cost me three more good men. Drop the laser."

I did so and backed up. "They weren't that good. They're dead, now."

His arm shook even more, and I was nanoseconds away from oblivion. With a growl that signaled he was barely in control, he said, "That was the final mistake. I shall kill you now and find someone with greater knowledge to perform this operation."

"Not likely," a voice said from behind him.

"What?"

Zitik turned around, his gun arm dropping a few centimeters. Nerfer had oozed his way in unannounced, the yellow dye he'd covered himself with gradually disappearing into his body. Bikor had failed to identify him in the ship, and in his natural form, my co-captain could go anywhere, unimpeded by a suit's constraints.

In a quick move, Nerfer's pseudopods shot out to grab Zitik's arms, immobilizing him then plucking his weapon away. He then heaved the bigger man into the air and body-slammed him.

Whoa! Nerfer was far stronger than he looked. Zitik seemed too surprised to do anything. Losing three of his best buddies could undermine anyone's morale.

"Not bad for a mold," Nerfer said in the most sarcastic tone possible. "You feel like apologizing now, or should I wait for your call?"

Zitik snarled, half in surprise and half in anger. His nose had been shattered, and blood covered his mouth and chin. He wiped it away, smearing the stains on the ground. "How did you get in here?"

"I rode out here," Nerfer replied and turned to me. "Rick, do you have my suit?"

"Yeah, you need it?"

"Save it until we get back."

He then handed me the gun. It was almost time to go, and my companions pointed at the exit. "Just a second," I said to Zitik.

Our jailer-turned-prisoner sat cross-legged, arms at his sides and a look of supreme hatred on his face. He might have been a scumbag, but I had to respect the fact that he wasn't a coward. "I am ready," Zitik said defiantly. "Do it!"

"Okay. Put your left hand on the ground."

After he did, I aimed the gun carefully, squeezed the trigger, and another blast of plasma blew his hand apart, leaving it a tangle of blood and destroyed flesh. He bellowed in a voice that cried to the heavens in agony and fell over, holding onto his mangled limb and writhing in pain. "You…you…"

"Yeah, me," I said, grossed out at what I'd done, but also incredibly pissed off that things had come to this. "Maybe I should blow off another limb. Maybe I'll let my girlfriend do to you what you wanted to do to her. How about that?"

Horror ruled in his eyes. "No, please. I surrender!"

Sure, he did. "Fine. I just spared your life. Remember this moment in time."

"Speaking of time, it's time to go," Nerfer called out with a sense of urgency. "I mean now, got it?"

Lynni leaned over to smack Zitik's face once — hard — with her claws. That tore open the left side of his face. He screamed and begged for mercy, while she straightened up to regard him with total abhorrence. "I need a shower. This place and that thing is filthy."

"Time to go!"

Nerfer sounded angry and somewhat desperate, so Lynni and I ran to the ship. Adrenaline working overtime, I got the start-up procedure in gear. Nerfer followed us, flowing over the side of the ship and settling behind the back seat. We had to hurry. Injury or no, Zitik wouldn't be far behind.

Once all three of us were in and just before the hatch closed, I fired a shot and blew open the door. The hatch closed and the engines caught.

"Punch it!" Nerfer cried.

Full throttle—yes! We shot forward, down the runway and into space, knifing through the inky darkness and back to our ship in record time. Once there, and once we'd gone through decontamination, I handed Nerfer his containment suit. He poured himself into it and took off for the bridge. "I'll handle the helm. They'll be coming for us. You two, relax."

"I can help," I said.

"Help me by relaxing."

Relax, hell! My adrenaline was spiking bigtime, and my stomach heaved, but it wasn't due to the shift. The memory of killing Bikor and his subordinate came back, along with the vivid picture of Zitik's mangled hand.

"Excuse me," I said and ran to the bathroom. Once there, I heaved my guts out and kept retching until my stomach was empty, and even then, I got the dry heaves.

After my gut calmed down, I rinsed my mouth out and went back to where Lynni was in the process of styling her hair behind her ears. "Are you all right?" she asked.

"Yeah."

"Good, I must wash."

She walked off to the bathroom. I watched her go, replaying the events of a half-hour ago in my mind. *I'm all right.* No, I wasn't all right. Saying so was the ultimate in self-delusion. Maybe I'd be all right—in time. Killing someone had never been on the menu. In spite of the old movies I'd seen as showing it to be heroic, in spite of reading my novels that depicted killing as an honorable thing, it wasn't.

In truth, it was ugly and evil, but at times, it was also necessary. My girlfriend returned, gently touching my face here and there. Once again, she seemed to be reading my mind, and in contrast to my blowing my guts all over the place, she seemed quite calm. "Rick, thank you for saving me. I do not wish to kill, either, but you did it for us, yes?"

"Yeah."

Another pithy answer given, something I'd have to work on. Lynni offered a gentle, understanding smile. "In our culture, we have a saying—'life comes before all'. That means while all life is to be respected, one's own life must come first. For if there is not life, then no choice can be made."

She shook her head. "Those creatures…they were loathsome. Even so, I did not wish to kill them, but your life and mine came first. So did Nerfer's."

While her words were delivered with good intentions, it still didn't change things. I'd need time to process this, perhaps work through a few nightmares, but I'd deal. In any case, my place was on the bridge.

Lynni stayed close to my side, and once we reached the command deck, the sound of the ship's engines coming online to blast us forward came through. "Are we safe?" she wanted to know.

"Uh, not really, no. Our ship can't go that fast."

"But you do have armor or weapons?"

"No."

Her response was to hang onto me a little more tightly. "Lynni?"

At first, she didn't answer, then her voice, muffled by her speaking into my uniform's sleeve, came out. "I should have opened myself up there."

Thanks for the vote of confidence. "It's going to be okay."

She popped her head out from under my arm. "How?"

Yeah, how? Before I could come up with a semi-convincing lie, Nerfer pointed to starboard. "Rick, we got company. According to the sensors, Mr. Stinky has his ship stationed less than four thousand kilometers away."

"And?"

"And he's powering up his weapons."

Powering up...

"Lynni," I said, "hang on tight."

"Why?"

Although I wasn't sure, something inside me said that we were about to take a trip. "Just...hang on." She already was, but a reminder wouldn't hurt.

"They're firing on us," Nerfer said in an emotionless voice. "Impact in less than a minute."

For what seemed like an eternity, the three of us watched our doom leap toward us in slow-motion. A blob of bright yellow light that resembled a supernova seemed to reach out for us. Its touch would be deadly, that much I knew. Nerfer inhaled sharply and Lynni gasped...

And exactly one-point-five seconds later, the ship lurched and shuddered. Lynni yelped in fear and pulled me closer to her. "What is happening?" she wanted to know.

"We're shifting," I said with a sense of wonder. "We're shifting!"

The yak-men had just fired upon empty space, and I was never so glad to get out of there. Lynni held on to me tightly, her breath coming soft and light in rapid pants on my neck. "Where are we going?" she asked.

"Anywhere but here is fine with me."

Chapter Eleven

Dead Zone

This time, the lurching of the ship was more severe. While Nerfer was safe in the captain's chair, the shaking took Lynni and me off our feet, and we ended up in one of the booths, upside down. Once all became still, we righted ourselves. "Any damage?" I called out.

"I am unharmed," Lynni said after patting herself all over. Once done, she gave a tiny sigh of relief.

"Fine here," Nerfer replied. "You doing okay, Rick?"

With a grunt, I got up, testing my limbs by shaking them out. Bruises aside, I was still intact. "I'll make it."

A glance out of the main window told me that wherever we'd landed, we'd entered a galaxy unlike any I'd seen so far. Every other place we'd been to, friendly or not, there'd been a palpable sense of life — a shining sun, planets that glowed in the darkness, stars that shone, beacons of light.

Not here. Not one star shone. Not one planet appeared green or blue or red, only black. A palpable sense of death emanated from every atom in this galaxy and seemed to worm its way through the hull of our ship and into my core. "Nerfer, have you ever been here?"

He shivered, as if touched by the hand of the Grim Reaper, a mythical figure from Earth's past. "No, and I hope that I'll never have to come here again."

Fine, if he didn't know, then ask for confirmation. "Computer, what is the name of this galaxy?"

"This area of space is known as the Prenimium Galaxy."

That was a new name, but on the other hand, we'd been in deep space for the past two years, farther than any astronomer or observatory had ever discovered or even surmised to exist. Every place was new. Our computer had charted those planets and galaxies, catalogued them and stored the information away.

Only those galaxies that could be considered living, though. This one was different. The computer had used the word 'formerly' — as in past tense, as in used to be. "Computer, how large is this galaxy?"

It gave me the information in its usual whirring, clicking unemotional voice. "It is approximately one thousand parsecs in size. One former sun, approximately eighty percent of the sun's size in the Sol System."

"Are there any Class M planets here?"

"None."

Wait! I'd said 'former'. "Uh, what about life on the other planets? If not carbon-based, analyze structure."

The computer whirred and clicked. Eighteen seconds later, it gave the readout. "There are no signs of life in this galaxy, carbon-based or otherwise."

No, no way, this can't be true. "Are you telling me the galaxy is dead?"

"There is no sign of life anywhere in this galaxy."

"The entire galaxy?"

"None."

Four letters to indicate that this galaxy was totally devoid of any corporeal forms of life. Nerfer turned to me with a helpless expression on his face. Lynni seemed stunned.

"How is this possible?" she asked in a whisper, one that denoted fear of the unknown as well as sympathy for those beings there that had died. "How can it be possible for any sector of space to have no life?"

Search me. Nerfer didn't help, either, but he spoke to the computer. "Computer, scan for any negative energy traces."

Whir...click. "Working," it replied in its tinny voice. "There are traces of dark matter, negative ion energy and another source, which this unit cannot identify."

Dark matter was one of the building blocks of the universe. Ion energy — we already knew what that was. But another source of energy that it couldn't identify...?

"Computer," I said, "Is there a sun, and if there is, how far are we from it?"

More whirs and clicks greeted my question. "Working...a sun once existed in this galaxy. We are approximately one-hundred-million kilometers away from it."

Was. Unnerved and yet curious, I asked Nerfer to set a course for the sun. "Once we're in range, just beyond its gravitational pull, stop and magnify the image."

"Will do, Captain," he replied, which gave me a temporary ego boost.

Lynni held my hand as he maneuvered the ship around an asteroid field. At our top speed, we'd reach the sun in about an hour. Along the way, we found six ships, all different alien designs, adrift on the interstellar tides. We tried hailing them, but the computer informed us that everyone aboard was dead.

Dead was one thing, but how had they died? The computer didn't have any data on that, nor did it have any data on where the ships were from or what kind of life forms had been inside. I asked Nerfer to get us close to one bullet-shaped ship that was drifting closer to our position than the other ships. "Why?"

"I want to take a look inside one of those ships."

An uneasy expression formed on his body. "You sure about this?"

I had to know. "Yeah."

He dutifully got us in closer, and through some fancy maneuvering, he managed to edge up to its side, although he couldn't dock with it. "Whatever you have to do, do it fast," Nerfer said. "I'll try to keep our position as long as I can."

While I suited up, Lynni watched me with an apprehensive expression working overtime. She asked then pleaded with me not to go. "I'll be back soon," I said. "I promise."

She kissed me before I put my helmet on. "Be careful."

Call that a given. Nerfer's voice came over the intercom. "I can't override their systems to open their hatch. You'll have to burn your way through."

"Acknowledged," I said and went to a storage room to find a laser torch.

Back at the airlock, once the doors opened, I floated over to the alien craft and cut my way through their hatchway. Their power systems were dead. Five aliens floated in the vacuum of space. Small creatures, they resembled monkeys to a great degree, but their faces and bodies were shriveled as though their essences had been sucked out.

"Hell," I whispered, then realized that hell had nothing to do with this. Some other unearthly force was at work here.

If the other ships' inhabitants were in the same condition, then that was something I wasn't prepared to see. Time to head back. Once I'd passed through the airlock and decontamination, I shucked my suit. Lynni had been waiting for me. "Was it bad?" she asked.

"It wasn't good."

We went to the bridge, and during our walk over, I wondered how everyone could just...die? None of this made any sense. Nerfer greeted me with a wave and said we were on course for the sun. I went to the computer and asked it to check things out. "Computer, confirm that there was life here before."

"Working."

It made its usual assortment of noises, then it gave out its findings. "Extrapolating from preliminary findings, the Prenimium Galaxy was once home to five Class M planets with a combined population of over thirty billion inhabitants. Those planets were once capable of supporting humanoid life. Only three of them contained humanoid life forms on them. The other two contained only lower forms of life — animal and vegetable matter."

As it continued to give its readout, a sense of horror as well as frustration filled me. That ship...those people...who or what could have done this? "Computer, can you tell me when life was here? By that, I mean how long ago?"

"Checking...rate of decay on each world indicates approximately thirty solar days ago. Sensors detect sizable populations on those Class M planets, bodies that have not yet been interred. Animals and vegetation are also present, but they are not alive."

I straightened up as an electric shock ran through my system. A month ago...

"Rick, I got something," Nerfer said as we slowly ground to a stop. "We're about thirty million miles from their sun."

"Can you detect any gravity? Any solar activity?"

"Nope."

He pressed a button on the console. "Here's why. I'm magnifying the image."

Beside me, Lynni gasped. The sun was burned out, a black husk that had somehow been drained of all its energy. "Ever seen anything like this?" I asked Nerfer.

"No," he said in a low tone that was filled with awe and not the least bit of terror. "It's like it's been...sucked dry."

Wasn't that theoretically impossible? It should have been, but then I reminded myself that I'd seen and encountered beings and worlds that went beyond human imagination. Moving trees. Walking slime. Alien beings that resembled yaks, stone monoliths, crab-people and more. Humans weren't the only form of life around.

As well, I'd just come from an alien ship where they'd been drained of their life forces, and the touch of Lynni's hand in mine made it abundantly clear that other kinds of life existed and that humans weren't the center of the universe. We never had been.

"Rick," Lynni said in a low voice, "we must leave this place of death. I do not have a good feeling about being here."

"I'm going to second that motion," Nerfer said as he nudged the ship into motion again. "I'm setting a course for the next galaxy."

The familiar feel of our vessel turning around made me long for an escape from this place, and the comforting drone of the engines gave me hope that our next encounter would be a friendly one. Anything had to be better than what we'd witnessed here.

As we cruised through the inky blackness, Lynni whispered, "Rick, may I stay with you in your room?"

We'd been keeping separate rooms since our first date. We both figured it was best for the galaxy inside her. Now, though, I didn't feel like being alone. "Yeah, please stay with me."

"Thank you," she whispered again as she linked her arm through mine and rested her head on my shoulder.

Her warmth comforted me, but only a little. I tried not to think about what had taken place in this region of the universe. It was too depressing.

Chapter Twelve

Death-verse

It took another day for us to leave this system. We encountered no other life forms, only dead worlds and drifting space vessels. At first, the computer gave us a readout, then I ordered it to stop. It wasn't worth it. Nerfer volunteered to remain at the helm and get us out of this place. Lynni didn't feel overly great about looking outside, and I didn't, either.

Fortunately, twenty-six hours later, my intercom buzzed. The clock on my nightstand read eight a.m. "What is it?" I asked after pressing the button.

"You feel like coming to the bridge?" Nerfer asked. "Computer's informed me that we're just about out of the Prenimium Galaxy."

Call that good news and then some. "On my way."

Lynni chose that moment to wake up, and after we took our turn in the shower, we went to the bridge-restaurant area, only to find Nerfer cleaning up the tables. With his back to us, he worked with a singular purpose, humming a tune. With his merriment, it was hard to believe we'd just been through a life-or-death situation. Maybe that was his way of coping.

He'd already done five tables, and when he moved on to table number six, upon closer inspection, he'd missed a few spots. Uh-huh…it wasn't worth bringing up, not now.

"You two okay?" he asked gruffly after turning around.

"We'll make it," I said. "You?"

He shrugged, his body undulating ever so slightly. "Sure. Going through that galaxy gave me a creepy feeling. Our species doesn't dream, but we do get visions."

That was a new one. "Visions of what?"

Nerfer grunted. "Of being alone. I'd hate to spend the next hundred-something years on this barge all by myself."

Yeah, he cared—only now did I realize it. "By the way, thanks for getting us out of Zitik's lair."

"No problem, kid," Nerfer answered, his gaze fixed on the sky. "Glad to help you out. But we got other problems to think about."

I followed his gaze. Unlike every other region of space that we'd been in, this area wasn't black. It was a horrid blood red, interspersed with streaks of purple and yellow lightning that lit things up then reverted to a rainbow of horror.

Lightning didn't occur in space unless it was some kind of solar storm. The computer confirmed that it wasn't a solar storm. However, it couldn't give us an answer to what it was, save to say that this galaxy exuded neither negative nor positive energy. Same deal with the purple or red hues. Where exactly had we landed this time?

Lynni stared at the scene, her mouth open, and Nerfer joined us. "Some light show," he murmured. "Ain't never seen anything like this, not in my lifetime."

Before I could consult the computer, it gave us a warning. "Vessels approaching, approximately three thousand kilometers from our position. They are closing fast."

Nerfer asked, "How many?"

"Three. Sensors detect they are approaching us from the ten o'clock, the two o'clock and the six o'clock positions."

I wondered how they could have snuck up on us without the computer giving us an earlier warning. That was something I'd think about another day. Lynni looked confused by the terms and asked, "What does the computer mean?"

"We're bracketed," Nerfer replied. "If we try to move, they might fire."

"Alien vessels are now less than one thousand kilometers from our position," the computer informed us. "They have halted their approach."

"Magnify image," I said. I had to get a better look at what we were up against.

"Magnifying."

There...there they were, magnificent, long, gull-winged ships that resembled fighters from one of the world wars in the twentieth century. Painted a bone-white color, they stood out from the multi-colored background of this section of space. "Can you signal them?" I asked the computer.

"Working. A signal is being broadcast, but they are not responding."

Wonderful. If they weren't answering, it was a sure bet they were hostile or had intentions of being so. Then, again, Kulida and his gang of ghouls had been friendly — and I'd fallen for their ruse.

Nerfer glanced over at me, his essence forming a puzzled expression. Clearly, he didn't know what to do, either. Lynni, though, had a different reaction. She gasped and put her hands to her head. "What's wrong?" I asked.

Her eyes turned up in her head. "I am…dizzy."

That was all she got out before she pitched forward into my arms, out cold. "Take her to the infirmary," Nerfer said. "I'll see what I can do here and join you as soon as I can."

I picked my girlfriend up and ran through the corridors to sick bay as quickly as possible. Once there, I laid her on the examination table. Lynni chose that moment to wake up. "Where am I?"

"The infirmary." Not knowing anything about Kagekian physiology, I felt helpless. "How are you feeling?"

That had to be the stupidest question of all time, even if it was the most obvious. "Tired and weak," she replied, her voice very soft. "It is hard for me to breathe, too."

We held hands, and hers, formerly so strong, felt limp. I hoped that a solution would present itself, but deep down, the feeling of hopelessness began to well up, and nothing could stop it.

Long story short — we were surrounded, my girlfriend was ill, and I wasn't feeling too great, either. It wasn't much at first, just a vague feeling of tiredness as well as irritability, but around my girlfriend, that irritability vanished. The lassitude remained, though.

Nerfer came down to the infirmary a few minutes later. "How are you feeling?"

I almost laughed at that—almost. Lynni did, though. It pumped up my spirits, but only temporarily. Nerfer nudged me in the ribs. "Gotta talk to you, kid, captain to captain. Bridge stuff."

His tone was sober, and his manner? I'd never seen him like this before. "Bridge stuff," I repeated.

Lynni waved us out. "Go. I will rest here."

Reluctantly, I left, and once we reached the bridge, I was out of breath and feeling worse than before. Whoever or whatever was doing this, they or it was doing it fast. Something was literally pulling the life from me. With an effort, I made my way over to one of the booths and sat. "So, what couldn't you tell me before?"

"This galaxy isn't good for us," Nerfer answered.

Since when was space not dangerous? Of course, there was inherent risk just being here. Meteor showers, comets, radiation belts, not to mention hostile alien races—the list went on. But simply being in space—that was a stretch.

"How can space be harmful to our health?"

Before he could answer, the interstellar com-link crackled to life. A querulous voice that sounded like the buzzing of an insect mixed with a paper shredding machine working at full capacity, spoke to us, and it sounded angry. "Alien vessel, you are in Verrillion space, claimed by our empire. State your purpose here. Do so immediately."

Verrillion? "Do we have any information on them?" I whispered to Nerfer.

He shifted his body from side to side, indicating no. Grunting from the strain, I got up and went over to the computer to press the com-link button. "This is Rick Granger, captain of the *Port Anywhere* space vessel, operating from Earth."

"You are in the realm of space that we claim as our own," the response came. "I am Commander Moskane. My flagship is to the right of your vessel. We have two other battle cruisers ready to destroy you, should you prove harmful to our kind."

It was as though he was following the bad ruler playbook. Identify first, then threaten, then open fire if he felt like it. Why did some aliens automatically assume that we were hostile? Since they had sensors, couldn't they read that we were sick?

"Uh, this ship isn't armed. I'm guessing you have sensors. Check for any weaponry on board. You'll probably find a few flare guns, one old-style rifle and some matches. Oh, and one Yelten pulse rifle that's in our landing bay. That's about it. While you're at it, scan our physiologies. We're sick and getting sicker."

"Scanning."

Silence fell, and I tried to remain upright, just in case they had the ability to see our bridge. Our screen remained blank, then an image flickered on it. Nerfer addressed our computer. "Increase resolution of image."

A figure appeared against a black background, but it was not humanoid in any way, shape or form. Its skin—if it could be called that—was a garish orangey-purple, it had a W-shaped face, slits for eyes, nose and mouth, and it seemed to shimmer in and out of existence. What kind of life form was this?

"It is true what you say," Moskane said in his querulous, buzzing voice. "Your ship does not carry any weapons that could harm our people."

"So—"

"Nevertheless, this is our galaxy. We claim it, and we will defend it to the death, if necessary. Inhabitants from the other galaxy tried to invade. More than five different races claimed scientific missions and sent their ships into that which we claim for our own. We did not believe them."

Another galaxy? "That wouldn't be vessels from the Prenimium Galaxy, would it?"

"Correct."

A cold wave of fear washed down my spine. They'd somehow infected and-or destroyed that galaxy, but why? "We also wish to know your vessel's secrets," Moskane continued.

What was he talking about? "What secrets?"

His voice grew higher-pitched and angrier. "Your secrets of propulsion."

Propulsion? We ran on ion-power engines. Ion power was nothing new for technologically superior aliens, and they possessed engines as well as weapons that were way beyond what Earth could produce.

"Commander, our ship runs on ion power. If you've scanned our vessel, then you know that we—"

"You *lie*!"

Apparently, not all alien races possessed a sense of fairness, decency or even advanced intelligence. I was getting tired of people being so uncooperative. More than that, I was simply exhausted as well as worried about Lynni. "Commander, we're not here to claim anything. We're not here to do any research. We're just passing through. If you let us out of your web, we'll be on our way with no harm done."

Moskane's eyes narrowed even more, if that were possible. "Very well. We will run more scans on your ship and think this matter over. For now, we ask you to wait an hour of your time."

The image faded. I turned to Nerfer, who was pointing at the computer. "Kid, you'd better listen to this."

"Is it good news?"

"No."

Marvelous, more good news. "Computer, what can you tell us about this galaxy?"

Hum and click, hum and click. "It is not compatible with human or humanoid life forms. Rather, human or humanoid life forms are not compatible with this section of the universe."

Moskane had practically spelled it out, but I had to know more. "Define 'compatible'."

The computer gave us the breakdown. Energy was the key, our energy, our life force, as it turned out. The Verrillion people fed on it, and not only their people, but their entire galaxy. "Sort of like…uh, energy vampires?" I asked.

I'd read about vampires in the old texts, and while they fed on blood, these aliens seemed to share the same traits. Damn, my earlier intuition had been correct. I hated being right.

"I don't get the term 'vampires'," Nerfer said as he scanned the computer readout. "But if you're asking does this galaxy feed on us, the answer is yes. I already see it in with your girl. Now, I see it in you."

Which made me wonder why my blobby friend was immune. "I'm not," he said after I'd posited my request. "I'm not feeling that well, either. If my suit were compromised, I'd probably be worse off than you and your girlfriend."

Okay, problem — explained — and I directed my next question at the computer. "So, is it the galaxy or the ships?"

It gave us its usual whirring and clicking. "This unit is unsure. It is picking up traces of negative energy from the alien vessels. It is possible that they are either emitting the energy itself or they are somehow magnifying the effects of negative energy within this galaxy. This unit is unsure."

More bad news. "Uh, computer, is there anything we can do to compensate for the energy drain?"

"Leave this quadrant of space."

Some help that was. "Let's try getting out of here," I said. "Screw Moskane. We stay here, and we die."

"Good idea."

Nerfer went to the controls and started to nudge us forward, but while the engines whined, we lurched forward then stopped. "No good. They've got us in a tractor beam. We can't move."

Wonderful. Using the engines was useless. They'd propel us at a reasonable speed, but it wouldn't be enough. No matter how fast we went, our life forces would leave us long before we cleared this galaxy's boundaries. There was no way out...

Unless we shifted. And, right then and there, it occurred to me that we'd always shifted in times of crisis. I had a theory, and while I wasn't sure, it made sense. "Computer, are the Verrillion ships still bracketing us?"

"Correct."

"Are their weapons trained on our ship?"

Click-click. "No. They appear to be waiting. But they have a force beam that is holding this vessel in place. Unable to analyze composition of the beam."

Naturally—nothing here made sense. "Open a channel and hail them."

As he did so, the door to the bridge swung open and Lynni staggered in, her face haggard and pale. "Hey, you should be in bed," I said, concerned for her well-being.

She shook her head, and her voice checked into the supremely frightened level. "I do not wish to be alone. Please...I must be with you."

It was impossible to send her away. She shouldn't have to witness this, but since she was here...

"Hailing frequency is open, Rick."

Nerfer nodded at me as if to say I was now in command. He would have to cede responsibility, but if not now, when? I took it on. "What is it, Commander?" I asked.

Moskane's voice, high, strident and demanding, echoed over the bridge. "I have consulted with the captains of the other ships. We have not changed our opinion of you or your kind. Are you going to surrender your ship's secrets?"

Well, that didn't take long. This Moskane's obstinacy was maddening, not to mention annoying to the nth degree. "You have a tractor beam on us. We can't move. You're also draining us of our life energies. We want to leave in peace, but you aren't giving us much of a choice."

By now, Moskane was downright pissed off, and his voice rose to a shriek. "Give us your secrets! We are prepared to find them out, and if we must board your vessel, then we shall. It will not be pleasant."

Screw this! They'd gone too far, and we had to get out of there. If we didn't, we'd die. My breath hitched in my throat, but I didn't dare let on how badly I felt.

Time to stand tall—literally. Nerfer did as well, and even Lynni struggled into an upright position.

"Moskane, take a good look at us," I said, now truly enraged at his obstinacy. "You're good at threatening others. Here's my ultimatum. If you want the secrets of this ship, you'll have to blow us up first or at least disable us. We're not turning spit over to you. Now, if you turn off your tractor beams and let us go, we might be able to come to an agreement. If you don't, we won't be responsible for what happens."

Sure, it was a BS statement. Sure, it was an empty threat. But he didn't have to know that, although from his harsh laugh, he'd already figured out we were as harmless as some baby animals. Even Nerfer gave me a questioning look of *what-the-hell?*

A snort of derision came from the enemy commander. It sounded like a squealing engine. "Your ship has no means of defense. You are no threat."

We were no threat, but they still wanted to destroy us. While hypocrisy should have been Moskane's name, I was too sick and tired to say anything save, "Oh, is that right?"

After I'd given him my clever comeback, I shut off the com-link. "Nerfer, can you run an electric charge through the hull?"

He shook his head as if unable to comprehend my idiocy. "Yeah, but—"

"Do it, and send a small charge into space, directed at their flagship. Just a burst. That'll be enough."

Lynni clung to me. Her face was ashen, her breathing, shallow. "What are you doing?"

"Wait for it."

A moment later, the outside of the ship lit up as Nerfer turned the juice on. Once he did, a blast of purple plasma came from the lead Verrillion ship. It seemed to head our way in slow-motion, then it sped up. The computer said, "They have ceased using their force beam."

Good news, but off to our right, another burst of purple plasma came in our direction. A nanosecond later, the computer announced, "Shift occurring. Shift occurring."

"Hang on," I said to Lynni, and we clung to each other, feeling the ship shake and shudder.

This was going to be close. I asked, "Computer, how long until the fire from the enemy ship reaches us?"

"Fifty-two seconds."

Oh, that was cutting it too close, and the energy plasma crept ever closer, undulating gracefully in space. The seconds passed...fifteen, fourteen...twelve...then six and finally...

A moment later, we got tossed hither and yon by the shift. When I picked myself up, I found that we were somewhere else, and my breathing returned to normal. Wellness spread throughout my body. A look through the screen revealed the welcome inky blackness of space, and I was never so glad to be away from that vampiric galaxy. "Nerfer, you okay?" I called out.

He was in the process of getting up. "Smart thinking, kid."

My girlfriend got to her feet, touching herself all over as if unable to believe she was whole and healthy again. "I do not understand. What happened?"

"It's the ship," I said, half in wonder and half in gratitude. "I didn't figure it out at first, but now, yeah. It only shifts when it senses it's being attacked. That's what my father built into the engine. It's a self-defense mechanism."

Actually, it was more like self-preservation, but whatever. Nerfer got to work right away, using his various extensions to check out, pull away, and repair what needed to be fixed. Lynni offered to clean up my room as well as the storage areas. "I am sure that something was knocked over somewhere."

She disappeared through the door before I could say anything. Nerfer watched her go with an expression of amusement then handed me a welder that wasn't much bigger than my hand. "Time to go to work, kid."

* * * *

Three hours later. My cabin.

"I am exhausted," Lynni said as she stepped out of the shower, a towel wrapped around her torso. While I'd been working on the bridge and elsewhere, she'd been cleaning up the cabins as well as the various storage rooms. "That galaxy we were in before. It was something I never want to experience again."

That summed it up. I took my turn in the shower, and when I came out, I quickly wrapped the towel around my waist. Even if Lynni was up for some fun, right now, I was too tired to do much else. Losing out on a potential chance or not, I slid under the covers and closed my eyes.

"Do you want to know something?" Lynni asked.

My eyes snapped open at her question. "What?"

"I know it is early in our relationship, but I wish to tell you something."

Lynni put her hand on mine. "What is it?" I asked.

Her face showed a multitude of emotions, and it was difficult to know what she was thinking. "Uh, Lynni, you can tell me. I'll understand."

She took in a deep breath and whooshed it out. "I shall, then. Even though we have not physically consummated our relationship, among your people, is it too soon for me to say that I care for you deeply?"

Call that a semi-surprise. I knew that she liked me, but this had gone to an entirely new and welcomed level. "Um, are you saying that you love me?"

Her eyes turned a brighter shade of orange. "Yes. I saw how you acted on that world with the trees. You risked your life to save me from those kidnappers on that space port, as did Nerfer. And now, you defied a superior force. You are brave and kind and good."

I wasn't all that, but at the same time, why argue? Lynni continued, her eyes glowing. "On Kagekia, we…we are not taught to suppress our feelings. If we like something or someone, we say so. Is that not more honest?"

"It is."

Lynni stroked my cheek and she put her face close to mine. "So, how do you feel about this?"

My lips stopped a fraction of a centimeter from hers. Sure, it was kind of fast, but we were young, on a ship together, and I'd never felt this way about anyone before, so what else could it be? "I love you, too."

"That is the correct answer."

Chapter Thirteen

Up For Grabs

Finding true love was one thing. Finding safety turned out to be another story altogether. It seemed that no matter where we went, trouble followed. After a forty-eight-hour period of relative calm, that being measured in no one dropping in unexpectedly, once we entered the Martanian Galaxy, the Drosh—a race of cyborgs—hailed us, demanded entry, and they were most definitely not into friend-mode.

They arrived out of nowhere in a kite-shaped ship that corkscrewed its way through the heavens. After we'd established a visual link with them, one of them said, "We are here to claim that green female you have with you."

Well, that was fast. This person was roughly my height and humanoid, but just barely. Most of his body was covered in metal. Tubes ran from his back and fed into his arms, legs, and a square-shaped hunk of metal that ran from his chin down to his navel area. To me, it looked like a power pack, although that was only a guess. The flesh that showed under his facial covering was pale white and unhealthy looking.

From behind me, Nerfer was quietly consulting the computer on the Drosh's physiology and murmured, "Keep them talking."

Keep them talking. Stalling for time wasn't one of my gifts, but I had to develop it—and fast. "Why do you want the female?"

"That is our concern," the first man-thing said, who'd identified himself as Penek.

His trademark was a tiny red crest on the top of his bald head. It was one of the few places on his body that wasn't covered by metal. It also made him look incredibly ridiculous, but it was doubtful that he cared. "We will destroy your vessel if you do not accede to our demands."

"Hold, please."

Hold, please—that had to be the stupidest thing to say, especially in a situation as dire as this one, but I had to stall for time, and those were the first two words that came to mind.

"You have one of your minutes to decide."

I cut the audio feed. We'd have to work fast. I turned around to face my girlfriend. "Since when did you become the most popular person in the galaxy?"

"Since I joined up with your crew," she replied promptly with a grin. "And as for my popularity, I hope it is only with you."

Her mood then sobered and with an expression akin to fear mixed with anger, she made a subtle gesture at the creatures on the monitor. "What shall we do about them?"

A grunt from behind us made me turn around. Nerfer said the computer had already analyzed them.

"Like we saw, they're mostly machine. According to the computer, they're humanoid, but the suits they're wearing? They're containment suits, sort of like what I wear. With them, they're about three times as strong as we are. Without them, my guess is that they're just as vulnerable as humans."

All right, that was a start. "And what will make them vulnerable?" I asked, then the answer came to me. It apparently hit Nerfer at the same time, as he grinned.

Acid. We had some stored on the ship. My father had used it from time to time in his experiments. Hydro-Fluoria was a stronger version of hydrofluoric acid, one of the oldest manufactured acids around. Engineers and scientists used it to dissolve various metals, so maybe it would work on our visitors' suits.

This acid was considered so dangerous that the concentrated form was never used. It had to be watered down, and even then, it was beyond lethal. The fumes alone could damage lung tissue. We'd have to be careful.

Nerfer knew where it was. He oozed away, saying that he'd get things ready. Our time limit was up, so I swiveled back to face Penek and clicked on the audio feed. "If you want the girl, come and get her. I'm no one's delivery boy."

"We will board your vessel."

That was exactly what I wanted. "Stand down, first. I don't like having guns pointing at my ship. They might go off."

Penek never blinked. "They are for our protection. We will be there shortly."

I should have known better than to trust a soulless cyborg. Whatever, they had the jump on us, so we waited. Good to his word, Penek's ship docked with ours and he came through the airlock along with four of his men. The computer readout indicated that they carried no pathogens, so that was a blessing. Lynni joined us, even though I'd asked her to wait in my cabin.

"My place is at your side," she responded defiantly. "If they kill you, they will take me, anyway. I wish to be with you."

No stopping her, and Nerfer met us at the airlock holding three plastic squirt guns. I'd brought them onboard, and sometimes my parents and I had water fights. It broke up the monotony of being in space and tending to the machinery twenty-four-seven.

Lynni pointed at the plastic pistols. "What is inside them?"

A faint grin formed on Nerfer's usually bland visage. "Some very nasty acid. You were right, Rick. This stuff is lethal. Just don't spray this on yourselves and don't breathe it in."

We were ready, and we each took a gun. I hid mine behind my back, finger on the trigger, ready to come out shooting, if necessary. Lynni and Nerfer did the same, and we put on our most innocent expressions.

Once the door slid open, Penek and his men strode through, and he pointed at Lynni. "Is that the female?"

Right to the point—that was Mr. Red Crest. "Yes, and you're not getting her."

He took another step toward us. "I think we will. She represents parts for us."

"Parts?"

"Correct...parts. We were once much like you, but our suits cover up our imperfections."

"Imperfections?"

A look of impatience crossed his face. "It was a disease on our world. That is all you need to know. The suits protect us, and we are of in need of parts, should our suits' systems fail."

Uh-huh. As they were more machine than man, they needed those additional parts to not only upgrade and augment themselves, but also for their survival. "And, uh, who's giving you those parts?"

"Someone you need not concern yourself with."

Uh-huh – again. I already knew, although I wanted to make sure. "Is his name Kulida?"

Penek blinked. Being thrown off-balance wasn't what he'd been expecting, and his gesture told me everything. How Kulida knew our location was beyond me, but that didn't matter. "Take one more step," I said. "Go ahead. Take one more step."

"What will you do?"

If that wasn't a cue, I didn't know what was. "Fire."

In unison, Lynni, Nerfer and I sprayed the invaders, drenching them in the fluid from our guns. At first, it had no effect, but then I yelled, "Aim at the tubes and the power packs!"

I meant the square metal boxes on their chests. We fired, and a puff of smoke came from the tubes. That was it. They must have been feeding either blood or nutrients — or both — to their bodily systems.

It was a mistake on their part not to have reinforced them. While the Drosh were advanced, they weren't indestructible. More smoke came along with the smell of metal being eaten through, then Lynni squirted a shot in one of the cyborgs' faces. He screamed and fell to his knees. A moment later, he collapsed, his body quivering.

We did the same to another one of his men, and his face melted. Penek didn't have time to think about it, as he subsequently let out his own shouts of pain. "What...what is this?"

"Self-defense," I said. "Give up now, and maybe we'll let you live."

His suit was smoking, and the stink itself of lethal acid escaped, making me cough. Nerfer went to rev up the ventilators, which took most of the dangerous fumes away. More moans came from Penek. While he may have been more machine than man, he was still humanoid enough to have pain receptors.

Parts of his armor began to melt, dripping on the floor and causing tiny holes to form. He tore the decaying armor off in a panic, leaving exposed, damaged, and raw flesh for everyone to see.

Before, he'd been a nearly indestructible cyborg. Now, he looked like less of an interstellar conqueror and more like a woebegone interstellar cast-off. With a piteous moan, he begged for mercy. "Wait, stop. We accede to your demands!"

I hadn't made any yet. His last man had his hands in the air, and he was quivering in fear. He wasn't about to make trouble, but just in case, I gave them a warning. "Nice to know. Here they are. One, you get into your ship and leave. We'll leave, too. Fire on us, and we'll disappear. Try to attack us, and we'll beam over some acid packs and burn all of you. Understand?"

"Yes."

Naturally, we didn't have that kind of tech available, but he didn't have to know that. "Good. Now, pick up your friends and leave. Don't come back. And tell Kulida to give up as well."

Penek bowed his head in defeat. "I shall do as you order."

Shortly after, they left, taking their dead comrades with them. Their ship disengaged itself from ours and swiftly moved out of range. Lynni breathed a sigh of relief once they'd gone. The ventilation system soon aired out the place, and it came as a relief to take in a deep breath without having to worry about being poisoned.

Even Nerfer opined that we'd been lucky, but a scowl formed when he saw the burned and scarred holes in the deck made by the acid. "I'll fix this then take the con," he said. "I've had enough of this spy and kidnapping stuff."

Lynni tapped me on the shoulder. "I think I need to lie down for a while. I am tired."

She didn't look tired, but then she arched her eyebrows...I got the message. "I guess I could do with a nap," I murmured.

With a playful expression at work, she led me back to my room. Once there, she kissed me fondly on the lips, lay down in bed and promptly fell asleep.

Yo-ho, the captain's life for me...

* * * *

Three days later

"We're entering another galaxy," Nerfer said as we cruised through space.

Our speed was constant—three-quarters light-year power. Our ship could go faster if we pushed it, but we never had. The shifting had taken care of that, although it remained a mystery of how exactly we could shift without incurring any damage.

The engines themselves gave no clue. "I really can't figure it out," Nerfer said as he exited the crawlspace from the engine. It was shielded, and a good thing, too, as it was incredibly loud. He eyed the machinery with admiration and a hint of fear. "Your ship works in strange and mysterious ways."

That was the only answer I ever got. I wasn't skilled enough to work out the whys, either. However, him mentioning that this was my ship — call that decent, and then some. I'd misjudged him. "It's your ship, too," I replied. "And I couldn't have done it without you."

He hung his head, sort of like the old-time cowboys doing their 'Aw, shucks' routine. "Good to hear," he said in a gruff tone then cleared what passed for his mushy throat. "Anyway, back to work."

Nerfer turned away before I could say anything. Maybe it was a little embarrassing for him, but he deserved all the credit in the universe. He'd saved my life a few times, and I owed him for it.

Our voyage continued. Lynni and I took our turns on the bridge, and I helped her learn more cooking skills. She quickly picked up what needed to be done and started cooking for me and Nerfer. "Y'know, this isn't bad," he said as he sampled a steak, medium-rare, that she'd prepared. "Not bad at all."

Modest to the max, Lynni bobbed her head and said that she'd had the best teacher around. Yes, call that another compliment. I'd take it, and for once in my life, I took a certain amount of joy as we cruised along. It had nothing to do with being in space.

It had everything to do with doing something I enjoyed, which was cooking. And, of course, being with someone who mattered to me counted for a lot—and Lynni most definitely mattered.

Then, of course, Nerfer would have to tell me that we were about to enter another galaxy. Immediately, I got a bad feeling. "Which one?"

A warning note sounded in his voice. "Alfarnan. I've been here before. Kulida and his gang frequent this area—that much I know. They could be shadowing us, although our sensors detect nothing in this area."

His words offered no comfort at all. While we had far-ranging sensors and a computer with a lightning-fast collection and retrieval matrix, we also had no weaponry to speak of, minimal shielding and our speed could only be described as pedestrian at best, compared to all the other ships out there.

In short, we were sitting ducks, as the old saying went. Not wishing to upset Lynni, I simply asked Nerfer to keep going and keep me posted. If we were very lucky, then we'd pass through this galaxy unmolested and uncontested.

A day later, our luck ran out. Shortly after we'd finished breakfast, the interstellar com-link decided to buzz us. "Might as well answer it," I said to no one in particular and clicked the button to open things up. "*Port Anywhere*, this is Captain Granger—"

"I am Osheerai, leader of the Blurd Empire."

His voice sounded tinny, almost mechanical, as well as harsh and unreasoning. If they were cyborgs, I wondered if we had enough acid...

"Respond!"

Demanding jerk, wasn't he? That order came from Osheerai, and he sounded more than a little impatient. "What do you want?" I asked.

His answer came swiftly. "Your surrender, first and foremost. I know who you are, and I know what precious cargo you carry."

Marvelous, more formal talk. Maybe it had something to do with the universal translator in my head, or maybe that was how all the bad guys talked. From Kulida to Penek, all the aliens, but especially the nasty ones, they had to carry a kind of bad-dudes manual.

Bad-dude rule number one—*thou shalt always speak in a semi-formal fashion, as it will terrify your enemies. Contractions in speech are not needed.*

"I will make this quick. Give us the girl or you will be destroyed."

Bad-dude rule number two—*thou shalt always threaten to destroy your enemies, for it will terrify them and cow them into submission.*

"Try it," I answered, attempting to sound tough and failing miserably at it.

A mirthless chuckle came from him. "I do not have to. Our technology is superior to yours in every way, and we will soon be upon your vessel. Do not try to fight us on that matter."

I muted the audio and turned to Nerfer. "Can the sensors pick up their ship?"

"No. Sensors show nothing. They must have a cloaking device."

Of course, they did. This was an alien galaxy and they'd discovered the secret of staying invisible. We were truly screwed, then a dull thud signaled that the Blurds had docked with us. I tried to shut them out, but the signal didn't work. "Do not try," Osheerai's voice said over the intercom. "Our technology exceeds most of the advanced species in this galaxy."

I stifled a curse at their efficiency. Osheerai hadn't been lying about their tech being superior. It most certainly was. They'd already overridden the computer, and a signal from the console said that they were already at our airlock.

I took off with Lynni and Nerfer close behind me in the direction of the airlock, only to find that they'd entered. Blocking it didn't work. They charged through to our side. "Guys, decontamination!"

Right, like they were going to listen. Rhetorical — not — and the door slid open on my side to reveal four tall, wraithlike beings in the realm of two meters who wore containment suits. "We are not carrying any pathogens, human," Osheerai said. "Rest assured we are not out to poison you."

Wait! How did he know I was human? Call me slow on the uptake, but it then occurred to me that he also knew Kulida and was working with him or working for him. Kulida was like an octopus. He had tentacles everywhere. That was how he and the other aliens knew us. We were now like hunted animals, and it wasn't a good feeling at all.

Osheerai leveled a long tube that resembled an empty bazooka but was probably lethal, all the same. I'd already seen too many aliens that possessed superior tech. "What do you guys want?"

He pressed a small button on the side of his helmet. It retracted, leaving only a small mask that covered his mouth. The rest of him, though, was a sight to see — slit nose, reptilian eyes that glowed purple and oversized ears that made me think elephant instead of humanoid.

"What do we want?" he repeated. "We are advanced beyond your kind in every way, and we want your surrender."

That was bad-dude rule number three—*thou shalt tout your technical superiority and state thine purpose immediately.*

Well, he'd already told us his tech was superior—which I'd figured out—and now, he'd told us to surrender. This was a person who didn't mince words. Using the universal sign, I put my hands up, and Lynni did the same. Nerfer didn't say a word, but he formed two pseudopods and raised them as well.

They had us. Now, it became a matter of what they wanted to do with us.

Chapter Fourteen

Captured

Since we were up against forces that we couldn't defeat, much less battle equally, time to go to Plan Two—only we had no Plan Two. Waiting for the shift to occur was futile. It wouldn't happen without some external impetus, such as someone firing upon us. We had no weapons on board with which to fight—and we didn't have enough acid.

In short, we were on our own. In the old days, people had called it weathering a storm. Nowadays, it simply meant putting up with a lot of crap, and in our case, the crap had a name—the Blurds.

"You may lower your limbs," the lead alien said. "I repeat, we are not out to harm you, unless you give us cause to."

Angry and yet determined to find out more, I asked, "Where are you from?"

"We are from a place that is so distant from this galaxy that even your sensors would not be able to detect it," another Blurd replied in an absurdly high falsetto tone. Maybe it was his mask or the voice synthesizer built into it — or both. Or maybe that was his real voice. It didn't matter. Trying to act tough against us voice-wise wasn't his forte.

On the other hand, he was armed. We weren't. Three thick fingers, each one about twice as thick as strongman's fingers, made up each hand, a sharp contrast to their spindly physiques. Their hands looked capable of tearing through anything, including metal.

Bottom line — we were screwed. "What are you here for?" Lynni asked.

"Since you have now surrendered, we want your secrets." He then stared at her, his cold, dead eyes raking her form as if undressing her then having their way with her, a look which repulsed me as well as pissed me off. "And we want you as well."

The Blurd leader whispered the word 'secrets' as if it was the goal in and of itself. It wasn't, and it gave me no clue as to what it really wanted. This was the second time I'd had to listen to someone demand that we give up our secrets, and I was getting tired of all this running around and even more tired of the bullshit subterfuge.

"Okay, start by telling me who you're working for. I already know, but I want to hear you say it. I'm Rick Granger. I'm the captain of this ship."

In response, the spindly leader eyed me as a scientist would eye an especially ugly specimen. "You are but a child, a boy."

Oh, here we went yet again. It took everything in me not to roll my eyes and jump up and down in frustration. While both those gestures were justified, they were also overused, and I didn't feel like playing into some kind of stereotype.

Seriously, though, what did they expect, some person in their fifties, some grizzled veteran? It seemed that the age stereotype was a universal concept, and it was pissing me off. "I'm almost eighteen. That's old enough—and you haven't answered my question."

He took a step toward me. "Who I work for is not relevant. Who I know, where I go, that is also irrelevant. What is of prime importance is my mission, and my mission is to retrieve the girl as well as learn your ship's secrets."

Bounty hunters? Interstellar bounty hunters as well as salvagers and thieves—great, something more I had to deal with. "And why do you want the woman?"

"Not her. What is inside her is that which we seek. Hand her over to us and we will go in peace."

Not bloody likely. I reached into my pocket and gently slid out the laser. It wasn't that powerful, and its range was only a few centimeters. If I could get Osheerai to walk close enough, maybe I'd have a chance.

"How did you know about the hidden galaxy?"

If ever there was a stupid question, well, that was it. I already knew, but I wanted to see their reaction.

And their reaction was one of amusement, as the Blurds guffawed with laughter, a high-pitched cackle of glee that they emitted in unison. Maybe they were clones, after all. However, this time, only the big-fingered leader replied after the laughter stopped.

"As I said, we are from a distant point in this universe, but our area of space is poor in natural resources on the planets we visit. Therefore, it is only natural that we seek the materials we lack from other sources."

Wonderful. In the entire universe, we had to run into hostile races. Why couldn't we meet any nice ones? At that point, my thoughts of science and peaceful coexistence went out of the proverbial window.

Angry and helpless, I took a step toward their leader, determined to get one shot in before he vaporized me. However, Lynni's strong hand kept me back. It amused the Blurds, as they laughed again at the sight of a woman standing up to them. Lynni didn't find it unusual, and with a snort of rage, she stepped in front of me to confront the Blurd leader.

"Do you really think you can control what is inside me?" she asked. "Do you? If you do, then I dare you to fire."

In a quick move, she grabbed the laser from my hand and unzipped her uniform. It fell to her waist. This wasn't part of the game plan, was it? "Uh, Lynni, you don't have to strip in front of —"

"Rick, be quiet."

I shut my mouth. My girlfriend continued to threaten Osheerai, shaking her fist at the alien leader, who took a step back in surprise. "What is this brazenness?" he asked. "We want what is inside you. We do not wish to take you, not in that manner."

Uh-huh, he wasn't in rape-mode. Good to know, and Lynni, her body quivering in rage, let her claws out. "Go ahead and fire. You will be the death of us all. The galaxy that you seek inside me is incredibly large and powerful."

His eyes held terror. "Wait."

Lynni held up the laser, flicked it on and pointed it at her stomach. She waggled it back and forth, and her tone sounded just short of menacing. "Even now, I feel it expanding. So, shoot me. Do you feel lucky?"

Did they?

Apparently not, as the Blurd leader put up his hands in surrender. "You would do that?"

"Yes."

He looked over at me. "Is this person your mate?"

Lynni swiveled her head around to face me with a devilish grin working. "Well, Rick, are you?"

What could I say? I felt my mouth work itself in a variety of positions until I got my voice working again. "Yeah, she is. And I'd listen to her if I were you."

Real fear manifested itself in the Blurds next words. "This...was unexpected."

If his response was unexpected, so was the jolt that nearly took us off our feet. I went to the wall-intercom and punched the button. "Computer, what was that?"

"We have been fired upon by another ship, one of Blurd design."

Osheerai took something the size of a pebble from his pocket and thumbed it. "This is your commander. Report!"

A strained voice responded immediately. "Apologies, sir. Our mechanics were checking our weaponry systems and they accidentally discharged a tiny amount of plasma. Our sensors show that the ship you are on was not damaged."

No, it wasn't damaged, but I knew what would happen next—and it did. The alarm went off, and Osheerai looked at me with apprehension. "What is happening?"

"Shift occurring. Shift occurring," the computer said.

Our adversaries looked around, confused. "What does that word shift mean?"

"It means," I said, pulling Lynni back—and she flicked off the laser and pulled up her uniform, "that this ship is going to move from this galaxy to another galaxy. We'll be safe inside here. I'm not so sure about your vessel, though."

Mr. Blurd turned to his friends, uttered a squawk of fear and they raced into the airlock. I shut it behind them.

"Thirty seconds before shift."

Well, that was a help, but they weren't going to make it. The ship began to shudder and Lynni and Nerfer held on to the rail. As I looked at the screen, the shuddering of the ship intensified. Osheerai and his men managed to make it into their ship, but a moment later, Port Anywhere gave a heave that took us off our feet.

When the ship stopped bucking, I looked at the screen. Most of the Blurd ship was gone, with only the nose-docking part remaining. Nerfer oozed his way over. "I'll get on that right now. Give me a few minutes to cut it loose."

After we got him through the airlock, Lynni and I checked things out in our rooms. Aside from the clothes and our belongings being tossed hither and yon, our abodes were largely undamaged.

But if our rooms were in good working order, the computer wasn't. When I asked it where we were, only garbled sounds came out. "The shaking must have damaged the voice circuits."

I found the repair kit, took out a screwdriver and a micro-laser, and I unscrewed the bolts on the console to take the cover off. A wire had come loose, so I carefully put it back into place and used the laser to solder it down.

Once I put the cover back on the console and screwed it down tight, Nerfer's grunt caused me to look up. "Okay, the Blurd ship is out of here."

Glad that was over. "I was fixing the computer. Thanks for getting rid of their ship."

Another grunt came from him. "I'm getting too old for this outside repair crap. You'll have to do it next time."

He sidled over to the computer to ask, "Where are we? Respond!"

Cheer down, bud, I thought. The computer clicked and whirred, then it intoned in its usual tinny voice, "Tirian Galaxy. Approximately ten billion light years from launch point."

Launch point meant Earth. I took over from my blobby friend. "Are there any habitable planets in this galaxy?"

Whirring and clicking noises greeted my question, then the computer spoke, and its next words chilled me to the bone. "According to the sensors and the insta-base, a number of Class M planets exist. They are home to the Gellenites, the Rattanians, the Findessi and —"

Rattanians? "Stop. Go back. Names of races in this galaxy."

"This galaxy is home to the Gellenites, the Rattanians, the Findessi and —"

"Stop."

That came from Lynni, who turned to me with a frightened expression working. "They are after me, and we are in their territory."

Yes, we were, and I wondered why the Rattanians had two worlds. We'd already encountered them before in another galaxy...then I realized that they must have conquered that world where we'd first met. If this was, indeed, their home galaxy, it wouldn't be long before the enemy decided to show its ugly head.

"Rick, look!"

That came from Lynni as she touched my shoulder and pointed straight ahead. Oh, hell, we were too late, as the air shimmered and Kulida and his two droids from our previous meeting—Frandil and Saddel—stepped through. I remembered them well. Their massive gray forms flanked another man with a short and slender form, a sad, beaten look about his face—and green skin.

"Father!" Lynni cried. "What have they done to you?"

"Daughter, I am fine," he said, but he said it in the weariest tone imaginable. Plain to see he'd been worked over with a few pairs of massive fists. Bruises dotted his face. Torture was never pleasant to see.

"Screw this," Nerfer growled. Never one to shy away from a fight, he quickly formed pseudopods and started forward.

It didn't help.

Kulida's men literally blew him apart. For a few split seconds, I couldn't believe what had happened. My co-captain—my friend—had been blasted into nothingness, and my mind froze in shock.

Shock gave way to muted rage. I kneeled to see if there was anything I could do. One of the blobs of matter quivered, then it lay still. Nerfer was...dead. Anger and vengeance surged in me. "You bastards! What in the hell did you do?"

I put my hand on another spot of his body that spattered the restaurant floor. No movement at all. For my friend, there would be no coming back from something like this.

A harsh laugh came in my direction, and I looked up, only to find the commander of the Rattanians wearing a fierce grin. "At the very least, he tried to defend this ship. You, Rick Granger, are but a boy and a supreme coward."

Coward? "Screw you," I snarled and rushed him. Nerfer's death demanded retribution, and I was determined to see that justice was done.

While my revenge was justified, rushing an armed madman who had backup turned out to be a stupid move. His men clubbed me over the head. Stars flashed, and I pitched face-first to the floor.

An ensuing cascade of kicks and stomps took the energy out of me. While one of the thugs held me down, the other patted my pockets and found the laser. He handed it over to Kulida, who examined it, flicked it on, smiled and subsequently turned it off. In a slow, almost insolent move, he crushed it and tossed it away.

"A clever toy," he said and signaled his men to move back. "But it was only a toy."

Lynni helped me to my feet. "Animals," she spit out. "You are lower than animals."

At her words, the enemy commander's smile segued into an even fiercer grin, something like a cross between a gargoyle and a Froog, a multi-faced alien I'd seen only in the database and had never had the displeasure of meeting.

"You may call us what you wish, and you may even attempt to attack me, if that is what you also wish," he said with the obvious relish of a sociopath who enjoyed his work way too much. "I would rather you do not, though," he continued. "I wish you to see what kind of magic I am about to wreak upon the universe."

He stared at Lynni. "Your name is Merlynni? I wished to make sure. When we transported you here before, we were not informed of your name."

She answered him with one word, the hatred evident in her voice. "Yes."

Kulida waved his hand in the direction of his hapless prisoner. "Good. As you can see, I have your father. It took my men a long time to find him, but it was well worth the effort. Outside of you, he is the only living being left from your world."

"What did you do?" Lynni asked, her mouth half open in a mixture of disbelief, fear and outrage.

The wannabe warlord-slash-world-conqueror Kulida leaned in, a wicked gash meant to simulate a smile upon his ugly mug. "We vaporized your world, of course. Your father is our prisoner. That should be clear to you. We will bring his equipment here in a moment. The transportation devices we purloined from Cradd and his men have proven to be most useful. We did not know that they operated on the brainwaves of the user. That is most remarkable."

He then turned to the scientist, who'd hung his head and was muttering softly to himself. "Well, shall we get to work?"

Chapter Fifteen

Showdown in Storage Room Nine

Kulida herded the three of us at gunpoint into a large storage room, number nine, which was located near the cargo bay. Lynni seemed to be in shock. Her limbs trembled as she walked, her mouth hung open and she stared into space, her mind blasted by the knowledge that her world no longer existed. Not even her father's comforting hand on her shoulder could invoke a response.

The Rattanian commander observed them without a shred of pity then turned to me. "I will have you know, Rick Granger, that I have been chasing this vessel of yours across the universe, and I am weary of the chase. It ends now."

Chasing someone had never been high on my list of priorities, and while half of me held a tiny amount of respect for Kulida's determination, the other half said his obsession was way off the charts wrong.

At the same time, I wondered how he'd been able to track me. The goons he'd hired had managed, but they'd been in the vicinity. However, how would they know who to look for? Could interstellar com-link devices travel that far? I wasn't sure — then it hit. "You put a tracer in Lynni's cage, didn't you?"

A glint of respect came to his eyes. "Obviously, you are not as unintelligent as I thought. That is correct. We installed a small tracking device into the cage we brought on our first trip here."

He huffed with what had to be disappointment. "Still, you cannot be that intelligent or that experienced. A good commander, one who prizes safety above all for his ship, would have jettisoned the containment unit into space long ago. Had I been in your position, I would have done so after freeing the Kagekian."

He stroked his chin as if musing on the vagaries of command. "Then, again, you had no reason to suspect that I would do such a thing. We have been through many galaxies and have scoured the universe in our quest to find you. It is fortunate that we have what you would call a wormhole device that cuts our travel time considerably.

"Additionally, we have allies on many worlds who provide us with information from time to time. You have already met some of them. While our tracking device does have its limitations, our wormhole device does not. It works on a certain frequency known only to us and our allies. Once they found it, they were most forthcoming with information as to your whereabouts."

If ever there was a burning indictment for not thinking things through, he'd just provided it, and if there was an award for being incredibly naïve, I would have won it, hands down. At his pronouncement, Lynni snapped out of her trance and turned to me with a stricken expression. "I am sorry, Rick. I did not know."

"No, of course you did not," Kulida continued.

He fixed his gaze on me and held his gun hand steady on all of us. "But here we are, and here you and your father are. If you wish to continue your corporeal relationship with him as well as with this human, then I suggest you keep your mouth shut and allow your father to work on you."

Lynni's father looked up, his expression one of anger as well as resignation. "If you wish me to work on my daughter, I must be allowed access to my equipment as well as a quiet place in which to perform the operation. It is a delicate procedure, and what is here is insufficient for my needs."

Kulida gazed around the room. "This place seems to be quiet enough. As for your equipment, you shall have it."

He clapped his hands twice and his disciples vanished into the ethers. They returned a few minutes later carrying a small machine the size of a coffee pot with three buttons on it, as well as something that looked like a laser scalpel.

Frandil carried a pair of surgical gloves and another object that resembled a pair of tweezers. "This is what you used, is it not?" the commander asked.

Lynni's father nodded. "It is. I will also need some anesthetic for my daughter. I do not wish for her to suffer any pain from the operation."

An ominous shadow swept across Kulida's face. Clearly, he was not pleased, but then again, he'd never struck me as the most patient person around to begin with. "I see. Well, we do not have any anesthetic on hand."

In a swift move, he threw a hook to her jaw and knocked her unconscious. She dropped like a rock to the deck and her father bent over her, rage seeping in to replace the mildness. "Merlynni was no threat to you. That was not needed!"

Rage flowed through me at Kulida's heartlessness. Since he had no compunction about using violence, I didn't have any, either. If the chance arose, I'd use whatever I could to destroy him.

I went over to pick up Lynni's unconscious form and place it gently on a table that one of the Rattanians had cleared. Once I'd laid her down, I started to charge at Kulida, only to pull up short as he leveled his gun at me. "I would not try it," the Rattanian commander said in a voice colder than ice. "You would not get far."

Seething, but also knowing he was right, I stepped back and felt someone's hand on my shoulder. It was Lynni's father. "I do not know who you are," he said. "But you do not have to die needlessly, not today. I have need of your services."

"Like what?"

He motioned toward the machine as he slipped on his gloves. "Turn it on. The green button—press it. It must warm up before I use it."

He bent over his daughter's body to unzip her uniform down to her waist and examine her torso. "What is your name?" he asked me while he worked.

"Rick."

"I am called Tranda."

Kulida grunted and stabbed his finger at the table. "Since the introductions have been made, I see no reason to prolong things. Proceed."

Tranda looked up, his eyes searching the room. "I will need a damp cloth for the blood."

I went over to a nearby shelf and found a clean rag. A washroom lay a few meters away, and I started for it. "Hold," Kulida called out.

An orange flame whizzed over my head, hitting the wall and searing it. That caused me to stop in my tracks and turn around. This jerk was making it incredibly difficult to keep my temper under control. "I'm just going to soak this rag, you moron. It's for the operation!"

The commander looked indecisive, and I had the feeling he'd deny my request just to be petty. Finally, he waved his hand at the door. "Go ahead."

I ran in to soak the rag then hustled back to where Tranda waited. "I'm ready."

"Put the cloth here," he said, pointing at a point just below her bottom belly button. "That is where I shall make the incision. It will not be a big one, but it will bleed."

Tranda turned to Frandil. "The pain will be bad. It may cause her to regain consciousness. You must hold her arms." Then he swiveled around to tell Saddel to hold her legs.

Kulida ordered his men to do so, and after they'd secured their holds on Lynni's limbs, her father twisted a knob on the machine and a light came out to bathe his gloves in a soft yellow glow. "What is that for?" Kulida asked with a mild tone of interest.

"It is a portable sterilizer," Tranda answered as he washed his hands under the light as well as the laser scalpel and the tweezers. "I must enter my daughter's abdominal cavity. I will do so now."

"Proceed."

Tranda flicked on the scalpel. A bluish-red flame leaped out, and he narrowed the beam to something less than the width of a needle. As he did so, the color changed to an almost incandescent magnesium white, and I had to shield my eyes.

Lynni's father obviously had stronger retinal protection than I did, as the brightness of the flame didn't seem to bother him at all. He cut into the skin below his daughter's bottom belly button. A tiny amount of red-green blood leaked out. She moaned but didn't wake up, although her body began to shake. Tranda started to murmur in consternation while I carefully dabbed at the blood. "What is it?" I asked.

"Something is wrong," he said in consternation. "I must hurry."

In a quick but smooth motion, he took the tweezers and clicked them together. They immediately lit up and began to vibrate. Slowly, carefully, he reached inside the slit, moved his hand around then nodded. "I am almost there. Hold my daughter steady."

We did, and the bile rose at the back of my throat. I'd never seen an operation done live before, and this was my first time to participate in one. It grossed me out, but at the same time, I couldn't afford to be squeamish. And...I had seen worse things.

Be strong, Lynni!

She moaned and began to regain consciousness. As she did so, she started to thrash around. "Hold her fast!" Tranda barked.

Kulida's men intensified their grips, and after a few seconds of uncertainty, her father gently pulled out a gray object the size of a pebble. Lynni moaned again, but she didn't move. Her breath came in shallow rasps, though. "What is that?" I asked.

"It is a stabilizer," he said. "It keeps that which is within her from shifting. It also prevents the sheath that covers the galaxy from breaking."

"That is all fine and good," Kulida said from his position. For emphasis, he waved the gun in our direction. "But I am still without my prize, and I have not come all this way for nothing."

What. A. Moron. "You'll get your prize, idiot," I said. "Hang on."

Wrong thing to say, as he walked over to shove his gun in my face. "You are this close to dying, Earth boy."

Tranda looked up and snapped, "I must have quiet!"

Kulida glared at him. "You shall have it. Continue working. Frandil!"

His subordinate let go of Lynni's arms and stepped over to his side. "Commander?"

"I shall take over for you in your duties. For now, go and break the bones of this piece of Earth-trash. As a reward, you may eat them."

That was something I wasn't ready for. Nevertheless, I waved Frandil forward. "C'mon, tough guy. Let's take this elsewhere. The sound of me smashing your head against the metal is going to disturb things."

Frandil growled, but Kulida interceded by pointing at the exit. "The stripling is correct. This demands quiet. Go to another storage room on this vessel and have your feast there."

The junior man already had a pistol in his hand. He motioned at the exit. I took him down the corridors, and as we walked along, I patted my pocket to make sure the jewel, the endra, was still there. It was. Maybe I'd get the chance to use it…maybe.

"Where are we going?" Frandil asked as he shoved his gun into the small of my back.

He kept jabbing me, just to get a reaction. He was taking me to my death, but I wasn't going to give him the satisfaction of seeing my fear, even though my heart rate had to be well over a hundred beats per minute.

His question came again, accompanied by a shot to the back of my head that staggered me. "Human, where are you taking me?"

Yeah, where were we going? Initially, I'd thought about taking him to the airlock and somehow tricking him inside, but that wasn't feasible. Then I had a thought and turned right at a junction.

"In here," I said and opened the door to storage room one where Lynni's containment unit was. The room also held several large crates full of parts, my parents' clothes, my barbells and dumbbells...and my old battle-practice droids. They sat against the wall, silent and waiting.

Frandil looked around as if getting his bearings, and that gave me all the time I needed to dive behind a pile of crates, a couple of meters from the droids, Huey and Dewey.

My Rattanian foe grunted in a mixture of frustration and rage. He hadn't been expecting me to hide, and what better place to do it? I'd hidden near my droids, and they provided the perfect cover. Somewhat taller than the Rattanians and incredibly powerful, both models operated on voice command, and I'd recharged their batteries only a month ago...

"Where are you, little boy?" Frandil called out in a mock-friendly voice. "I will make your end merciful and quick. You cannot beat me. You are small and weak. You have no chance."

That may have been true, but it wouldn't stop me from trying. First off, I had to disarm him, somehow. What could I use as a weapon? I looked around... *There!* A stray five-kilo plate. It was heavy, solid and best of all, potentially lethal.

Grabbing a small plate of crumpled metal, I tossed it to my right. Needless to say, it was the oldest trick in the book. My hope was that Frandil hadn't read that book.

He fired his pistol in the general direction of the sound, vaporizing the metal. While he went forward to check it out, I crept from my position, and once he heard me, he spun around. At the very instant he did, I swung for the fences and bashed the wrist of his gun hand with the weight plate. The weapon went flying.

"You insect," he ground out as he rubbed his wrist. "I will not need a weapon to destroy you."

Oh, damn, here it comes.

While the blow would have broken the bones of a human, it probably only bruised him. In a quick move, he lashed out with a kick to my hand that knocked the plate loose and sent it spinning over to the far corner. A right hook to my left temple staggered me, and he followed that up with a kick to my midsection that put me down.

Crud, he would have to be well-trained. Remembering my lessons with the battle droids, I rolled with the kick, got up and, when he moved in again, I replied with a kick of my own that caught him on the left knee and he staggered. I followed that up with a straight shot to his mouth and he fell back against one of the crates.

As I strived to keep composed, it occurred to me that while he was strong, he wasn't invulnerable or invincible. Still, he was an adult, he had the edge in power as well as training and he didn't so much as acknowledge my ability. Instead, he sneered, shook his leg, spat out a mouthful of blood then, with a cry of rage, he came at me again.

In a flash, he switched fighting methods and used palm-edged strikes as well as hurling elbows when he got close enough. He moved much faster than I expected, chopping hard at my shoulders, arms and neck, hoping to land the killing blow.

In turn, I blocked most of his strikes, but a few got through, enough to rattle me. As much as they hurt, they helped to fuel my anger. I replied in kind, trying to figure out his defenses.

Damn it, he switched styles again, shifting to fighting at close quarters, using his elbows and knees — but always with the same combination. Left elbow in, right block and left knee.

I did my best to counter what he threw at me, ducking and popping my elbows up and out like a counterpuncher would do in boxing. Right kick, leg block, duck and lash out again!

It seemed to work at first, but he was too strong, and he continued to hammer away at me. His shots got through to my face and I felt blood flowing. A moment later, drops of it splashed on the floor.

Still, I managed to stay cool, pain or no pain, which was one point in my favor. Frandil, on the other hand, grew increasingly frustrated when I didn't fold. "Keep punching, big man," I grunted out. Waves of agony assailed me, but I wouldn't give it — or him — the satisfaction. "You can't beat me."

"We shall see. I shall cut you up with my hands and eat your heart!"

He bent over to whack away at my head and neck, and that was mistake number one. He should have stayed upright and used his superior reach to wear me down.

Mistake number two came due to the positioning of his hands. He weaved them in a rough circle in front of his face, but he neglected to keep his elbows down to protect his neck and chest.

Timing…timing…it was everything…and I saw my opening. He was right in front of the battle droids. They stood, ready and waiting, two meters behind him. "Ready," I gasped as a particularly heavy strike caught me in the sternum.

In response to my voice command, the droids' sensors lit up. All right — go to phase two.

"You are ready for what?" Frandil asked as he unleashed a one-two strike to my face and left shoulder. He then made his last and biggest mistake of bending over to leer in my face, the expression of a bully who enjoyed inflicting pain. "Tell me, what are you ready for?"

"More fun."

In a quick move, I snapped my head up to connect with his jaw. The impact rang my bell and lights flashed in front of my eyes. Frandil let out an *urk* and staggered back. A right shot to his face with my palm shattered his nose.

Blood spewed out like a geyser, fountaining over the floor. Frandil bellowed in pain and brought his hands up to protect his face. Not a wise move on his part, as it left the rest of his torso unprotected, and with the last of my strength, I yelled and launched a dropkick to his chest. The impact plus the surprise sent him reeling into the embrace of the droids.

"Grab him," I ordered, and they did just that, wrapping their machine-like clamps around his wrists and ankles and lifting him off the floor.

He struggled to get free, but as strong as he was, those droids were used to lifting hundreds of kilograms, far more than he could, and their gripping power was immense, five times that of a human's. Frandil wasn't human, but that didn't matter. He wasn't going anywhere, and his eyes bugged out in surprise. "What?"

I bent at the waist, breathing heavily, and trying not to bleed. Futile, really, so I shoved the pain aside. Time to finish this. "Hold him and move half a meter to your left," I ordered Huey. With Dewey, I repeated the order but told him to move to the right. Obediently, they pulled hard on his arms and legs, stretching him out.

Frandil's face was a mask of blood. Through it, his eyes shone with nervousness as he glanced at the droids then at me. "What are you going to do?"

If he couldn't figure it out, then there was no hope of helping him. In fact, help was the last thing on my mind. Still struggling to regain my breath, I panted out, "You know, I like history. In the old days on Earth, they called this 'drawing and quartering'. You said you'd cut me up with your hands and eat my heart."

"You—"

"I don't have a sword to cut you up with, but I think my droids can do the job. You understand where I'm going with this, don't you?"

The big mercenary looked left and right again, comprehension slowly creeping into his eyes. His lips quivered, and even though the thought of what was about to happen made me queasy, this was what we'd come to. No backing off now. "Huey, move back another half a meter."

Huey did, his gears slowly grinding.

"Now, Dewey, move back. Half a meter will do."

Dewey did as I commanded.

"Now, both of you together — march."

By now, Frandil's arms and legs had been stretched taut, and he obviously realized what was going to happen. He struggled, but to his credit, he didn't beg. He did gasp out, though, "I will...kill you."

"Maybe tomorrow."

With that, I ordered the droids to keep moving. A horrible tearing sound came, one of splitting flesh, the rending of muscle tissue and the breaking of bones and ligaments from their foundations. Frandil began to scream.

Then he shrieked.

Once.

Silence. I turned my head away and said, "Stop."

Turning away didn't hide what I'd seen. Five pieces of Frandil lay quivering on the floor and the area was awash in his blood and spilled out organs. Gorge rose in my throat then the bile, along with the contents of my stomach, came up.

I couldn't help it. I retched, spewing everything out, and once I'd finished, I took in a deep, shuddering breath to compose myself. Killing Bikor was one thing, but that had been to save Lynni's life. Now, I'd done this to save mine. Killing was an ugly, evil thing, but in this situation, it couldn't have gone any other way.

This mess could wait. For now, I picked up his gun and made my way back to where Kulida was. Stealth and guile — use them to creep up on the enemy.

So much for stealth and guile, as when I poked my head around the corner, the muzzle of Kulida's gun greeted me. *Crap.*

The alien leader wore an expression akin to stone. "I should have suspected that my man failed. He has never taken that long with anyone."

In a quick move, he plucked the gun from my hand, then he stepped back to inspect me, assessing the number of cuts and bruises on my face, along with the blood. "You are more resourceful than I thought, and I will admit that you are not a coward. Go to the doctor's side. I have finished assisting him for now, but he may need additional help."

After I did so, Tranda asked me to wipe the blood from the incision away, and once the area was clear, he pulled a transparent, smaller-than-pinky-sized purple oval-shaped object from Lynni's gut and held it up to the light. "I have it."

It was the galaxy and it quivered, perhaps because Tranda's hand was tired—or perhaps it was due to something else. A tiny amount of blood seeped out from Lynni's incision, and I gently dabbed at it. She sighed and passed out again.

No one bothered looking at her, save me. They were more interested in staring at the galaxy. Although it was covered with blood and bodily fluids, it glowed with life and purpose. "It is a marvel," Kulida whispered in the tone of someone truly awed.

"It is," Tranda responded as he bent over his daughter's form to examine the cut in her abdomen, which was still leaking blood. "It has all the energy it needs to revitalize any dead solar system and perhaps the life within that system. That is why I created it."

A sharp breath came from Kulida. "A king's ransom. It is beyond remarkable. I will take possession of it now."

Tranda shook his head and spoke without looking up. "Not yet. My daughter's wound must be cleaned and closed. I had to leave an infinitesimally tiny portion of my creation within her. It was inside her too long and has become part of her. Therefore, some of it must be left to stabilize her system."

What?

I peered at her stomach, and sure enough, a tiny star winked at me as it circled around her inner organs. "Stand back," Tranda said. He reached up with one hand to position the sterilizer's ray upon Lynni's incision. His other hand clasped the galaxy-sheath firmly. "It will take only a minute."

Another grunt of frustration came from the massive man. "I have waited long enough as it is."

However, Tranda refused to be cowed. He stared at the larger man with a hint of steel replacing his former compliance. "You could wait for a minute or for an eternity, but in any case, you will not do anything."

Kulida blinked. "How so?"

Tranda quickly changed the laser scalpel's strength. He gently played it up and down the wound, closing it off, then he moved the sterilizer's rays up and down Lynni's torso.

Once done, he turned it off, stood up from his daughter's body, and he held the encapsulated galaxy between his thumb and forefinger, waggling it back and forth in front of Kulida's face. The capsule was quivering faster. "You will need to use your portal device and use it quickly. We will leave together. Then you shall have your prize."

"That is not good enough," Kulida replied, now with a sneer on full display. "You will have to do better than that."

It had come down to this standoff, but I had one trick left to play. In a quick move, I took out the endra jewel from my pocket and held it up. As expected, the Rattanian commander turned around at the sudden movement and he fired, as did Saddel.

Bad idea, as the jewel absorbed the energy and reflected it back upon Kulida's right hand—his gun hand. A horrible cry of pain came from him as the energy seared his flesh, causing him to drop his now-useless gun as well as the portal device. The reflection of energy did far worse to Saddel, as it fried him in his tracks. Only ashes remained, dancing in the air briefly before drifting to the floor.

A horrid smell of charred flesh filled the room, and I knew that I'd be having nightmares about this for a long time. Still, I kept it together, snatched up the portal device and sidled over to Tranda. "We have him."

Our Rattanian adversary wasn't going anywhere. He sat on the ground, holding on to his half-melted appendage. Kulida then started to curse my name, my family's heritage and the inhabitants of the universe.

Much as I wanted to beat his face in, that would have to wait, as Tranda shook his head and muttered something about leaving. "Leaving?" I asked. "Why do you have to leave here? I mean, you're going to take Lynni home, and—"

"No, it is not that. And, in any case, I cannot return to my galaxy with my daughter. I told Kulida the truth before. I must go somewhere else…now."

"Why?"

He showed me his creation. Uh-oh, this wasn't good. It was vibrating faster and harder, making a faint humming sound, and a tiny crack had appeared. A bit of light showed, and even though it was than a millionth of a millimeter, its incandescence almost blinded me.

"The protective covering was damaged when I extracted it from my daughter's stomach," Tranda said as he shielded his eyes. "The stabilizer prevented it from expanding inside her stomach, but it is useless now. The galaxy will expand."

Wonderful. "Can't you stop it?"

As the humming from the miniature galaxy grew louder, so did the note of urgency in his voice. "No. We do not have much time at all."

Tranda looked at the portal device in my hand. "Give it to me," he said. "As this piece of offal has said, the portal device operates on the brainwaves of its user. I will take this creation of mine as well as our foe to a place where we cannot hurt anyone, although I do not know where."

I did. We'd come from a dead galaxy, and since there was no life there, perhaps his artificially constructed galaxy would have a chance. "Sir, I have an idea." Then I told him the coordinates.

Tranda nodded. "Then, that is where I shall go."

"Father!"

Lynni had woken up. She tried to get off the table, but her wound still must have hurt terribly, as she fell back with a scream of pain. "Father, please…do not do this!"

"I have no choice," he said with a sad smile. "I have created this, and in doing so, I have also created misery, although that was not my intention. Now, it is time to rectify my mistake. When I open the gateway, I will enter first. Toss in the Rattanian scum next."

He looked at me with finality in his eyes. "Rick, I do not know much about you, but I must trust you. Please…take care of my daughter for me."

With that, he opened a portal and stepped in, clutching his creation to his chest. Kulida was holding his hand and cursing, but he managed to get up to throw an awkward left hook at me, which I ducked. "I would rather see you die along with me then go to my hell alone," he said as he threw another hook.

He kept attempting to land a blow but stopped when I kicked his maimed and ruined hand. A bellow of agony erupted from him. He sank to his knees. We were running out of time, as the light inside the portal grew brighter and Tranda's voice urged me to hurry. "Rick, there is no time."

"Yes, there is no time," Kulida said. "I will —"

"Burn," I finished for him then launched another kick to his face that catapulted him into the gateway.

Just before it closed, a brighter-than-bright flash went off, practically searing my eyeballs, and the portal closed in upon itself with a loud snap. Lynni let out a moan then began crying. "My father…he is gone."

I went to her side and gently held her around the shoulders. "I'm sorry."

She continued to sob. "You know what he did."

I knew. He'd opened his creation in the area that I'd mentioned. How that would affect the orbital and gravitational fields in that sector of space was anyone's guess. However, considering there was now life where none had been before, perhaps that would turn out to be a good thing.

All I knew was that Lynni and I had survived and that would have to be enough.

"I'm sorry," I repeated. "Can you walk?"

The incision to her stomach had already healed. She heaved in a deep breath and whooshed it out. The tears still fell, but she said, "I will be fine, thank you," and reached up to caress my face. "Our race heals quickly. I am fortunate that way."

We were both fortunate, and she still had a star within her, a marvel in and of itself. Still, I'd lost a good friend in Nerfer, and while I wanted to have some time to mourn his loss, the intercom blared out a warning. "Earth vessel, this is the Rattanian flagship, Grytan. You are to surrender the girl. Put our commander on."

Aw, not again! I punched the intercom button. "Grytan, this is Rick Granger, commander of *Port Anywhere*. Your commander is dead."

Silence reigned, then the other man's voice came, filled with fury. "Then prepare to die."

I looked at the screen and saw a yellow charge building from the nose of the vessel that hung off our starboard bow. Lynni clung to me. "What will happen?"

"Nothing good."

Or maybe something would, as the computer intoned, "Shift occurring. Shift occurring."

"I have to see this," I said, and we took off to the restaurant. It had the best view, and while the ship heaved to and fro, we stayed on our feet.

The shift must have affected the Rattanian vessel, as it rapidly moved off. A moment later, the stars whirled and spun, and we arrived at our destination. Plates and cutlery littered the floor, and after one final forward heave in which the stars seemed to flash before our eyes, things settled down.

"Where is this place?" Lynni asked.

Good question. As I looked through the viewing screen, a sense of familiarity hit, and with it, my heart began to beat faster. It couldn't be, but it was! The stars seemed to be in their former positions, there was a sun...

Immediately, I checked with the computer. "Give me a readout of this system. Is this Sol?"

The tinny voice replied, "Affirmative."

Hope took flight and my pulse rate escalated. "Give me a readout of the planets closest to this sun."

"Mercury, Venus—"

"Stop."

By now, my heart was beating faster, and it seemed too good to be true. "Hey, Lynni, I know where we are."

"You do?"

I did. Outside of the computer telling me about the sun and the first two planets of this solar system, the constellations—Big Bear, the Little Dipper, the Big Dipper, and all the rest? They were where they should have been.

The computer only underscored what I'd known all along, and after three years, a series of adventures and the death of my parents as well as surrogate father and friend, a pink blob named Nerfer, a sense of completion overwhelmed me.

"We're home."

Chapter Sixteen

A Message from the Past

Lynni asked the obvious as she stared through the screen. "Are you sure?"

"I think I'd know. The stars don't lie."

My answer, while it might have sounded arrogant, it wasn't, not really. I'd seen those constellations from the viewpoint of my telescope at Salt Flats, and I'd seen them from the vantage point of this ship the first time we'd broken free of Earth's atmosphere. No way could I have made a mistake.

She wandered over to the porthole and gazed at the greenish-blue bauble below us. "We are in orbit now. It is a beautiful world, much like mine was."

Lynni sounded wistful and way beyond heartbroken. She had a right to be. Her world was gone, while mine remained.

And it was true—Earth *was* beautiful, but only from space. When I'd been there, the surface depicted a much different, harsher—and sometimes, crueler—reality, at least, in my experience. I wondered if telling her was the best way, but after giving the matter some thought, no. It wasn't worth it.

However, maybe a trip down to the surface wasn't such a bad idea. I'd been away for a fairly long time, so perhaps things had changed in a more positive fashion. While I pondered the ins and outs of arriving home, there was something I had to do.

"What shall we do now?" Lynni asked as she looked down at her blood-smeared jumpsuit. "I must change."

My suit was filthy as well, and I still had to clean up the mess I'd made in the storage room where body parts were scattered. "Okay, there should be a spare suit in your room. I have to do something first. Then I'll meet you on the bridge."

Lynni nodded and ran off to her room, while I went first to clean up where Huey and Dewey had helped me, then to the storage room where Lynni's cage was to search for the tracer. Patting it here and there yielded no bumps or protuberances. I felt inside, but there was nothing save the metal itself. If the tracer was inside the cage, as Kulida had said, there was no time to take the damn thing apart and search for a mechanism.

Bending over and grunting from the load, I dragged it to the cargo bay, shoved it in the waste disposal chute and ejected it. It would now drift forever on the tides of space.

No sooner had I closed the airlock doors when the computer hailed me from an intercom. "Warning, warning."

Warning about what? "Computer," I said. "What's wrong?"

"A security light has gone off in your cabin."

Security light? It was probably a burned-out wire, so I jogged along the corridors to my cabin and found a red light blinking from the ceiling. What else could be up there, except wires and metal? Did we somehow pick up an alien that was about to ingest us all or use us as host subjects? Was there a fire? I didn't smell any smoke.

To that end, I grabbed a chair, stood on it and removed the panel. I poked my head cautiously through the opening and found a seven-by-seven-centimeter metal box blinking at me. It emitted regular pulses of red light, and it played up and down my face as if linking my image to that of someone in a database somewhere.

"What in the hell is this?"

Retrieving the box didn't involve any danger. After examining it thoroughly, I realized that it wasn't a bomb. It was an old-style recording device, pre-twenty-second century. Someone had pre-recorded a message, and it was timed to replay itself at this day and hour.

There were only two buttons on the machine, one for 'play' and the other for 'rewind'. I sat on the bed and pressed the play button. My father's voice came through.

"Rick, if you're listening to this, then I'm dead and you're now the owner as well as the captain of the vessel, along with Nerfer, if he decides to stay on. I'm sorry about not getting you back to Earth. I know that your mother and I promised you. It hurt me to break that promise, but there was nothing for us there."

Nothing for them there? Anger surged to the forefront. He'd only stolen two years out of my life, so, nothing there? For him, maybe, but for me?

A second later, a measure of reason crept in. My father was right, to a degree. The only person I'd ever had a connection to was Sarah, but any feelings I had for her were gone.

As for my life on Earth? Well, I'd had a home, but it had been a home in name only. Solid ground, terra firma, a chance to walk on grass or dirt—that was all. I'd never had many friends or any kind of permanence. I'd only deluded myself into thinking that I'd had a kind of permanence in Salt Lake City or Chicago or any of the other places my parents had lived.

Once I'd left Earth's confines, and once I'd experienced life up here, in a sense, nothing had changed. I was just as rootless on my home world as I was in space. Like Lynni, I'd become an orphan of the stars.

I pressed the play button again.

"Let me explain," my father said.

While this must have been recorded at least a year ago, it sounded like it had been done only yesterday. My father sounded hopeful at that point. Perhaps all scientists did when they were on the verge of discovering something great.

"When I rebuilt this vessel, when I installed the hyper-shift engine, I had the idea that it would come to be used as a port, a waystation. That was my dream, to have a place where different people from all worlds — if life existed out there — could get together and talk. That's what my dream was. When your mother and I met years ago, and just after you were born, it became her dream as well.

"I hadn't figured out how to actually build the hyper-shift engine. That is, I'd made the calculations, but it was your mother's genius that brought my concept into reality. Once we'd constructed it, once it was online and working in conjunction with the ion engines, we knew that our dream of seeing the universe could become a reality."

And all this time, I'd thought my father had been the main designer and that my mother had just been his assistant. Incorrect assumptions about who did what aside, his message about meeting others, having *Port Anywhere* become a waystation—now, it resonated with me.

Journey among the stars, meet different races and become friends and allies—that concept had been the ideal of many philosophers and writers from long ago. When television had been around in the twenty-first century and before, there'd had been shows depicting just such things. They showed different races working together and living together on various kinds of spaceships, and that seemed fine as far as it went.

Reality, though, painted a different picture, and a note of disappointment and sadness coated his next words. History often showed that in the battle of dreams versus reality, the latter, combined with practicality, always won out. My late father's voice continued his speech…

"It was a naïve hope, and, as it turned out, it wasn't the government's dream. They wanted the hyper-shift engine your mother and I had designed to use for their own purposes, mainly as a way to star-jump from quadrant to quadrant and galaxy to galaxy. It's like a wormhole, only safer.

"Factually speaking, it is its own wormhole. It just doesn't project one. Anyway, the armed forces wanted to use it not only as a means of exploring space but also as a weapon of war, to literally get ahead of or behind their supposed enemies.

"Naturally, your mother and I protested. We'd intended that engine to be used for peaceful purposes of exploration and only that. We were supposed to go out and meet new life. That was what our mission was all about – or what it was supposed to be all about."

Here, my father's voice became impassioned, and a hologram of him leaped up. As it did, tears involuntarily sprang from my eyes. He'd been healthy then, even though he'd clearly missed my mother. The pain of loss showed in his eyes, and if I'd looked in a mirror, I knew that I'd see the same pain of loss in mine as well.

He talked about the officials in the government coming to him as well as my mother, cajoling, begging, wheedling and finally threatening them to hand over their ideas about constructing hyper-shift drives for Earth's spaceships, specifically, warships.

My parents had been the only two people around with the knowledge of how to construct such engines. With their help—or so the government officials had thought—the US would become preeminent again.

The military applications had been staggering. On Earth, hyper-shifting meant that they could simply walk into any country and dominate. By the same token, they could take that idea to the stars—go anywhere, be in ten different places at once. Control of the universe would be theirs.

Long story short, my parents had refused to go along with the US government's perverted dream, even after being threatened with significant jail time. Those individuals in power, though, had taken their revenge, as for a period of about a year, my parents had been relegated to serving as backup technicians on other projects.

My parents had acceded to their demands, but all the while, they'd planned for their eventual jump to the heavens. That they'd succeeded was remarkable, considering that they'd been watched the entire time.

Call me naïve or just plain stupid, but I'd never realized the scope of the government's plans. They were into control, plain and simple, and my parents had refused to go along with the program. No wonder my parents had preferred space...

"So, I decided to make a radical shift, if you will, in the engines."

My father's tone turned practical here, more realistic. He'd known what the government was up to—and he'd played along. The government and military personnel had never recognized that he was also playing them.

"I still worked on the hyper-shift drive for our vessel, and I also drew up some plans for the government, if only to placate them. I needed access to materials and alloys and power sources that only they possessed. It meant giving up my ideals for a time.

"At any rate, once your mother and I were allowed back into the regular program, we continued our work on the hyper-shift in secret. You see, for regular orbits and cruises, the ion engines will work just fine. The shifting that you will experience is something I built into the system of the vessel, not only the computer, but also the entire ship.

"Before today, it was geared for the shifts that have occurred. I'm sure you've noticed that the system couldn't be altered. I did that for a reason. Life is a chance, after all, and I believe that chance usually favors the innocent. Perhaps that's a naïve assumption. We always made the jump, and the shift only happened if a hostile force tried to invade. The sensors on the ship saw to that."

And I'd never suspected that, either, until we'd been directly attacked. The sudden jumps we'd made had been due to someone firing upon us or near us, as when Kulida had attacked his Yelten foes. That jump—and others—had gotten us out of there immediately, off to another distant galaxy, another experience and another adventure. It was randomness to the nth degree, but it was also randomness with a plan.

"*Rick, by now, you're probably back to Earth. Again, that's what I designed the ship to do – to send us here and there across the universe for a two-year period. From this point on, the ship will respond to your command to randomly shift or not. The computer will recognize your voice and only yours, so it's up to you whether you stay on or quit.*

"*It's your decision, and I realize now that I shouldn't have decided your future for you. That's something no one should do for anyone else, even though you were only fifteen when we started out. We thought your dreams would become our dreams, and we were wrong.*"

I stopped the recording at that point. My father was correct, of course. At first, his dreams as well as my mother's dreams had never been mine – never. Time, though, turned out to be not only a healer but also a changer, and my thought processes had changed in the most significant of ways. Meeting Lynni had altered them even more. "Dad," I whispered. "Dad."

On went the recorder again.

"*Rick, if you decide to return to Earth and you no longer need the ship, go to the command console on the bridge. Simply say the word 'hyper-shift' and that's it. From that point on, your voice will override any sub-commands on the computer. Those two words will automatically shut down the shift and freeze the engines, although the ship will still have power. The life-support systems will continue for two hours, which gives you more than enough time to pack what you need.*

"*From that point on, you can take the scout ship back to Earth. Before you leave, though, say the words 'destruct code seven-a' into the command console. The computer will do the rest. That will cause the ship's engines to overload and explode within thirty minutes.*

"Once that command is given, there's no way of stopping it. I designed that backup system so that our tech — your mother's and mine — wouldn't fall into the wrong hands."

By now, I was crying harder and made no effort to wipe away the tears. His next words made me bawl my head off and I didn't care if anyone heard or saw. This was too important.

"Son, no matter what, I love you, and your mother loved you as well. Be strong, be brave and come what may, always know that we tried our best to inculcate a love for the stars in you."

The message ended after that, and the hologram of my father faded from view. I clicked the machine off and kept sobbing. I'd cried only twice in the past two years, both times for my parents. I cried for them and for the lost years I had. They'd done what they'd done out of love for me. I understood that now.

One question remained — that of whether to go back to Earth or not. That was something to discuss with Lynni. I put the box under my bed, away from prying eyes. In the future, perhaps I'd listen to it again, just to hear the sound of my father's voice. But, for now, I had other things to do, and so, after I changed clothes, I got up and headed back to the restaurant.

Chapter Seventeen

Where Do We Go from Here?

Lynni was still in the process of cleaning up the place. She'd mopped the floor where Nerfer's remains had been. Just seeing the clean floor made me think that it would take some time for me to process his passage. I'd deal with it.

As I waited, Lynni tossed some shards of plates into the garbage, wiped a few tables and that had been that. Once she heard me come in, she turned around and tossed a rag at me. "Your eyes are red. Are you all right?"

Maybe I would be—in time. "Yes. How about you...your stomach, I mean?"

"I will be fine. As I said, our people heal quickly."

She went to a booth to sit and relax, and the computer chose that moment to inform us that our orbit was stable. Up to that point, stability hadn't been a factor in my life, but now, with Lynni here, perhaps things could change.

No, strike that—they already had changed, and in only the best way. Nerfer's words about relationships came back to me. I now understood that concept could be applied to anything.

"Kid, it ain't always where you're going. It's where you are at that point in time and who you're with. That's the important thing. Once you know where you are, you'll be able to figure out where you're going. Understand?"

Now, I did. His wise counsel, as well as the counsel of my father, had given me all the information I'd ever need. Oh, and if what my father had said was true, then I'd be able to control where we went.

"Rick?"

Lynni called me over and entwined her seven fingers, the digits so slender as well as powerful, gently around my hands. "Yeah?"

She pulled me down to sit with her and kissed me fondly on the lips. "I think I did a good cleaning job."

"You did. Thanks."

"I am sorry about your friend."

Yes, so was I. "I'll deal with it. I'm sorry about your father."

Tears showed in her eyes, but she inhaled a deep, shuddering breath then let it out slowly. "I will…be all right. I must grieve on my own time. Thank you."

A note of uncertainty entered her voice as she waved her hand at the inky darkness beyond the screen. "Will you communicate with the people on your world?"

Did I want to? Since my first year on this ship, I'd thought of nothing else save returning home, but at the same time, with her in my arms, nothing else mattered…

A second later, a man's voice crackled over the interstellar radio. "Unidentified vessel, respond!"

Lynni gave me a semi-hopeful look. In my case, I still felt wary. After going through what I'd gone through, witnessed the death of my friend and the needless death of my girlfriend's father, there was good reason to be skittish. Nevertheless, I got up and went over to the radio to flick it on. "Uh, *Port Anywhere* Restaurant. Can I help you?"

"This is Captain Jason Collins, from Earth's planetary defense system. I'm in charge of the *Balaron*. We're off your port bow about one thousand kilometers away. We detected your vessel's sudden entry into our area of space...and did you just say you're a restaurant?"

He sounded incredulous, but then again, many people had, at least the first time they'd met us. "Uh, yeah."

I looked out of the window. Nothing but space, but when I magnified the image, sure enough, a vessel that bristled with weapons hung off our port bow. The computer then informed me that sixteen other vessels were in orbit around the Earth. Collins' voice came again. "What is your name?"

"Richard, er, Rick Granger. My father was Orville Granger. My mother's name was Mary. We left Earth two years ago."

Silence...then, "I'll check the names with our database. What are your intentions?"

Lynni gazed at me and mouthed, "What will you do?"

Oh, right, answer the questions. "Well, my girlfriend and I were about to have lunch. Do you want to join us?"

A sputtering reply came our way. "I don't think you understand. By my question, I mean, what are you going to do? The central government here asked us to investigate. Shall I assume you're friendly?"

What kind of a question was that? "Sure. Like I said, our ship left Earth two years ago. You said you'd check your database, so go ahead and check it if you don't believe me."

I then gave him the registration number of our vessel. Couldn't they see things for what they were? After all, I was still a citizen of the Earth, so they couldn't really blow us out of the sky, could they?

Well, they probably could, but *would* they?

As for Lynni, would she be welcome among Earth's people? There was only one way to make sure. Lynni waved in my direction. "Hold, please," I said into the receiver and went over to her side. "What?"

"Are you going to go to Earth?"

Her voice was full of hope as well as heartbreak. Her species mated for life, and even though we hadn't gotten to that point—yet—there was no one else I wanted to be with. I could handle the fangs. Same deal with her claws…and her ears.

Her skin, though, emerald and translucent and still full of stars and wishes of the universe, well, that was something not many people would feel comfortable with. I did, but that was me, and I was biased.

"First, we need to talk to this Collins guy."

Her eyes, large and soulful, regarded my calmly, but underneath, there was a smidgen of doubt and more than a smidgen of anger. "I see."

Perhaps she did. "Lynni, it's just lunch. After that, we'll talk it over, you and me. Then we'll decide, okay?"

She nodded. "I understand. It is only natural to be among your own kind."

No, she didn't understand, so I cupped her chin with my hands. "Well, yeah, but listen…I've been up here two years, and I haven't really lived anywhere else in that time." God, I sounded desperate, so I tried to make things clear. "Lynni, we're good together, but I was born here."

A tear slipped from her right eye and trickled down her cheek. "Would I be welcome on your world?"

My girlfriend was far more perceptive than I thought. "You're welcome in *my* world. Isn't that enough?"

She shook her head sadly. "Perhaps not among them."

With a sigh, she got up and pushed past me to the cooking range. Her voice sounded lifeless. "I shall prepare something for our guest. You should welcome him at the airlock."

No arguing with her on this. I went back to the radio. "Are you still there, Captain Collins?"

He sounded shocked as well as surprised. "Yes. Uh, Captain Granger, we ran a check on your vessel. Our records show that you're seventeen. We also found out that your vessel was an experimental model. It wasn't supposed to go that deep into space."

Again, someone had to bring up the age thing, and I was getting tired of it. "Yes, I'm seventeen, and as for your question about my ship, it works. Trust me on that. We've been to a lot of galaxies, and we've got records of where we've been, so while I'm a kid to you, I guess I have the experience. Are you coming aboard?"

"That was my intention."

From the tone in his voice, saying no wouldn't have worked. I stole a look in Lynni's direction. Our eyes met, then she turned away. Wonderful, I'd finally made contact with my own people and hurt my girlfriend in the process. Hopefully, I could work things out. "Have you got the coordinates to dock with us, Captain Collins?"

"Send them, please."

After I'd sent everything, he acknowledged my reply and said he'd come aboard — alone — in roughly twenty minutes. "See you then," I said and clicked off.

Lynni waved me out. "I shall be here."

It seemed that Kagekians had to stew first and perhaps forgive later. I was learning that the hard way. With a feeling of trepidation as well as resignation to the situation, I went to the airlock. Soon, Collins docked with us. A dull thud signaled our locks had clamped down on his ship, so I pressed the button to pressurize the airlock.

After he'd stepped through, and after I'd activated the decontamination procedures, he shucked his space suit to reveal an orange uniform with a blue Earth logo on the left breast.

"Decontamination — complete," the computer announced.

I opened up. Collins was a small man in his late thirties, around a hundred-seventy-five centimeters with a lean physique, a closely shaved head of brown stubble and a sallow complexion. "Captain Jason Collins," he said as we shook hands. "Nice to meet you."

"Rick Granger. I'm the owner of this place."

He wore a dull copper bracelet around his right wrist. "Translator?" I asked, motioning to the device.

"Yes. Just in case we meet any critters that aren't from around here."

Uh-huh.

He glanced around at the ancient outfitting's of the ship, muttered something about a tin can, and I led him to the restaurant. He would have to insult the ship, but I let that pass. It wasn't worth making a fuss about.

"Oh, my girlfriend is there," I said as we walked along. "She's an alien, but she's not a critter."

I half-expected him to snicker, and, true to form, he didn't disappoint. Only coming from him, it came out nastier than I'd figured. "I suppose she's got claws or fangs?"

Considering he'd used the term 'critters', I had the feeling that he wasn't going to be good company. Still, he was a visitor — a human visitor — and custom demanded we welcome him. "Actually, she has both. I hope Earth is open to aliens living there."

He didn't reply, but then again, I hadn't expected him to. We entered the restaurant where Lynni had already finished preparing our noon meal of braised beef, vegetables and a salad. She'd set the table as well, along with a pitcher of water and two glasses. Collins' eyes widened at her appearance. He stopped dead in his tracks, but he soon recovered, bobbed his head then introduced himself.

"It, uh, smells good," he said as he sat down. He still glanced at her with uncertainty, though, as if expecting an imminent attack.

"It tastes even better," she answered.

Lynni took a seat in a nearby booth and waited. Collins cut into his meat and wolfed down a large mouthful. "This *is* good. We don't have great food on Earth anymore."

"No?"

He grunted. "No. Things have changed a lot."

After pouring himself some water, Collins went on to tell me about me about the various races that had visited Earth over the past couple of years. Some races had been friendly, but only a few.

"After your vessel left our solar system, more and more aliens decided to drop in. Some were humanoid…many weren't. Some were friendly, but a few decided to shoot first and talk later."

He shoveled in another mouthful of his lunch and chewed thoughtfully. "And?" I asked.

After gulping down more water, he said that Earth people had opted to get tougher.

"Tougher," I echoed.

"Meaner, too. That's how it was. I don't expect you to understand."

Upgraded tech, better space fighters and planetary missile defenses had provided a solid shield for Earth. After a few skirmishes and one outright bombing mission that had wiped half of Russia and most of China off the map, Earth had finally prevailed.

His face took on a determined look, but behind that, there was something else, something darker. "We had to use up a lot of our resources. It wasn't something we wanted, but we ended up gearing our planet for war. For now, that's how it has to be. We're still not number one in the universe, but then again, we never were. We realized that after our first skirmish with a race called the Cloradians."

"Ravagers," I mumbled.

He nodded. "I see you've met them."

"Sort of. Not my kind of people."

A harsh laugh came my way. "Our thoughts exactly. To be honest, our experiences taught us that we needed a much tougher policy to keep Earth safe. If anyone who isn't Terran doesn't disable their weapons once they enter our space, then our fleet will drive them off.

"Even if they come with peaceful intentions, all alien visitors are automatically quarantined. Their weapons are taken away. We keep them in quarantine for a month, just to determine if they carry any pathogens deadly to our kind."

Our kind. He went on to say that the leaders of Earth — the Council, he called them, with a capital C — had decided that Earth was only for Earthers. "We've allowed some of the aliens to stay. We watch them. We have to in order to ensure our survival. If you want to say it's xenophobic, go ahead. That's how it stands."

Xenophobic — as I'd feared, the shift in mindset and action had, indeed, occurred — and not for the better. It showed in Collins' face and in his voice.

He went on to say that he was surprised to see me so close to an alien. "Uh, she's sitting right here. You can talk to her, too, if you want. You've got a translator. Her name is Lynni, and she's my girlfriend. And she doesn't carry any pathogens. Trust me on that."

While she did carry a star within her, it wasn't worth mentioning. For his part, Collins chose to ignore my statement, and his next words ruined it all. "Glad you've got her trained well."

Talk about a major cringe moment, and Lynni got up, glaring at him in anger. With a hiss of rage, her fangs came out, as well as her claws. "I am no one's pet!"

Startled, Collins dropped his fork and shied back, but then she retracted her fangs and claws and strode out of the room, spitting expletives at a rapid-fire rate.

Our visitor watched her go with an expression akin to fear, but underneath, something else lurked, something dark, and I didn't like it one bit. "That was unexpected," he murmured, and while someone might have expected him to sound contrite, he didn't sound that way...at all.

Screw that — he'd meant every word. "What else did you think would happen?"

"Huh?"

Either this guy was insensitive or a bigot — or both. My guess went in the direction of him being both. I put down my fork and let loose. "You're an idiot, you know that?"

"Hey —"

"You came here, insulted my ship, and you just insulted my girlfriend. Lynni's not a pet. She's a Kagekian. That's how she looks. You don't like it? You don't have to. But you don't have the right to come in and insult her...ever."

Collins blinked. "I didn't know. I thought you hired her as —"

"A slave?"

He didn't reply, so I continued, leaning over to stare him in the face. "Collins, this is my ship. Got it? *My* ship. *My* restaurant. And she's not my slave. She's my girlfriend, like I've already told you. This is year 2134, not 1534. So, yeah, you could blow this ship to smithereens, but that won't make me change my mind about her — or about you."

Now he got defensive and stabbed his forefinger on the Formica. "In case you haven't figured it out yet, kid, this is Earth you're orbiting. You're welcome to stay. It's your planet, after all."

Once again, he just had to go with the 'kid' stuff, but before I could answer, he pointed at the viewing screen. "My ship is waiting, but as for her, if she comes with us, then she'll have to be interned along with every other alien life form that's down there. Considering she's been with you and you're still healthy, I'll see to it that she gets out in forty-eight hours. That's our policy, so either you take it or leave it."

He picked up his cutlery again and started back on his meal. *Insensitive prick.* I didn't have to think about his offer. "I hope you enjoyed your lunch."

Immediately, he stopped eating, his veneer of confidence shattered. It was as though he couldn't believe anyone would turn down his generous offer. In a quick move, he tossed his utensils on the table and stood. "You'd better be sure about this. Think about it. This is your world."

"I'll show you out."

Wordlessly, we went to the airlock. Once he'd donned his suit, he exited and never looked back. A bump seconds later signaled that his ship had uncoupled with our dock, and it slowly disappeared into the dark and off the radar.

Back at the restaurant, Lynni was in the process of washing the dishes. With quick, deft movements, she soaped the knives, forks and plates then ran hot water over them to rinse off the suds.

Once done, she jammed them into the rack and strode over to a booth to take a seat. Yes, she was pissed off, but then she blew out a deep breath and waved me over. I joined her. Neither of us spoke for a few minutes. Finally, she asked the most obvious question. "He has gone?"

"Yes."

Lynni blinked. "You are not going back to Earth?"

"No."

Her eyes glinted their unearthly orange. "Because of me?"

A puff of air escaped my lungs, and it seemed to signal the biggest decision of my life. "Because of a lot of things. I have my Earth here."

Lynni's mouth opened and closed spasmodically like a fish that had been tossed onto land. "I do not understand. This is what you wanted. You wanted to go home. You told me so."

True, yes, but that was before I found out that racism and xenophobia hadn't been eradicated like I'd hoped it would be. It was a sudden, bitter pill to swallow. What I was about to do—it meant giving up my heritage. It meant giving up everything I'd been born into.

But at the same time, there was someone sitting across from me who I didn't want to give up—not now, and not ever. And I was still me, a human, and no one and nothing could ever change that. "Like I said, Lynni, my Earth, my world, is with you. If you want it to be, that is."

In a sudden move, she leaned over the table and kissed me firmly on the lips. "I want it this way." She then added with a touch of sadness, "And, I have nowhere else to go."

No, she didn't. We were both orphans of the stars, but even orphans could find homes, and that meant making our home here. As I was about to take her in my arms, though, the interstellar com-link crackled to life.

"This is Captain Collins. I've just been in touch with the Council on Earth. They've instructed me to impound your vessel. You and your passenger will accompany me to Earth."

Impound *my* ship? So, it had come to this. My decision to stay up here had been a good one. "Granger, respond!"

Impatient jerk. I pressed the button. "Hold, please." If that didn't bug him to no end, nothing would.

"Now, wait..."

Too late. He'd have to wait, and while I was mentally smiling as well as cursing him out, the computer spoke to me. "Captain Rick Granger."

Oddly enough, it didn't use the monotonous tinny voice it usually employed. Instead, it sounded like a mix of my parents' voices. Perhaps their personalities had been ingrained in the ship. That was for another day, though. I had time. "Yes?"

"What are your orders, sir? Shall we shift?"

Oh, man, I'd forgotten that I was now in charge. Lynni glanced at me. "What does it mean, Rick?"

A smile came to my face. "It means that we can go wherever we want. Are you ready to leave?"

A tiny smile came to her face. "Whenever you are."

I motioned to one of the tables. "Park it. This is going to be sudden."

She slid into a booth and held onto the table while I turned to the computer. "This is Captain Rick Granger. Commence shift."

"Preference?"

It didn't take much thought. "Random."

As if to underscore my statement, the loudspeaker blared, "Shift occurring. Shift occurring. Please stay calm. Shift occurring."

After I'd mentally counted off forty seconds, I pressed the interstellar com-link. "Collins?"

"Yeah?"

"Bye."

Then I clicked off. Randomness was the key. In their own way, my parents had been simply random people. Truth be known, I was beginning to understand why they had liked being that way — and I was starting to like the concept as well.

I made my way over to where Lynni was. Our ship began to shudder. My girlfriend grabbed onto me. The heavens tilted, the stars spun, one more upheaval then…silence. Lynni let go to ask, "We are… Where are we?"

We'd stopped in orbit around a greenish-blue planet roughly the size of Earth. Way up ahead, a brilliant sun shone out. Nothing around us, only space and more space, and it felt good to breathe here. "Computer, where are we this time?"

"Antlia Galaxy. Approximately three-thousand-eighty-four light years from previous position."

"Are there Class M worlds here?"

"Three. We are orbiting one now. Display is up."

A moment later, a hologram leaped up that showed the planet we were orbiting along with two other places to visit. All of them had oxygen-nitrogen atmospheres, humanoid life — we'd visit. We had all the time in the world now.

Soon after I'd established our position, a crackle came over the interstellar radio. I pressed the receive button and the translator kicked in. "Hello?"

A crow-like voice spoke. "This is Fruid, leader of the Ulinian people. Our sensors detected a sudden intrusion into our space. You are in orbit around our world. State your name and your purpose here."

Friend or foe — that was the question. "My name is Captain Rick Granger. I'm in charge of this vessel. It's called *Port Anywhere*. We're in the food service business."

Silence, then his voice came again, somewhat puzzled sounding. "We do not understand. Please clarify your vessel's purpose."

"We, uh, we're an eating establishment, a restaurant. We prepare meals for travelers. We're not here to hurt anyone. If you scan us, you'll find that we're not armed."

"Scanning."

A few moments later, Fruid resumed talking, and he sounded surprised. "It is as you say. Our sensors detect that there are only two occupants on your vessel."

"That is correct, sir."

More silence, then, "This is most curious, but you are welcome here. We would like to sample your wares if that is within your mission's parameters."

It was. I sent the coordinates, and Fruid said he'd send a delegation of five within a few minutes. "We have scanned the area in which you and the other person with you are standing. From our preliminary findings, it seems that our physiologies are similar to yours. Anything you prepare will be acceptable to us."

"See you soon…and thank you."

I breathed a sigh of relief. They could have blown us out of the sky, but they'd decided not to. Perhaps Fruid and crew understood the concept of trust, something my own people had failed to learn. We'd be okay. If we had the place open to all, played favorites to none, our lives here would continue.

And we could go here, there and everywhere. Lynni squeezed my hand and pointed to the sky. A vessel — long and oval-shaped — was fast approaching. "Us," I said, as we looked at the oncoming ship cutting through the inky darkness.

"Us," she echoed. "I do not understand. Do you mean 'us', as in lifetime mates?"

Lynni's question wasn't unexpected. She'd always been direct, and now, even more so, since we'd eventually take our relationship to the most intimate level. "Yes, I do, but I'm wondering about that star inside you—"

"It is stable," she cut in with a coy and somewhat devilish grin. "I do not think any physical contact will damage me."

"Are you sure?"

The grin spread. "There is only one way to find out."

Truthfully, it was something I was looking forward to, but in the meantime, we had guests to serve. I leaned over to kiss her on the cheek then whispered one word. "Breeto."

Us.

Want to see more from this author? Here's a taster for you to enjoy!

The Menagerie
J.S. Frankel

Excerpt

Karen Fox rubbed her right leg — the bad one — sighed, and figured that she might as well get out of bed. Hospital beds weren't all that comfortable, so she turned over onto her left side, slid out of bed and stood up. She gripped the cool tiles with her toes while she teetered unsteadily for a moment. Once she regained her balance, she limped over to the window. Scents of summer — fir and pine trees, hollyhocks and azaleas — drifted in through the window along with the sounds of shouting. She muttered, "It *would* be a nice day today."

Today was the middle of July, the time was around noon, and although the Portland weather was hot and dry, a cool breeze swirled around her. It was different from the air conditioner. It was natural and pleasant, whereas the air-conditioning unit put out a steady stream of dry air that made her cough. Pleasant or not, it didn't matter. Instead, she shifted her gaze to the sky and prayed for rain.

Since being brought here roughly two months ago, Karen had grown to despise sunny days and hate the summer season. What she hated more than anything was the idea of people going around in shorts and tank tops and riding bikes and everything else sixteen-year-old kids did when they were fully capable.

Now, all the fun of life had been taken away and she just wished — selfishly so — for it to rain and dampen everyone else's fun. Let Mother Nature do her worst and not just rain but storm. Bring on a flood, a volcanic explosion or something else equally dire. If she couldn't enjoy life, why should they?

"Don't be selfish," she whispered a second later, and took back her wish. Thinking about it, it was just plain mean. Even if life didn't work the way she wanted it to, she couldn't go around blaming anyone for what had happened. Part of her said that it would be fun. Everyone deserved a little misery in their lives. However, the other part, the rational and decent part, said no.

"Hey, what's up, Megan?"

The question floated up to Karen's position, and she followed the source. There, a few people she knew from her school rode by and she moved away from the window, flattening her back against the wall. Doubtful they saw her, as she was on the second floor, and who looked up while riding along, anyway?

After sneaking a peek, she saw their bicycles disappear down the road and breathed a faint sigh of relief. The breeze blew some strands of her long, dirty blonde hair around her face and she brushed them away with an impatient flick of her hand.

Letting out a series of grunts as she moved back to the bed, she winced with every step. The accident had been a bad one. She'd been in the back seat of her father's car, enjoying the ride and then…then the bright light had come from the onrushing car. She'd heard her mother screaming, her father yelling "Get down!" and the sound of metal being crushed...

* * * *

May fifteenth, two months ago

"You've had an accident," one of the nurses told her in a kindly voice. A middle-aged woman, heavy with a tangle of dyed black hair, she wore a strained smile.

"What happened?"

Karen's first words...accident victims always said that, didn't they? This had been her first real accident. Biking and running and roller skating had always been part of her life. Bruised knees and elbows came with it, but now, this was major, so she asked the obvious question.

The lights in the room were dim and shadows lurked in every corner. Moonlight came through the drawn shades. A smell of antiseptic hung in the cool air and stabs of pain lanced through every fiber of her being. Her right leg hurt and had a heavy cast on it, suspended by a sling that hung from a support bar attached to the bed. Thick bandages had been wrapped around her right forearm. An intravenous tube ran from a bag in an overhead support and fed into the vein in her right arm.

She didn't take much note of that, though. Instead, she focused on the pain. Her right cheek hurt monstrously, and bringing her good arm up to feel her face, her fingers encountered more bandages.

"You were in a car accident," the nurse gravely intoned. "You don't remember it, do you?"

"Not much," said Karen, struggling to think. "Where are my parents?"

"I'm sorry."

Just two words, but they carried a lot of meaning, and the meaning knifed into Karen's head with all the immediacy of a thunderbolt. A second later, the tears began. "I want to see them," she sobbed out. "Where are they?"

As she struggled to get off the bed, the nurse gently pushed her back and said, somewhat reluctantly, "They're...in the morgue. You just had an operation and you need to rest."

"I want to see them!" Karen screamed and once more tried to get up, lashing out with her good arm. Her fist connected with the nurse's cheek. She heard the nurse grunt then another nurse ran in, a needle at the ready. Karen felt it stab her arm then...nothing.

Waking up the next day, pain still there but somewhat more manageable, Karen noticed the sun streaming in and she felt a little stronger. The nurse whom she'd belted walked in with a massive bruise on her cheek, but a professional smile in place. "Are you feeling better?"

"Yes." Karen nodded and mentally steeled herself for what she was going to ask and what she had to see. "I'm sorry about hitting you."

The nurse inclined her head slightly. "You were upset. I understand."

It was good that someone understood. "Can I...see my parents now?" Karen asked in a faint voice.

"I'll get the doctor."

About the Author

J.S. Frankel was born in Toronto, Canada, a good number of years ago and managed to scrape through the University of Toronto with a BA in English Literature. In 1988 he moved to Japan and started teaching ESL to anyone who would listen to him. In 1997, he married the charming Akiko Koike and their union produced two sons, Kai and Ray. J.S. Frankel makes his home in Osaka where he teaches English by day and writes by night until the wee hours of the morning.

J.S. Frankel loves to hear from readers. You can find his contact information, website details and author profile page at https://www.finch-books.com

Sign up for our newsletter and find out about all our romance book releases, eBook sales and promotions, sneak peeks and FREE romance books!